CW00468017

ALMOST DARK

By Mark Hardie

For Debbie

PROLOGUE

I

Standing on the observation platform, she turns away now from the mouth of the river and gazes into a darkness illuminated by the lights of Canvey Island, the distant floodlit cranes of the London Gateway container port. From here, she cannot see the Crowstone. Though she knows it is there, in the dark. To her left, the rides of the Adventure Island amusement park lie still and silent. Lifting her face to the night sky she closes her eyes. Allows the needles of cold rain to chill her forehead. Run down her cheeks. Moisten her dry lips. She can still hear the voices. The voices of the dead. The voices that have urged her to follow them through the chrome gate. To clamber up onto the wall of the observation platform. To balance, one foot on the wet handrail, the other braced against the shifting glass panel. She feels a sudden rush of vertigo, sways precariously over the inviting rain-soaked pavement seventy feet below . . .

II

She becomes dimly aware that she is lying on the ground. Her breath comes again now ... ragged ... uneven. She has no idea how she got here. The ground beneath her face damp ... cold ... the sharp edges of gravel embedded in her cheek. Her fingers and the palms of her hands, at the same time, numbed ... yet stinging ... as if from a fall. Her head swimming. A dull pain across her kidneys. Her right trainer lost. She can smell damp earth and mulching vegetation ... can hear a susurration of leaves ... the plaintive call of a crow. And then, footsteps ... the crunch and pop of grit beneath a heavy tread. A mud-spattered workboot appears close to her face. She can make out ... laboured breathing ... a stream of muttered obscenities. Rough hands turn her. And something makes her close her eyes ... Denial? Fear? Self-preservation? Whatever it is, her resistance is minimal ... ineffectual. And as her other running shoe is removed, her track suit bottoms and underwear yanked down, as it begins ... she hears ... as if from a distance ... a piteous mewling that she only vaguely recognises as her own . . .

PART ONE

DAY ONE

Detective Constable Catherine Russell almost made it all the way along the passage to the Incident Room. Almost. The Nick, all-but-deserted this early in the morning. The phones silent. The hallway only partly lit. But she made the mistake of pausing, just for a moment, outside the half-glazed door to Detective Chief Inspector Roberts's office. The room beyond was in darkness. But Cat was certain she'd heard music coming from inside. A classical piano piece – Debussy, perhaps? Not that she was any great expert on the subject, and it was just *so* unexpected, so out-of-place, that it stopped her in her tracks. It was so surprising that she dithered; her right hand raised, in two minds about tapping gently on the window, wavering as to whether to go in –

Suddenly the music clicked off. 'Russell? Is that you? I need a word.'

Roberts. He must have recognised her shadow through the pane of frosted glass. Cat glared accusingly at her raised right hand. As if it might have acted on its own volition. As if it might have deliberately set out to betray her. Now, it moved to the door handle and turned it. And she pushed the door open and went inside.

'Put the lights on, would you?' Roberts said. When she switched them on Detective Chief Inspector Martin Roberts knuckled his eyes, then made a desultory effort to pat down his thinning red hair. Cat wondered for a moment whether he might have just woken up. Whether he might have spent the night there. He *had* appeared pretty uptight of late. Even more impatient than usual – something she hadn't thought possible – then again, with Roberts it was difficult to tell, he was always irritable, always looked like he'd slept in his clothes. Yawning, moving a hand – too late – to cover his open mouth, he nodded at one of the plastic visitors' chairs, 'Take a seat.'

Inwardly Cat cursed herself. What had she been thinking? What had she imagined might have been going on? That someone had broken into the Nick, made his way to the Detective Chief Inspector's office and then, maybe, halfway through ransacking the place, the culturally-minded burglar had paused to hear his favourite piano concerto?

'As you know,' Roberts said, 'DS Pearson is attending Magistrates' Court this morning in regard to the Ryan Yates case. I understand that your name's down this week as "Disclosure Officer"?'

'Guv,' Cat nodded.

'Have you acted as Disclosure Officer before?'

'Not yet, Guv,' Cat shook her head, 'We've only recently set up the rota.'

'Okay,' Roberts nodded, 'As I'm sure you are aware' – *but, no doubt you're going to tell me anyway*, Cat thought – 'one of the responsibilities of the Disclosure Officer is to produce the 'Schedule of Unused Materials' in order to comply with the 'Criminal Procedure and Investigations Act, 1996'. Because?'

"'Anything related to an investigation,' Cat quoted, 'which the Police will not be using as part of the prosecution has to be passed on to the Crown Prosecution Service. Anything which might assist the defence or undermined the prosecution has to be highlighted and shared with the trial defence team." '

Roberts eyed her suspiciously, searching for any hint of sarcasm. Not finding any – maybe it was too early in the morning, maybe he wasn't quite awake yet – he added, 'Look, we all know how fucking tedious it can be. Which is why everyone has to take their turn. Right? But I want the paperwork watertight on this one. I want it completed well before it goes to Crown Court. And I ... don't ... want ... anything ... missed. Understood?'

Cat nodded again, 'Guv.'

'Everyone appreciates,' Roberts said, 'that even a fairly straightforward murder case generates a huge volume of unused material; exhibits, witness statements and so on. As you know' – Cat held her tongue. Best not to push her luck too far – 'recently there have been a number of high-profile prosecutions that have proceeded to trial, only to be thrown out because full disclosure has not been forthcoming. If you feel you need some help,' something like a smirk passed briefly across Roberts's face, 'I can always get DC Gilbert to give you a hand.'

Cat was shaking her head, 'No, Guv. I'm sure I can manage.'

'Detective Chief Superintendent Curtis,' – this delivered like an announcement of the discovery of foot fungus – 'is up before the promotion panel in the next few weeks for the Assistant Chief Constable's job. Word is, he's a shoo-in. Which means, of course, that up until the interviews he'll be more of a fucking pain in the arse than usual. Now, with any luck, he'll get the job. In which case he'll be moving to Chelmsford and won't be sticking his nose in our business anymore. But, until then, any sniff of a slip-up, and by that I mean, if he has even the slightest concern that there's a possibility that anything might reflect badly on him, and we'll all suffer.'

Rumour was – that is, Pearson had told her – that Curtis already wanted to get rid of her. Had tried to get rid of her following the death of DI Sean Carragher. Admittedly this had only come to her second hand, from a conversation Pearson had supposedly had with Roberts, but if it *were* true … this, then, was by way of a coded warning.

2

Ryan Yates stood in the dock. Experiencing a dizzying panic. The acerbic taste of bile in his mouth. Aware of the acrid tang of his own sweat. The soreness under his armpits. The clammy shirt clinging to his back. The trousers sticking to his thighs, bunching behind his knees. He was momentarily disorientated. Breathless.

On entering the court he'd been taken back in time. To a *somewhere* he couldn't quite place … a somewhere he might have visited while at school … a vaguely remembered auditorium, a school trip to some airy and radiant theatre for a Christmas pantomime, a modern church at harvest festival. But to a memory of a better, brighter, time. Now, though, despite the high vaulted ceiling, the freshly whitewashed walls, it seemed suddenly claustrophobic. Airless. Hot. He felt ignored: the Magistrates, on the high stage to his right, gathering together their papers, slipping them into briefcases; the bewigged barristers immediately in front of him, standing up from their desks, flapping their black gowns, turning to the opposing benches, chatting amiably. The atmosphere at once all genial bonhomie where, moments earlier, it had been adversarial and antagonistic. Most of all, though, he felt abandoned, the visitors' gallery opposite conspicuously empty.

Ryan Yates had neither followed the arguments, nor the exchanges between the two counsels. He had simply, as he had been instructed, spoken clearly. Answered the questions to the best of his ability. Or had tried to. But his explanations had quickly become confused; the sequence of events muddled, the narrative disordered, the details misremembered or contradictory. The story, as a result, had been unconvincing . . .

Ryan looked down at the plexiglass screen in front of him. At the smear of fingerprints, the downward trail of – now drying – saliva, the smudge of coagulating blood. At his hands; the chewed and ragged fingernails, the knuckles blanched from gripping the narrow, wooden ledge beneath. He felt something being clamped uncomfortably around his wrist. A bulky metal handcuff. A green nylon rope in a plastic sleeve. A second handcuff on the wrist of a woman who must have entered unnoticed through the side door of the dock. Her face impassive, her eyes wary and unsympathetic, "SERCO" stencilled in black on her white short-sleeved uniform shirt. She tugged gently at his elbow, and then he was being led away through a door at the back of the court . . .

Then he was in an interview room. Somewhere beneath the court. The room the same as all the other rooms he had been in since his arrest. The walls painted off-white, or beige, or magnolia. He wasn't quite sure what this particular colour was. The floors linoleum. Green, or blue, or cleaned, polished and scrubbed over the years into some indeterminate shade of grey. Leaning again on a tabletop of scarred and scuffed wood. Or grey Formica. Sitting in a moulded plastic chair with metal legs. This one, like all the rest, orange. Ryan felt oddly detached. As if present, in the room, and yet at the same time somewhere else. As if he might be watching another person. As if he were both participant and observer. Watching a scene which a part of his rational mind was able to simultaneously elucidate and interpret. A scene where a running commentary was being provided by what might have been the replaying of another, different, remembered conversation . . .

'It's like everything's like ... kind of ... all flat or something?' Donna Freeman had confided to him, at another time, in another place, 'Like it looks all three-D from a distance, but if you look closer it's as if it's all been painted on or something.'

'You mean like one of those painted backdrops in a theatre?'

'Yeah, that's it, like it's all just scenery?'

'A *trompe-l'oeil.*'

'A what?'

'A *trompe-l'oeil,*' he had said again, 'It's French. It means "deceives the eye".'

If Donna Freeman had been *here*, or even if they'd been just sitting on the bed in his room, just sitting, having a fag and talking, she would probably have given him one of those looks. One of those looks that said he was being a pretentious twat. Might've even rolled her eyes. But because they weren't, because of where they were, and maybe because she'd felt kind of safe, she'd said,

'Sometimes it's like what you see isn't what's actually there … as if behind everything is … something else'.

Donna hadn't said what that *something else* was. Hadn't been able to say what it was. Hadn't quite had the right words. But he'd imagined that that *something* might have skittering claws. That that *something* might have sharp teeth. That there were countless numbers of that *something* and they were blind and pink and hairless and jostling and clambering over and over one another. That they were gnawing at that soggy and insubstantial fabric. And that someday they would all come tumbling through . . .

They had spent most of that night at the Abigail Burnett Children's Home, talking. Or, at least, Donna had spent most of the night talking. Ryan had spent most of it listening. They had been lying together in his single bed, spooning, Ryan snuggling up to Donna's back. A few minutes earlier they'd been having sex. Not because either of them really fancied the other. Not even because they'd wanted to do it that much. But more because everyone else had been doing it. The sex hadn't been that good – *he* hadn't been that good – and he didn't think either of them had enjoyed it much. He *knew* that Donna hadn't enjoyed it much, because after it was all over, she'd said, 'Can't see what all the fuss is about.'

Later, she'd told him how she saw things – people especially – not as a *trompe-l'oeil*. But – and he'd imagined here some kind of innate and unconscious *camera lucida* – more as if a second, *true,* image of someone she looked at was superimposed over the surface of their outwardly-visible features.

'It's like the two faces exist at the same time? Like . . . '

'You mean like that thing that happens sometimes with old photos? Like a double exposure?'

'Yeah, whatever,' she'd said. But, then, with her head still on the pillow, still facing away from him, she'd nodded, 'Yeah, that's it, a double exposure.'

They'd just laid there then. Not talking. And, at the time, hadn't he felt a bit sorry for her? Hadn't he thought that it – all the things Donna had confessed to him – might all be a bit sad? But he'd tried to be sympathetic, too. He was sure he'd tried to be sympathetic. But he definitely remembered feeling a bit afraid of her, as well, if he were totally honest. Scared of her mental illness. He'd *always* been terrified by any thought of mental illness . . .

'Ryan?'

This is how it had been. Suddenly arriving at a location with no real idea how he'd got there. Abruptly *present* in the middle of a conversation. Dimly aware that he'd been asked a question, had been asked the same question more than once. He had a vague recollection of having been searched again. Of having his tie, belt and shoelaces taken from him.

'Do you think,' Ryan hesitated, 'that it's possible to, like, catch madness?' he asked the woman. The woman appointed as his solicitor. The duty solicitor at the police station when he'd first been arrested. For a moment she looked totally confused. Then, exasperated. Dismissing his question with an irritated shake of her head, she asked a question of her own.

'Do you understand what just happened, Ryan?' Asked again. Because now she was sitting down in the chair opposite, had a briefcase open on the table, was scribbling some notes on a pad.

'No,' Ryan said. Shaking his head. Looking down. Away. Running his thumb along the edge of the table.

Tapping her fingernails on the tabletop, she said, 'Look at me, Ryan', then, when he didn't look up, more insistently, 'Ryan ... look ... at ... me.' Reluctantly Ryan looked up and she said, 'You shouldn't be here. Given what happened.'

Her eyes drifted to Ryan's restless fingers; rubbing at the grubby bandage on his left wrist, scratching the itchy stitches underneath, worrying at the lifting and curling corners of the dirty surgical strip.

'We . . . ' the solicitor said, ' . . . that is, I made an appeal to the Court, the Judge, that you are what the Crown Prosecution Service term, a *mentally disordered offender* . . . ' Ryan had heard the phrase before. Still wasn't quite sure what it meant. Wasn't really sure that it actually applied to him. 'You understand why we asked for this, don't you, Ryan? That this can influence the Court's recommendation on whether to prosecute or divert . . . ' And Ryan still wasn't completely convinced that all of this might not be about someone else.

14

Had hoped all along that someone, somewhere, had made some awful mistake. That *all* of this might be about someone else and that it would soon be all over, ' . . . that it can affect the decision on whether you are fit to plead . . . ' But his solicitor seemed to think it important that he should pay attention. So, for her sake, Ryan tried his very best to follow what she was saying. She had a nice voice. Sort of ... musical. Soft. And lilting. So, he kept finding himself listening to the rise and fall, the cadence, and not quite able to grasp exactly what it was she was saying ... 'That, most importantly, it could determine the length of the sentence. You understand all that, don't you Ryan? I mean, I did explain all of this before.'

Ryan didn't understand. But it didn't seem right to say so. Not again. So instead he nodded as if he did. The solicitor nodded back. Pleased with him. 'Good. I thought you would; judging by your exam results, you're a very intelligent young man. Now, that appeal has been unsuccessful – and, ironically, the fact that you *are* obviously very intelligent has rather counted against you in this – but I've made another application to the Court, asking that you undergo a *proper* psychiatric evaluation. If we can establish that you have a significant mental illness – significant enough to meet the legal criteria – and I still think we've got a reasonable chance of this, then this can still be weighed against the seriousness of the offence and the possibility that it will be repeated. At the very least we may be able to delay proceedings. So, you can stay longer on remand. That's what you said you wanted, right?' Ryan nodded. 'Good,' she nodded encouragingly at him again, 'you're much better where you are . . . '

Ryan didn't think he was much better where he was. The only thing that made it in any way bearable, was that, since he'd slit his wrist – and he hadn't even done that right, apparently; slashing across rather than along and opening the veins up properly – he was in a cell on his own. But it didn't make it any *better*. Nothing could make any of it any *better*. Ryan shook his head, shook the thoughts away. 'My Mum didn't come.'

Not really a question. Ryan knew that the solicitor had tried. She'd told him so. She had tried her *very* best. Texted. Phoned. Written letters. Even gone to the house, she'd said. But his mother had refused point blank. Didn't want to have anything to do with him anymore, she'd said. The truth was, his mother hadn't wanted anything to do with him for a long time, had she? But you'd have thought she could have made the effort. You'd have thought *somebody* could have come. Ever since this had begun, though, his mother had acted as if Ryan had brought dishonour on the family's good name. Like he'd sullied the family's reputation or something. She'd even given an interview to the local paper; saying how shocked she was, how she couldn't believe *her* son could be capable of anything like that, how ashamed she was. As if his family had any reputation. Except with Social Services. Except for being trouble. Except for his mother being a total fucking-waste-of-space . . .

'Are you okay, Ryan?' the solicitor asked.

And without looking up, Ryan squeezed his eyes shut. And nodded.

3

The Civil Service. A complete misnomer, of course. The outward civility a thin disguise for ruthless ambition. The processes, the procedures, the protocols a cloak for the almost constant intriguing, political manoeuvring, and ruthless backstabbing. Admittedly, it was all very well-mannered, all very polite, all very British. She had always been of the opinion that, at the point any organisation reached a critical mass, its primary function, its overriding preoccupation, became solely the perpetuation of that organisation. Her particular subsector of the Civil Service, namely MI5, was no exception. The service performed no longer determined by the national interest, but rather by the self-interest of its officers.

This was, she suspected, the reason she had received the rare summons to the top floor. Why she now sat in one of the cosy leather armchairs in the office of Sir Douglas Langham. Service legend had it that Douglas Langham – as was – had earned the knighthood by 'throttling' a sexual scandal involving someone in direct line of succession to the throne. The Deputy Director General of the Domestic Security Service stood now with his back to the room, silhouetted against the plate-glass window, making a show of gazing reflectively over the view of the Thames. This, after all, was how one measured the success of all the years of politicking, scheming and machinations: on which floor you were situated, the quality of the view, the dimensions of the office, the proportion and character of the desk behind which you sat, the depth of pile of the carpet. Even the way the tea and biscuits were served; exquisite bone china cups and saucers, an array of artisan cookies on the low, lacquered coffee table, was an implicit barometer of status.

'I understand, Geraldine,' Langham said, that you've been looking into an issue in … where was it now?'

'Southend-on-Sea, Sir Douglas'– Always 'Sir' Douglas. After all, what was the point of a title if one didn't insist on people using it? – 'It's in Essex?'

'Ah … quite so.'

Sir Douglas clearly didn't have the faintest idea where Southend might be, and probably only the vaguest of notions regarding Essex. But, she suspected, he knew exactly what she had been doing there. From this point on, their conversation would be a matter of public record. In as much as the minutes of the meeting – complete or otherwise – might possibly be filed retrospectively. Depending, of course, on how advantageous this would prove for Sir Douglas. Her eyes slid across to the occupant of the other cosy leather armchair; Penelope Redmond. The Personal Assistant to the Deputy Head of the Domestic Security Service. His 'wife in the office', and, as the gatekeeper between Sir Douglas and any supplicant seeking admittance to the inner sanctum, one of the few people in the organisation who actually wielded any genuine power. Anyone having the temerity to challenge the authority of 'Lady Penelope' would quickly find any career aspirations they harboured swiftly and irrevocably crushed. Penelope: sensible shoes, yellow cotton shift dress with a motif of roses and forget-me-nots, bullet-proof make-up, was perched on the edge of her seat, a reporter's notebook

18

balanced on her knee, an expensive silver Cross pen ready in her hand.

Turning her attention away from the personal assistant and back towards Langham, Geraldine said, 'There are – or were – two issues, Sir Douglas. One, I believe, has been satisfactorily resolved. The body of Beverly Marsh, aged sixteen, was discovered on the beach at Southend-on-Sea on the morning of Thursday, 31st March 1966. In the course of the investigation a folder containing the transcripts of sessions held between a psychiatrist, Doctor Angela Fitzgerald, and the person now known as Richard Lennon, the man who had initially been charged with the murder, came into the possession of the Essex Major Investigation Team. As there was good reason to believe that further examination of the information contained in the folder might result in doubt being cast on the original conviction, the folder was sequestered on the grounds of "national security"–'

'1966?' Langham asked, 'Wasn't that around Dickie's time?'

Dickie. Sir Richard Fennybrook. The former head of the Domestic Security Services. Who just happened to be the grandfather of Simon Fennybrook, the current head of MI5. No such thing as social mobility in the Security Service. It was fair to say that, in all areas of Government, nepotism had always been, and would always be, the order of the day.

'Poor old Simon,' Langham said, turning from the window, and looking anything but sympathetic, 'the last thing he needs, what with all the fuss there's been about the outsourcing of services. Ah, tea, splendid! Geraldine?'

19

'Please,' she said looking over at Penny, who already had the teapot in her hand ready to pour, 'White. No sugar.' Best not to pass up the offer of a cup of tea. Very bad form. Sure sign of a Bolshevik.

'At the time the folder was sequestered, the Major Incident Team requested the return of the victim's clothing, in order that they might undergo forensic examination.'

'The results of which was what?' Langham asked.

'No useful DNA was recovered from the clothing supplied.'

Langham picked up a cookie from the coffee table, took a bite, then chewed reflectively, 'And the other matter?'

'The death of Michael Jason Morris– '

'Is he one of ours?'

'Michael . . . ' she said. Noting Langham's use of the male pronoun. She wondered if this was genuine ignorance. Or a deliberate distancing of himself from any personal knowledge of the transgender former operative, ' . . . has been employed by the Security Services. But purely on a freelance basis.' Meaning: If required, any evidence of an association between Michael Morris and the Security Services could be swiftly excised. Langham nodded, 'Carry on.'

'By attending certain entertainments in Southend, Michael Morris was endeavouring to discover the exact level of involvement and, as a consequence, the potential security risk posed by one Layla Gilchrist.'

'Layla Gilchrist?' Langham asked.

'Layla Gilchrist is a former intern at the House of Commons. She is suspected of attending, or possibly even organising, numerous questionable "entertainments" in grace-and-favour properties in and around Westminster. These entertainments were thought to be frequented by various government ministers and high-ranking civil servants. She has subsequently relocated to Southend-on-Sea where she was, until recently, employed as the manager of *Iniquity*, a local sex shop. It was believed that she might have been organising the same type of private entertainments in Southend that she was suspected of providing in Westminster.'

She waited while Langham took a clean linen handkerchief from his trouser pocket and blew his nose. Then added, 'The body of Michael Morris was later discovered on a nearby beach. The exact circumstances and location of his death are unknown. It is thought, however, that in all probability he died of manual strangulation at one of these parties and the body was later moved. Anthony Derek Blake has since confessed to the murder and is currently in custody at HMP Chelmsford awaiting trial.'

'What do we have from inside the investigation?' Langham asked, 'I take it we have someone inside the investigation?'

'We do,' she nodded, 'Anthony Blake's girlfriend is currently under the care of the local Social Services department, and may be being questioned by the Child Protection team. Ms Gilchrist has gone to ground.'

'That is' Langham folded the handkerchief and put it back into his pocket, 'unfortunate.'

4

Cat Russell sat at her desk in the Incident Room. Her pen hovering over her notepad; unable to concentrate, unable to think, unable to do anything. Just … waiting … and there it was. Again. Admittedly, despite the best efforts of several desktop fans, and even though the weather outside was dank and miserable, the room was still hot and stuffy. That never helped. And it had been a while now since she'd been out for her lunchtime fag, though probably not long enough, just yet, to justify her going out again for another. But the thing was, once you'd heard something, something that occurred at a relatively regular interval, but not quite regular enough that you were able to treat it as just more background noise, once you'd realised just how bastard irritating that thing was, then you just *couldn't* ignore it. For this reason, about a minute or so later, when it happened again, Cat decided she just had to say something. Taking a deep breath, putting down her pen, looking up. She asked, calmly, she thought. Reasonably, in her opinion.

'Do you have to keep doing that?'

Detective Sergeant Frank Pearson, in the chair opposite, hand over his mouth, mid-yawn – mid-another-bloody-yawn – frowned, dragged his eyes reluctantly from his computer screen, and turned to her, 'Doing what?'

'Making that noise.'

'What noise?'

'*That* noise. I mean it's not bad enough I have to sit here and listen to you swearing under your breath every five minutes because the computer system doesn't work. Or doesn't work how you seem to think it should – without having to listen to that noise.'

Pearson looked at her as if he hadn't the foggiest what she was talking about, '*What* noise?'

'*That* noise,' Cat said. Again. Irritated at having to repeat herself. Because he had to *know* he was doing it, didn't he? 'That noise you make every time you yawn? Like a … dunno, it's like halfway between a gasp and a sigh? Combined with a sort of groan. If you *are* going to insist on yawning, you could, at the very least, do it quietly.'

Pearson did sigh now. Heavily. Then shook his head. As if she might be imagining things. Made a face – long suffering – as if *this* was the sort of nonsense he had to put up with all the time.

Properly needled now, Cat said, 'Look, I'm sorry,' though she wasn't, 'but I've been sitting here listening to it for the best part of a fucking hour now . . . ' She saw him surreptitiously lift a cuff and check his watch – the old-fashioned Timex on a battered leather wriststrap – no doubt doing a rapid calculation of how long it had been since her last cigarette. Then he looked up, nodded an acknowledgement, 'Alright. Fair point.'

It *was* an apology. Of sorts. But the sort of apology that was only offered in a bid to keep the peace. The sort of apology, in her view, that wasn't really an apology at all. God,

24

the 'patience', the 'forbearance'. He could be so bloody … patronising at times.

Almost immediately, though, she felt guilty. Cat admitted to herself, reluctantly, that she may have been a little abrupt with Pearson. Alright, she might have actually been downright rude. This *wasn't* who she was. Not really. Or not the person she *wanted* to be, at any rate. Why was it that, despite her best intentions, she could never quite be the person she was inside? The kind person. The forgiving person. Why couldn't she ever just say something *nice*? Or at least just bite her tongue? Show a little self-restraint for once? After all, it wasn't really the yawning that was bothering her, wasn't even the tedious admin, it was that bloody text she'd received just over an hour ago.

Cat looked across the Incident Room now. At Wendy Simpson. Before her maternity leave, the Team Analyst had been the epitome of calm composure. Ever since her return, though, she had appeared nervous and preoccupied. Cat *had* put it down to her having to spend the day separated from her new baby. But why then did she appear so reluctant to go home? Why was she staying late every night, still at her computer after everyone else had left?

At Detective Constable Peter Gilbert. Gawping vacantly at his screen, absent-mindedly strumming his bottom lip. By all accounts he was extremely bright, had the makings of a decent copper, but these mannerisms, along with his general naivety, his readiness to blush at the slightest provocation, inevitably left him open to no end of piss-taking from the rest of the team.

At Detective Sergeant Alan Laurence. According to Pearson, Laurence had, in the past, been a diligent, conscientious copper. But in the time she had worked on the Major Investigation Team, Cat had seen precious little evidence of it. Laurence now seemed to be just killing time until retirement when, word was – Pearson again – Laurence was going to open a rescue home for donkeys with his missus. Nowadays, it seemed, Laurence preferred to stay in the Nick, on the phones or computer. Forever on his mobile, half-turned away from the room, on one personal call or another. Never without a folded copy of the *Racing Post* in a jacket pocket. At the moment, though, Laurence was pretending to be engrossed in something on his computer, smirking to himself, shaking his head and obviously earwigging on their conversation. Laurence had observed more than once that they 'bickered like an old married couple'. Sensing her eyes on him, Laurence looked up. Cat glared at him, 'giving him evils', until, embarrassed, he turned away.

Well, absolutely no chance of nipping out for a quick puff now, Cat thought. She'd definitely *have* to leave it a reasonable amount of time, a good hour probably. Just to prove a point. Just to show that she didn't really need one that much. Part of her was relieved. It meant, at least, she could put off dealing with that text. The text she had yet to reply to. The text she wasn't sure *how* to reply to. The text, in truth, she wasn't sure she even wanted to reply to . . .

5

Ryan Yates was sitting on a mattress. A thin, blue plastic mattress laid on wooden slats. The wooden slats screwed to a concrete bench. The concrete bench in a room only five foot by five-foot square. Sitting … because he couldn't do anything else. Sitting. And staring. At the off-white, concrete walls. The grey linoleum floor. The heavy metal door. Sitting. Waiting for prison transport. This wasn't the first time Ryan Yates had made this journey. The journey from dock … to interview room … to holding cell. And he could remember each time. But mostly, he could remember that first time, remember that first journey in exquisite, excruciating detail . . .

Shuffling down the concrete steps in the loading dock. Wearing the same cheap suit, he was wearing now. The suit that had been bought at Primark especially for his court appearances. Shivering against the cold. Stepping awkwardly up into the prison van. His hands cuffed in front of him. His too big and beltless trousers working their way down his hips. Having to grip with his toes in order not to leave his lace-less shoes behind. Then making his way down the central aisle to be placed in a metal box. Each successive space into which he had been placed throughout that day had been smaller than the last. This one about three feet square. A window high up to the outside. Dim light through frosted glass. He had stood for a while at the locked door, staring through a second window into the van's interior. In the drab, grey light from outside, the feeble illumination of the lamp in his cramped cell, Ryan could just make out other prisoners, at other windows. But as the engine started and the van began to rattle and shudder . . . as it pulled away, hitting every bump and pothole in the road, and Ryan had been buffeted from one wall to another, he'd finally been forced to sit down . . .

Clutching the edges of the seat. Experiencing that familiar light-headedness. That same cold sweat pricking his body. That unmistakable trembling in his fingers. His toes again numb and tingling. The walls closing in. His mouth suddenly dry and a constriction in his throat. A tightness in his chest. He made an effort to relax. To focus on his breathing. Counting as he slowly took in a lungful of the stale air ... one ... two ... three ... four ... holding it inside ... one ... two ... gradually letting it out again ... one ... two ... three ... four. Repeating the process. And again. And again . . .

He'd felt his respiration gradually return to normal. His heartbeat slow. The walls of the metal box start to recede –

Then ... from some hidden speaker inside the van ... deafening electronic dance music. And, suddenly, all of the lights went out . . .

That first time. He'd been *so* glad when, in total darkness, inside his tiny metal box, he'd felt the van finally lurch to a halt. The engine stalling and starting up again. Outside; metal doors opening. The van edging forward. A set of doors closing behind them, a set of doors opening in front. The van edging forward again and stopping. The metal doors closing.

That first time. He'd been so … fucking … grateful … to be out in the open. Shuddering with the cold. His teeth chattering. And not really caring how much his shoulders ached from being in the same position for so long. Or that his wrists were chafed from the handcuffs. So grateful that he was indifferent to the aching in his legs from his attempts to stay on the metal seat. Unconcerned by the bruising on his knees from bumping the metal walls of his cage.

He'd watched the light drain from the sky. Stared at the metal gates through which they'd passed. Barely acknowledging the guard as she gently touched his elbow and turned him towards a single-story red brick building. And he had been thrown back in time to the toilet block at his old Infants' school –

Kneeling on a puddled and slippery floor, his cheek jammed against the ridge of a stainless steel trough, staring into a round drain hole dammed by a partly-dissolved square blue urinal cake, ears ringing from the repeated blows to the side of his head, the smell of piss and disinfectant, the taste of blood –

The toilet block at his old Infants school … except for the barbed wire on the roof. The metal bars at the window.

That first time. Standing inside that single-story red brick building. He'd been uncuffed. Patted down again. Had his details noted and his photo taken. Then, he'd gone into a small curtained cubicle where he'd been made to remove his clothes. Lift his penis and testicles. Bend over and cough. Where he was given grey boxers, two grey t-shirts, a grey sweatshirt, grey track suit bottoms. And a pair of black plimsolls. Where he had watched his court clothes being put into a large, clear plastic bag by one of the guards. Had been issued with his ID.

Ryan slipped the card out of his pocket now. Stared down at a laminated surface which held a printed name, a date of birth, a pale, terrified face which he barely recognised as his own. And, partly obscured by his smudged and sweaty thumbprint, a prison number. He realised, maybe for the first time, that this is what he had become. What he was. All he was.

6

The back of Cat Russell's hand went automatically to her mouth as she found herself stifling her own yawn. Caught herself making *that noise* now. But that was the thing about yawns, once one person started yawning it was contagious. The action confirmation of just how monotonous the Job could be. Most annoyingly, it was corroboration of the other thing Laurence always said: that she *"had been working with Pearson so long that she had started to pick up his bad habit"*.

Christ, to think it was barely four months ago that her career had appeared to be hanging by a thread. Only four months ago that the death of a colleague, a supposed friend, whose body had been found in the shell of a burnt-out car on the seafront and her association with the man, Detective Inspector Sean Carragher, had left her career in the balance. Detective Chief Superintendent Andy Curtis had wanted her dismissed. Roberts had had to fight hard to keep her in the Force. Even now it seemed that, for some, for DCS Curtis at least, her professional reputation remained tainted. She had spent a long time agonising over whether she really wanted to carry on as a police officer. Eventually, after much soul-searching, she had decided to stay. Somehow, though, during those lengthy and tortuous deliberations she had managed to forget the grinding routine, the endless bloody paperwork that the job sometimes involved. Cat put the *Schedule of Unused Materials* to one side and riffled through the papers on her desk. Then she looked over at Pearson.

'Do you have the Post Mortem report?'

'No,' Pearson said, 'I thought I'd given it to you.'

'Well, I don't have it here.'

'Maybe I left it on the printer,' then pushing himself out of his chair, 'Hang on.'

Standing up, Pearson saw Peter Gilbert turn swiftly away. He had caught the young Detective Constable on more than one occasion mooning over Cat. Had given him a conspiratorial wink. Smiled to himself as Gilbert reddened. Shook his head as Gilbert, staring fixedly at his computer, did an unconvincing impression of it never having happened. Pearson crossed the room, noticing as he passed that Gilbert had a packet of menthol cigarettes and a disposable lighter ostentatiously on display on his desk. Maybe he thought that it made him seem more grown-up. More likely he hoped that he might someday pluck up the nerve to join Cat outside for a smoke. Pearson picked up the post mortem report from the printer.

'What are you smiling at?' Pearson, flicking through the pages, glanced up to see Wendy Simpson looking at him.

'Nothing,' Pearson shook his head, 'You're looking–'

'Knackered,' Simpson cut him off, 'is what I'm looking.'

She was, he had to admit, looking very tired, 'Baby not sleeping through yet?'

'No,' this time it was her turn to shake her head, 'we're lucky if we get a couple of hours a night.'

'I've got to admit,' Pearson said, 'I *was* surprised to see you back so soon.'

Simpson shrugged, 'I was getting a bit bored at home to tell the truth. Plus, there's the money to consider. You only get full pay for eighteen weeks. After that its Statutory Maternity Pay, which isn't really enough to live on. We couldn't afford for me *not* to come back to work really.'

Pearson knew for a fact that Ronnie, Simpson's husband, was a gambler. Worse, a loser. A low-life, 'Who's looking after . . . '

'Lily.'

'Lily,' Pearson nodded, 'Sorry. Someone did tell me.'

'Ronnie looks after her during the day. He's really taken to it. A proper homemaker he is. He does all the housework, the feeds, the nappy changing, you know ... I mean I love my baby, of course I do, but by the same token I need *something* to keep my brain ticking over . . . '

Across the room, Cat pretended she wasn't watching. Wasn't bothered by how Pearson and Wendy Simpson interacted. Wasn't interested to see if there was anything still between them. Didn't care if the rumours of them having had a 'thing' in the past might be true. By the time Pearson came back and dropped the post mortem report on her desk she was already busy looking busy. She made a show of indifference. Didn't look up, made a point of not catching his eye. Simply said instead, 'Thanks.'

She picked up the report and started to read . . .

Firefighters had been called to a blaze in a large Victorian property in Westcliff. The building, in common with houses of a similar size in the area, had been converted into a number of bedsits. A man's body had been recovered at the scene. As with most incidents of this nature, the most likely cause of death was originally assumed to have been 'smoke inhalation'. The death had been re-categorised as suspicious following the search of the premises when a laptop charger was found plugged into the mains, but no computer could be located; the initial line of enquiry being to treat the death as a possible 'burglary gone wrong'. That was, until the results of the *Examination by a Home Office Pathologist*.

Cat paused. Reflecting, once again, on how swiftly a brutal and callous murder could pass into the commonplace. How quickly, as a serving police officer, you could become inured to the horrific and sickening details of another's death. But was it only the repeated exposure to such events that left her feeling … well, nothing? Or was it the nature of the victim involved? When photographs are recovered from the deceased's flat containing graphic depictions of sexual abuse, wasn't it only human to find it difficult to have any sympathy? Only normal to feel a reluctance to investigate the case with the usual diligence and professionalism? To wonder whether the sick bastard might have had it coming. Cat glanced across

34

the desk, as if Pearson might be able to read her thoughts. Pearson, however, was covering his mouth with a hand. Stifling another yawn. Making a pretence of glancing over at the wall-clock, in reality though, Cat was sure, checking if she might have noticed. Concerned, no doubt, that there might be another sarky comment coming his way. This time, Cat let it pass.

The deceased was later identified through a DNA match as Clive Townsend. The thirty-eight-year-old former Senior Care Assistant at the Abigail Burnett Children's Home. A man who had been implicated in the sexual exploitation of the vulnerable, and in some cases under-age, residents. A man the police had been trying to find for some months. Though, as they had found during the Michael Morris case; alter your appearance, change your name, acquire a false identity through a passport or some other official documentation, and it was all too easy to disappear into the anonymity of bedsit-land.

Cat looked down again at the report. The body had been partially destroyed by the fire. However, this had failed to conceal a blunt force trauma to the skull. What appeared to be abrasions on the victim's wrists compatible with being restrained. And thirty-four anti-mortem puncture wounds consistent with sustained and deliberate torture.

7

Ryan Yates was still sitting on the same blue plastic mattress. Had been sitting for hours now. Sitting and waiting. Sitting and staring at the heavy metal door. The inset observation panel occasionally sliding to one side. A pair of eyes peering in from the gloom beyond. Sitting. And listening to the noises outside. The footsteps. The muffled conversations. The heavy doors clanging shut. Palms slapping against metal. The raised voices. The cursing. The whining. The wheedling . . .

That first day, there had been another room. The walls the same colour, or some minor variation on the same colour. A version of the same indeterminate shade of linoleum on the floor. That day Ryan had been sitting on another moulded orange plastic chair. Waiting to be processed with the other prisoners from the van. He'd been staring at the scuffed and faded lino when one of them had sidled over. Slumped into the chair next to his. Then leant over. Leant a little too close. Encroached a little too far into Ryan's personal space. Even from the corner of his eye Ryan instantly knew him for what he was. Recognised the gaunt features, the poor complexion, the decaying teeth. Had seen plenty of his type before. Seen them curled up on benches in shelters on the seafront. Seen them huddled on flattened-down cardboard boxes in shop doorways. Seen them on filthy sleeping bags in foul-smelling and dimly lit subways. A junkie. A 'bitty' in the Nick. The name for any user. Or ex-user, come to that. Because, whether they'd kicked the habit on the outside or not, a couple of weeks back in the Nick and they'd be using again.

'What're you in for?'

Ryan looked up. Noted the right-hand scratching unconsciously at the inside of the left elbow. The agitated bouncing of the left knee. The teeth. Not just bad, but completely missing on one side.

'Clark!'

Ryan looked past him, to the prison officer who, until now, had been leaning against the wall; bored, arms folded, eyes invisible under a peaked cap, beer-gut straining a short-sleeved blue shirt, a set of keys in a ziploc bag hanging from his belt, but had now seemingly taken an interest.

The other man followed his gaze, said, 'Yes, Mister Murray?'

'I've got my eye on you, laddie.'

'Yes, Mister Murray,' turning away, muttering under his breath, 'Fucking Jock.' Then, to Ryan, 'They tell you not to say anything, right?' Clark asked, 'Not to tell anyone any of your business? Only everyone always finds out. One of the guvs –' he nodded over at the screw, Murray, disinterested once again, his attention now elsewhere – 'will blab. Besides, if you don't say anything, everyone assumes you're a nonce anyway. It's only the nonces who won't say what they're in for . . . ' Clark stared into his face. Waited. And then pressed, 'Is that it? You a nonce?'

Ryan had to look away. Down again at the scored linoleum floor. Considering his options. What would actually happen if he did say what he was in for, would it give him an added kudos? Would the other prisoners leave him alone then? Would they give him a wide berth? He didn't think so. More than likely it would mark him out as a target for every would-be hard man in the Nick wanting to make an instant reputation for himself. When Ryan looked up again the other man's face was only inches from his. Ryan could feel Clark's breath on his cheek. Could smell the combination of festering digestive juices, crumbling enamel and cheap tobacco.

And … that first time, he'd made his first mistake. Had said, 'Nicking cars? Aggravated TWOCKING?'

'Yeah,' Clark said slowly. Nodding, 'that's the other thing all the nonces do. Ask any nonce what he's in for – ' still nodding, like he'd had his suspicions confirmed, like it all made sense now, ' – and they'll say some kind of motoring offence.' Clark's yellow eyes had searched Ryan's face then. As if he might read something there. As if his real crime, that of a 'kiddie-fiddler', might be written there for everyone to see. Then he'd sat back in his chair. Folded his arms across his chest. Nodded at him. A knowing smirk on his face, 'I know who you are. I've seen you in the papers. Ryan, right? Ryan Yates.' He let it hang there for a while. Waiting for a reaction. Waiting for Ryan to say something. And Ryan saying nothing told him all he needed to know.

'Listen,' Clark said, casting a look over his shoulder at the screw, shuffling a bit closer, 'you ever want a smoke … gear, y'know? Spice? You come to me, okay? I'll put you right. I've got some on me right now.' A wink. Another look back over his shoulder. Then nodding again. This time towards his lap, 'You just got to practise coughing,' Clark nudged him with a bony elbow, 'know what I mean? Nobody's looking too closely up another bloke's jacksy, right?' Clark attempted a smile. And failed. The half-smile, the half set of teeth, the half a mouth, only succeeding in making him look sly.

'A couple of weeks in here, and you'll be smoking it too, whatever you think now.' Seeing the look on Ryan's face he added, 'It's alright, it's in a plastic bag.' He left it a beat. Two. Then smiled again, 'Only joking. No point. You never know what Nick you're likely to be sent to and some of them have the BOSS chair. The Bodily Orifice Security Scanner? You've heard of that, right? The papers go on about people smuggling stuff in. The prisoners, visitors, all that. Or it's all about drones and all that shit. You know where all the stuff comes from? Drugs, phones, all that? I mean how you going to fit an *iPhone* up your bum, right? You know where it all comes from?' After a second or two. After he had waited for Ryan to say something and he hadn't, Clark said, 'It's the screws, right? Who else can come and go as they please? So, you just got to find the ones who don't mind doing you a favour – '

Mercifully, Clark had been interrupted by one of the prison officers calling them to order. They had been led out then. Out into the courtyard. Out into the rain. Walking single file behind the same fat, bored screw. Another screw at the rear of the line. Clark falling into step behind him. Walking too close. Talking. Forever-fucking-talking. Even then, Clark had been forever-fucking-talking, Ryan wishing he'd just shut the fuck up. 'You'll get used to it soon enough,' Clark was saying as they were led through two more gates and emerged into another courtyard, 'Not that much different from school, really.' But it wasn't much like any school Ryan had ever been to. Granted, there were tarmac football pitches. Some metal-framed gym equipment vaguely reminiscent of a climbing frame. But the buildings to the left, to the right, and directly in front all had bars at the windows and barbed wire on their roofs. They went through another set of massive metal gates and into the building at the end.

That first time, Ryan had stood in prison reception. At a hexagonal desk enclosed with plexiglass and flanked on either side by doorways to the wings of the prison. Had watched in disbelief as someone in an electric wheelchair had entered the doorway to the left, the wing for 'vulnerable prisoners'. Ryan had stood in line and asked to be put on medication. Explaining to another disinterested prison officer behind the glass that no, he wasn't actually on medication now. That the reason he wasn't on medication now was … well, he didn't really know why he wasn't on medication, but he thought that it was probably a good idea that he went on medication. That, no, he couldn't actually say exactly what medication it was that he wanted to go on. Watched as the screw wrote down his request on a form. Listened patiently as the screw told him that they couldn't prescribe any type of medication before he'd undergone a mental health assessment. That, no, he didn't know how long that might take or when, exactly, Ryan might get the medication. Had been reassured that it was all in hand, that all the details had been noted and would be passed onto the relevant people. Only to

41

find out later that the request had been lost. Or misplaced. Or mis-filed. In any case, not available, but if he could give them the details of the medication he wanted, that it would be noted down again and passed onto the relevant people in order that he could then be scheduled for an assessment by a mental health practitioner.

That first time Ryan had been led to the doorway on the right – *Induction and Remand.* Had waited for another eternity in another identical, featureless room to be led to … his cell.

During socialisation, '*Soash*', he'd gone onto the landing. Because? Because he hadn't known what else to do.

'Got any burn?' Clark had asked. Almost as soon as he'd left his cell. And when Ryan had looked blank, said nothing, Clark had said, '*Burn*? Baccy? Ciggies? Fags? It's called "*burn*" in here. You got any?'

'So, have you got any burn?' Clark had asked on the way to the Library. 'You must have *some* baccy,' Clark had said, as Ryan had left the Library. After being told that no, they didn't have any of the books and magazines he had looked for on the shelves. Why? Well, either because someone already had them out. Or, more likely, they just didn't have them. Because, to be honest, most of the people in the Nick, even those who might *want* to read a book, couldn't *actually* read that well. And yes, they might be able to order those particular books and magazines, but he'd have to fill out some forms. And no, they didn't know how long it might be before they arrived, or if they would come at all, whether they would even be deemed acceptable. 'Go on, do us a roll up,' Clark had badgered on the way back to his cell.

Until, that first time ... he'd made his second mistake. Finally caving in to Clark after he'd hung around on the landing. Just outside the open cell door. Asking repeatedly for a smoke. Clark just wouldn't fucking leave him alone. Wouldn't stop asking for burn. So, he'd made his second mistake. He'd given him one of his pre-made roll-ups. Then none of them would leave him alone. Wouldn't leave him alone all during socialisation. Wouldn't leave him alone, even after he'd asked one of the guvs to 'bang him up'. So, on that first day, on so many, many days afterwards, he'd laid in his cell. Laid on the thin blue plastic mattress on the metal frame bed. Listening. To the tapping on the cell door. The whining, 'Roll me a ciggy under the door ... ', the metal being slapped. The wheedling. 'Come on, I know you've got baccy ... ' The banging fists. The cursing. 'Slide a ciggy under the door, you fucker, or I'm gonna stripe you up next soash ... '

Ryan was back in the prison. On another thin blue plastic mattress. On a metal frame bed. Sitting. Looking around his cell. A cell measuring twelve foot by eight. The walls magnolia. Another lino floor which had once been blue. Or grey. The half-open sash window. Flaking and pitted black metal bars set into the sill beyond. A small desk on which stood a kettle and a portable telly. A porcelain sink with metal taps. A steel toilet with no seat. A mirror above and a flush button to one side. And that was it. But it was his. And his

43

alone. And if he asked one of the guvs to bang him up, he could lie on his bed and read a book, and no one would bother him. The one place that, after lights out, he could find some peace. A place he didn't have to share with another living soul. For the time being. Ryan fingered again the bandage on his wrist. Scratched at the stitches beneath. It wouldn't be that long though, he thought, before it would be decided that he was well enough to share with someone else . . .

8

Ruth Pearson glanced down momentarily, running a fingertip distractedly around the rim of her wine glass, and Pearson took the opportunity to study her face. She was looking much better, he thought. His wife. His soon-to-be-ex-wife. His *very* soon to be ex-wife, unless he was greatly mistaken. Her suggestion they meet for a meal had come totally out of the blue. It could only possibly be in order to discuss a divorce. For him, now he'd removed his wedding ring, that final, irrevocable separation had already moved that step nearer. Even in this light he could still see the ghost of its presence. The faint trace of an indentation. The parallel grooves cut into the flesh. The pallid skin and a definite sparseness of hair compared to that of his other fingers.

Ruth's hair, he noticed, was uniformly dark again. The traces of grey gone. Black dye applied to the pixie cut. A little mascara accentuating her large brown eyes. There was colour, too, in her cheeks. Even if it was artificial. But the very fact that she had bothered with make-up at all was a good sign. There had been a time when she wouldn't have left the house without at least a bit of mascara and lippy. And then there had been a time, too long a time, when she hadn't bothered with make-up at all. Hadn't been bothered with anything. Hadn't wanted to leave the house. Hadn't wanted to leave her bed most days. It had been those eyes that had first attracted him.

'Stop staring, Frank,' Ruth said, still gazing into her wine glass. Then looking up, making an effort at small talk, she asked, 'So, how's the boat coming along?'

In his mind, Pearson pictured the cabin cruiser. As it had been. Secured under a blue tarpaulin. Standing among the overgrown grass and litter blown onto his front drive, 'I flogged it.'

'Really? Why?'

Pearson made a face – a grimace, sort of, as if that might explain it all – and scratched and earlobe. 'It ended up being more of a burden than a hobby. I never seemed to find the time to work on it.' Not quite the whole truth. That had been part of it, admittedly. But mostly he'd needed the money. He'd been paying both the mortgage on the house and the rent on his flat. Despite the fact that his brother-in-law had moved in with Ruth. Terry Milton owned a club in town. But somehow, he always contrived to be skint. Worse than that, always seemed to owe somebody money. So, Pearson had carried on paying for the house. So that Ruth hadn't been upset. So that she hadn't had that, at least, to worry about. As a result, Pearson's savings, what savings he'd had, were all but gone now. So, he'd had to start selling off some of his possessions. And the relics of his many failed hobbies seemed the obvious place to start.

'Well,' Ruth said, 'you never were much of a handyman, Frank? I was the one who did all the stuff around the house, if you remember?'

Pearson winked at her, 'You know I've always thought of myself as more decorative than practical.' It was nice to see her smile again, he thought. It seemed to have been a very long time since he'd seen her smile.

The moment was interrupted by the arrival of their food. Pearson had opted for tapas. Because he hadn't had much of an appetite. Wasn't sure he'd be able to eat much of anything if his supposition proved to be true. Ruth had been happy to go along with his choice. They spent some time now transferring their food from the serving dishes onto their own plates. There had been an awkward moment when Pearson had wondered whether he should do this for her, wondered if he still had the right to do this for her, and had, finally, decided against it. They ate in silence for a while. Making only the occasional comment on the quality of the food, whether or not it was quite as good as they remembered. They had often eaten here. In the summer the restaurant, situated on the seafront, looked out onto the beach. Tonight, Pearson could make out little beyond the darkness of the plate-glass walls, other than the area of decking lit by the outside lamps, their dim reflection in the tidal pools of the mud flats, and the garish illumination of the distant pier. It wasn't until they had almost finished that Ruth, dabbing at her lips with a napkin, said,

'Sorry. I haven't asked how you are. After … your Mum. I haven't spoken to you since the funeral.'

Pearson reached for his drink, the half of Peroni he'd been nursing all night. He slowly took a mouthful, and then put the glass carefully back on the table, shrugging, 'Alright, I suppose.' Across the table, Ruth stared at him. Waiting for him to elaborate. Pearson cleared his throat, 'I'm supposed to feel some sort of grief, right?'

'And you don't?'

'Well,' Pearson looked down for a moment into his half-empty glass, 'not in that way. I feel sad, obviously. Melancholy. Down. All of that. But actual grief?' He shook his head, 'I dunno.'

'So,' Ruth said, 'you're feeling guilty about not feeling more?'

Pearson drained what remained of his beer, shrugged again, 'I suppose.'

'You can't make yourself feel something you don't, Frank. And, let's be honest, she wasn't the easiest of people to get along with.'

'You two used to get on,' Pearson said, nodding across the table, 'back in the day.'

'I suppose so,' Ruth admitted, 'till she took against me. For what, I've still got no idea.'

Pearson picked up his glass. Tipping it up, letting the last dribble of warm beer fall onto his tongue, before replacing the glass on the table, 'Did she ever say anything about my Dad?'

Ruth frowned. Thinking. Then, shaking her head, she said, 'Not that I recall. Where's all this coming from, Frank? You've never been that bothered about your Dad before.'

'So, she never said anything about Jack Morris?'

'Being your Dad?' Ruth asked. Clearly surprised. Pearson said nothing. 'So, let me get this straight,' Ruth said, 'you want to know if Jack Morris is your father? Is that it?'

'No,' Pearson said, 'I want to know that Jack Morris is *not* my father.'

'Whatever put *that* idea in your head?' And when Pearson again said nothing, 'Why don't you just ask him?'

'He wouldn't tell me,' Pearson said, 'Not the truth. He might *say* he was. Because that way he'd think he had something over me, that he might be able to take liberties. Or that he might be able to call on me for the odd favour. Or just to annoy me because he knows how much I'd hate it.'

Ruth finished her wine, 'You can't just look it up on the DNA database, I suppose? He must have done *something* dodgy.'

'Drink-driving. Lost his license.'

'Okay. And you'd be on there because you're a police officer, right? So, your DNA can be ruled out at a crime scene or whatever?'

'It's not that easy,' Pearson shook his head, 'there's all sorts of red tape. Plus, everything's audited,' Pearson sighed, 'Never mind, it was just a thought.' He nodded at her empty glass, 'D'you want another?'

'You going to have one?'

'Better not. But I'll have a coffee.'

'Alright,' Ruth said, 'I'll have a coffee as well.'

A few minutes later, frowning, absent-mindedly stirring her coffee, something clearly on her mind, Ruth cleared her throat, placed the spoon deliberately back into the saucer. Then looking directly at Pearson, she asked, not unkindly, 'I think it's time we got that divorce, Frank, don't you?'

Though he'd been expecting it, the words still hit him like a punch to the chest. He realised now that when he'd received the invitation, the phone call, some part of him – maybe only a small part – had been hoping that it might signal a reconciliation. Ruth picked up the coffee glass. Cupping it in both hands she took a sip and then said, 'I think it's time, Frank. If we left it to you, nothing would ever change.'

'Yeah,' Pearson reached for his own coffee, 'what is it you called me? "Saint-fucking-Francis-of-the lost-causes"?'

Ruth smiled, 'I *did* apologise.'

'I always thought that being pig-headed was one of my *better* qualities.'

'You're a good man, Frank. Too good for me–' She held up a hand to forestall any argument, '–Let's not have *that* conversation again. The trouble is, you mistake looking after people for love. You've gone through your entire life collecting waifs and strays.' She shook her head, 'Sorry.

That's not fair. I think we loved each other. Once. But it really is time to call it a day and move on.'

Pearson sipped his coffee. Then asked, 'So what do you want to do?'

'First, we need to sell the house. You can't possibly afford to keep paying the mortgage and the rent on your flat.' Coffee still cupped in both hands she took another sip, 'So let's sell the house. Split the money, straight down the middle.'

'Look, I can't be arsed with all that paperwork,' Pearson said, 'You do all the legal stuff. Just send me any papers that need signing ... and *you* keep any profit.' Before she could object, he went on, 'You're going to need a new start, right? A deposit on a flat? Plus, you're going to have to find yourself a job. You're going to need some money behind you for all that, right?'

Ruth was nodding her head now, 'I was thinking of going back to teaching English Literature.'

'Trying to get teenagers interested in books? Christ, and *I'm* the one who's fighting lost causes ... I'm only joking. It's a great idea,' And then, 'Look, sell the house and you keep whatever money you make. I've already got a job, a place to live ... you know it makes the most sense.'

Reluctantly she nodded, 'Okay. Thank you.'

Pearson stared past her. And at the reflection of himself in the black mirror of the plate glass window. Suddenly everything fell away, and all was clarity. He had a fleeting presentiment of some future darkness. A foreshadowing of some catastrophic event that had yet to occur. A feeling that he was somehow outside the restaurant looking in. Inside, seated at the tables, were the insubstantial and transparent ghosts of diners, all of whom seemed to be engaged in their own private and silent conversations of which he could never be a part–

' "The pier is Southend. Southend is the pier",' Ruth said.

'Eh?'

'John Betjeman,' Ruth said, 'nodding through the window, 'One of the trains on the pier – the old trains, you know the open ones? – was named after him.'

'Really?'

Ruth shook her head, 'Don't you know anything about the town you live in?'

Pearson, still slightly unnerved by his premonition, had something else on his mind. 'If we do sell the house,' he said, 'What happens to Terry?'

'Don't tell me you're worried about my brother?'

'No,' admitted Pearson, 'but obviously you will be.'

'Not really,' Ruth said, 'Let's just say … we've had words. And not just about you paying the mortgage. That was part of it. But there's been *other* things … like him not telling me he's up to his eyeballs in debt. Again. To be honest, I've had just about enough of him. So, we had some massive row. I haven't really seen that much of him since. I've heard he's had the rubbish cleared out from the flat above the club and all-but moved in . . . '

Terry Milton was hiding something. Pearson knew it. Had known it for a long time. He hadn't done anything about it, up until now, for fear of upsetting Ruth. But Ruth seemed a lot better, and if she and Terry weren't really talking, if they'd had a falling out ... then perhaps this was Pearson's opportunity to find out exactly *what* his brother-in-law was up to.

9

Terry Milton checked the rear-view mirror. Just in case anyone had seen him. Swinging the car – too quickly, at too-acute an angle – into the parking space; mounting the pavement, clipping a lamppost, bumping back down the kerb, colliding with the car in front. And finally coming to an abrupt, shuddering halt in the street outside the club. He was over the limit. Way over the limit. If he was breathalysed now, he'd lose his licence. He'd been drinking. Of course, he'd been drinking. He was always drinking. But sitting alone, with the bottle of single malt and a shot glass, in his wood-panelled office, he hadn't noticed quite how drunk he was. Sitting. And brooding. About just how unfair his fucking sister had been. Going on and on about Pearson paying the bloody mortgage. About how Terry must be 'doing alright for himself'. About how he had the club and he must be earning a decent living. About how he should be able, *eager* even, to pay the bills or at least contribute *something*. Going on and on. Until Terry had lost his rag. Told her that no, he wasn't 'doing alright for himself'. Far from it. That no, he couldn't afford to pay the fucking mortgage, didn't have the money to help with the bills. Didn't have *any* fucking money at all. That, in fact, he owed money. And he wanted to tell her then just what sort of trouble he was in. Tell her everything. And if she'd said that they should go to the police? Then, fine. He *would* have done it. He would have done whatever she'd said. Except that she wouldn't let him say any of it. Didn't want to listen. Didn't want to know. So, eventually, he'd just slammed the phone down. Then he'd sat in the office behind the club.

Brooding. And drinking. Getting angrier. Until finally he'd had enough. Had decided to take advantage of the fact that Ruth would be out. Had decided that he would go to the house and get his home cinema system. Not that he'd ever put it together in all the time he'd lived there. But fuck it, it *was* his, right? By the time he'd got to the house, though, he'd calmed down a bit. Alright, he'd still taken the home cinema stuff; the Blu ray player, the speakers, some of the other bits and pieces, but in the end, he'd decided to leave the flat-screen TV. Couldn't leave her without anything. Besides, it had been heavier than he'd thought. And awkward. Too awkward for him to carry to the car on his own –

The girl appeared, out of nowhere, suddenly present at the driver's side window, shouting, 'I know what you've been up to!' Banging on the car roof, trying the door handle, 'I know what you've been doing!' Rapping on the glass with her knuckles, pointing an accusatory finger at him, 'I know what you *are*!' Him, locking the doors. Shrinking away from the window. Her, screaming, 'Don't look away from me!' Scrabbling at the door handle again, 'Don't fucking ignore me!' Him, looking wildly around the street for any possibility of help. Her, banging her fist on the side window, 'I know what you *are*!' At the same time, him, not wanting anyone to see. Not wanting anyone to know. 'You dirty bastard! I know what you are!'

And so it went on. Her, battering the car roof, hammering on the side window, jabbing a finger, yanking at the door handle, yelling. For what seemed, to him, like hours.

Though, if he were honest, it was probably only a few minutes at the most. Those few minutes spent cowering inside the car. Terrified of someone who was little more than a girl. Waiting for it to stop. Waiting for her to go away. And then, as suddenly as it had started, it ended. And the girl was gone . . .

Terry sat behind the wheel of his car then. Staring wildly in turn; through the driver's side window, the front windscreen, the passenger side window, checking in the rear-view mirror. Then, panicking in case his view might be obscured in some way, twisting in his seat, craning his neck to stare out through the back of the car. Before starting the whole process over again. Finally, with an effort of will, clutching the steering wheel, his knuckles blanching, his heart racing, his breath coming in ragged gasps, he managed to stop himself. Not quite believing what had just happened. Again. After a minute, two, he released his grip on the wheel to run a meaty hand down a face dappled with cold sweat. He looked out now through the side window, and to the relative safety of the club. Still a good twenty yards away. Then glanced towards his jacket on the front passenger seat. Thinking about the phone in the inside breast pocket. A no-thrills pay-as-you-go containing only one stored number. The phone had been delivered by a courier. And almost as soon as he'd unpacked it, he'd received a call, been issued instructions. The mobile was to be used only once. In the event of it being used, it would be collected by a courier, who would issue him with a new phone. And the most important instruction of all, the one repeated slowly, and several times: the mobile phone was only to be used in the case of an absolute emergency.

Terry checked the street again. Looked out through the side window towards the club. Stared down at the jacket, the phone, on the front passenger seat: this *was* a fucking emergency, wasn't it?

10

Pearson had dropped Ruth off at the house, headed back to his own flat. Distracted. Tired. Still feeling slightly hollowed out from the conversation at the restaurant. He had pulled up outside his place in the Mondeo, opened the drivers' side door and got out, was leaning back in to retrieve his dark woollen overcoat from the front passenger seat when he heard the voice.

'Good evening, Detective Sergeant.'

A voice he recognised. Female. Cultured. Clipped. Unemotional. Pearson backed out and slammed the door. Turning to face the woman he knew only as 'Graham'. The operative of MI5 who had intervened a few months earlier to shut down two concurrent investigations being carried out by the Major Investigation Team. Her brown frizzy hair again pulled back from her face. The complexion a little paler, the freckling across her forehead a little less distinct than he recalled. Then again, it *was* winter. Her expression, though, was exactly as he remembered; composed, dispassionate, impassive. In their prior, though admittedly brief, acquaintance he had found her almost impossible to read. Despite the years spent in interview rooms. Probing for the lie. Watching for that negligible flicker of emotion, that slight hint of a reaction, the celebrated 'tell'. The garish orange nail varnish and lipstick she wore no mere affectation, he suspected, but rather an added distraction to conceal even the subtlest unguarded reflex. Even the striking violet eyes behind the steel-rimmed glasses, he supposed, might only be coloured contact lenses.

'Evening,' Pearson nodded a greeting. Casually scanning the street for any unfamiliar cars. She wouldn't have come alone. She would have protection of some sort. Ex-Special Services in all likelihood. No more than two, he guessed. Though, let's face it, one would probably be more than enough to incapacitate him.

'Before you ask for whatever it is you're going to ask for,' Pearson said, lifting a hand to his mouth to hide a stifled yawn, 'and that's obviously why you're here; some information you want, some favour you want doing, but something you, no doubt, want to distance yourself from ... I've got to warn you, I'm not sure that I'm particularly interested in helping out the Security Services. Given what happened with the Beverly Marsh case . . . '

When Graham said nothing, Pearson decided to take a shot in the dark. Now, *there* was an unfortunate turn of phrase, Pearson thought, for his subconscious to come up with, given the circumstances. He felt his scalp crawl. The physical manifestation of the imagined red dot, the laser-guided sight of a high-velocity rifle, as it tracked across the back of his skull, and he was unable to stop himself once again nervously surveying the street.

'That clothing we requested,' Pearson said, 'The clothes Beverly Marsh was wearing at the time she was killed? It seems to me that it was all a little too straightforward; we mention that they're missing, have been missing, in fact, for the best part of fifty years and within forty-eight hours they suddenly reappear. Just as, coincidentally, you said they would. We sent them to forensics for DNA testing, of course, and found *nothing*. But you already knew that, didn't you? You must have already had them tested yourselves. So, either there was nothing to find in the first place … or, and this is the more likely, they're *not* the clothes Beverly Marsh had on when she died.'

'Is that your price?' Graham asked, 'The answer to that question?'

'I'm not making any promises.'

Graham made a show – at least as much as she was capable of making a show – of considering the matter. Finally, she said, 'As an indication of good faith I will answer your question. The clothes are by the same manufacturer, and of a similar vintage and style as that worn by Beverly Marsh. But, no, it is not the actual clothing that she was wearing at the time of her death. And yes, of course, we had the original items tested. As a further show of good will, I *will* make a promise. You will receive the results of the forensic analysis carried out on the clothing of Beverly Marsh, Detective Sergeant, if that's what you really want.'

'How can I trust you?' Pearson asked, 'Why would you do that now? Why reveal the results now, when you were obviously so keen to keep them to yourselves before?'

'Let's just say … it serves our purpose.'

Pearson shot a cuff and checked his watch. Cast a glance at his front door, wondering if they'd been inside.

Were still inside now. Rifling through the bedside drawers, lifting the mattress and searching under the bed, going through the kitchen cupboards. Noting the unmade bed, the pile of dirty clothes in the corner of the bedroom, the unwashed plates stacked in the kitchen sink –

'There is,' Graham said, 'another matter I can help you with,' and when Pearson turned, once again, to face her, she said, 'The issue of your paternity? I know it's a matter you've considered yourself, whether or not a certain local businessman is your biological father?'

Pearson tried not to react. Tried not to register the shock he felt. Tried to arrange his face into something resembling indifference. But wasn't *quite* sure he'd managed it.

'But how, exactly, would you go about finding out?' Graham asked, 'A simple match of your DNA run against the DNA sample taken from Jack Morris when he was arrested for drink-driving, of course, could establish any familial connection. But I'm sure you've considered the implications, Detective Sergeant. You couldn't possibly justify an official request. By the same token, it would be difficult, if not impossible, to ask for a match off the record, even if you do know someone who owes you a favour. No, unfortunately, it's not quite that straightforward is it?' She waited a beat, then, 'For *you* that is.'

Pearson considered the offer. The two offers. Wasn't quite sure, even in his own mind, which of them held the most sway. In the end perhaps it was the combination of both that, as he suspected Graham had known they would, proved just *too* hard to resist. Pearson sighed, 'Okay. I'm listening.'

'Shall we walk?' Graham asked, 'It's getting a little chilly.'

Pearson shrugged on his overcoat, jammed his hands into his pockets and fell into step beside her.

'You have to understand, Detective Sergeant, that the days of the monolithic structures of state apparatus are all but over, even for the Russians. There are, as a result, certain agencies attached to the British Government –' she raised a palm, '– whose very existence, let alone the exact terms of reference under which they work and the scope of such work, obviously have to remain classified.'

'Agencies,' said Pearson, 'that can legitimately be denied to exist by the British Government?'

'Because,' said Graham, 'to all intents and purposes, nobody in the British Government – and we are, of course, talking only of the political aspect of Government here– '

'That part of Government that is directly accountable to the electorate you mean?' There *might* have been a faint change in her expression, the merest flicker of amusement at his naivety. Pearson almost had to laugh himself.

'In fact,' Graham continued, 'there are very few people at all who know of their existence. And, before you ask, no, they don't have names. If they had names, they could hardly be kept secret, now could they?'

Pearson examined the logic of Graham's argument. As soon as any department of government had a name, Pearson reasoned, it would, by necessity, be allocated a cost-centre code and an authorised budget. Immediately putting it under the supervision and scrutiny of the Treasury. And, by extension, any junior ministers or civil servants currently charged with implementing the sporadic attempts at cost-cutting in Whitehall. Any one of whom might just start asking awkward questions . . .

Pearson could not dispute the logic in the statement. The logic was unassailable. But it was the insane logic of the uncaring and faceless machinery of state. The kind of logic that had, in the past, made other people, 'ordinary' people, expendable, worthless. The kind of logic that had loaded people onto cattle trucks, had herded them into the showers, had reduced the act of genocide to calculations of efficiency and throughput.

'Budgetary restraint,' Graham said, 'value for money, competition, Sergeant Pearson. That's how Government is run these days. National security is no different. And because everything is assumed to work better with a little competition. Each agency is free to pursue its own particular interests, within certain strict fiscal obligations of course, in the belief that the most favourable outcome will be the inevitable result – '

'Your role,' Pearson broke in. Making a point of checking his watch, 'Has nothing to do with ensuring value for money though, has it? I'd say it's more like . . .

housekeeping? Your job is to come along after these various "agencies" and clear up their mess, right?'

'It's true to say that this same arrangement of separate agencies also allows a certain degree of . . . "latitude" . . . as to how results are obtained. Certain shortcuts might end up being taken, corners may end up being cut– '

'Yeah,' conceded Pearson sarcastically, 'I can see how that might happen.'

'This approach may also cause certain other . . . operational issues. The perception of pressure sometimes results in what might, on later reflection, come to be regarded as ill-advised or hasty decisions–'

'Or,' Pearson cut in again, 'as any normal person might see it, morally dubious judgements. As in the case of Michael Morris. That's what this is all about, isn't it? Let's not lose sight of the fact that one of these "ill-advised or hasty decisions", as you put it, resulted in the death of an actual human being.'

'That death, whether you choose to believe it or not,' Graham said, 'will continue to be a matter of deep regret. Nevertheless, the fact remains that Michael Morris died before he could find out anything. Or, at least, before he could pass on any information that he might have had to us.'

'And what, exactly, were you hoping to find?' And when Graham wouldn't answer, Pearson said, 'Okay, look, it's getting late. Let's try a different question: What *is* it that you want from me?'

'Just do your job, Detective Sergeant,' And then, 'Wherever it may take you.'

At some unseen signal, at least no signal that Pearson had noticed, a black car with tinted windows appeared as if from nowhere.

'There's someone involved in these parties, isn't there?' Pearson asked, 'a senior police officer ... someone high up in the Government ... or both?'

The front passenger door opened, and a man got out. Cropped sandy hair. Green eyes. A pale complexion. Hard. Athletic. Even under the jacket Pearson could see he was heavily muscled. He looked Pearson up and down, assessed the threat, dismissed it, and moved on. Checking up and down the street before opening the back door for Graham.

'One more thing,' Pearson said, 'as a "show of good faith?' Already half inside the car, Graham turned back. 'What's your given name?' Pearson asked, 'I presume you have a given name? You can't just be called "Graham".'

She gave it a few seconds thought. Calculating the risk inherent in such a disclosure. Then said, 'Geraldine.'

As Pearson watched the car leave, he allowed himself a half-smile.

DAY TWO

11

Picking up the pack of menthol cigarettes and disposable lighter, cupping his hands to hide the flame, he sparks up and takes in a lungful of smoke, then drops the packet and lighter back onto the top of the dashboard, his eyes never once leaving the view through the passenger side window. This morning he has been lucky. He has been able to claim a rare empty parking space. Gain a vantage point that affords a clear, unobstructed view of the buildings opposite. A row of large, semi-detached Victorian houses which have been converted into flats. He has allowed himself plenty of time. Time enough to fill the polystyrene take-away cup on the front passenger seat with dog-ends. He sits for a while then, as he has sat since the first cigarette smoked shivering in the chill of the pre-dawn: the fixed stare through the side window, the fierce draw on a filter-tip clamped between taut lips, the agitated flicking of ash into the makeshift ashtray, the irritable exhalation of smoke through his nostrils. Smoking. As the persistent drizzle of the night slowed and then gradually faded away. As damp leaves stirred in brief eddies of wind. Smoking. As bathroom lights snapped on behind frosted glass, as streetlights blinked out and a pallid morning seeped across the sky. Smoking. And waiting . . .

He ducks down now over the steering wheel and risks a glance through the front windscreen. Storm clouds are gathering, once again, on the horizon, threatening further rain. He is sure that no one has left the house but is still unable to stop himself checking the time on his phone. Looking up he sees, on cue, the front door open and Cat Russell step out onto the street. She is wearing her customary black trouser suit and white blouse. A mode of dress that is meant to convey that she is professional, capable, in command. He, of course, knows different. She takes an elastic hairband out of the side pocket of her jacket and twists it over her dark, shoulder-length hair. Arranges it into a loose ponytail. She scans the sky doubtfully, then looks past him and up the street. Headlights appear in the rear-view mirror, a dark blue Ford Mondeo drives past, then pulls up at the kerb. She opens the passenger door and gets in. Drawing angrily on his cigarette, he follows the progress of the car along the street, watches it stop at an intersection, the righthand indicator come on. Then the Mondeo turns right and disappears. Pinching out the cigarette and dropping it into the polystyrene cup, he starts the engine . . .

12

There was a tentative knock on the open door of the Incident Room, a clearing of a throat, then an uncertain female voice asked,

'Erm, I'm looking for a Detective Sergeant Pearson … or a Detective Constable Russell?'

Cat glanced up from her computer screen to see Pearson rising from his seat, quickly tucking in his shirt and straightening his tie, a soppy grin spreading across his face, 'That's us. How can we help?'

Cat's gaze shifted to the doorway. The woman was beautiful. This was a word, Cat had to admit, that she had seldom used in her life about another woman. Had seldom used in her life about *anything* at all come to that. But it was undeniable. She *was* 'beautiful'. Mixed race, her long elaborately arranged plaits were drawn severely back from a face with the sort of bone structure that meant she would remain extremely attractive well into her old age. Her most striking feature, however, was a pair of almond-shaped eyes of an extraordinary near-amber. Although she, in contrast to the vast majority of even moderately good-looking people in Cat's experience, seemed completely oblivious to just *how* stunning she looked. Hugging anxiously to her chest, instead, perhaps the biggest handbag Cat had ever seen.

As Pearson approached, she held out her hand, 'Detective Constable Campbell. Would it be possible to find somewhere a little more private?'

'Sorry about the mess,' Pearson said as the three of them entered the interview room and he turned on the lights. To see polystyrene cups, plastic sandwich containers, sweet wrappers and a blackened banana skin abandoned on the scuffed wooden table. He gathered the debris together and dumped the whole lot into the waste-paper basket.

'No problem,' Campbell said, 'it's just the same at our place. She set her heavy bag down on the floor and taking a small leather wallet out of her coat pocket, she removed two business cards and placed them on the table. Cat pulled up a chair and sat down, picking up one of the cards, reading: Fadziso Campbell. Detective Constable. Child Protection Unit.

'My family's from Zimbabwe originally,' Campbell said, 'my mother's family anyway, so she wanted me to have a Zimbabwean name. Fadziso roughly translates from the Shona as "one who brings happiness". I'm actually from South London. Peckham, born and bred. The Campbell's from my dad's side. About the only *decent* thing he left us, to tell you the truth. But something, for which, I am eternally grateful given the trouble people have pronouncing my mum's maiden name – sorry, I'm talking too much, it's always the same when I'm nervous – could talk the hind legs off a donkey, me.' She took off her coat, folded it and laid it on the table before sitting down, 'Everyone usually just calls me Fay.'

Fay Campbell took out a slim laptop from her bag and then began to fossick inside. 'Ridiculous isn't it?' she asked, catching Cat's amused expression, 'It's way too big. I can never find anything in the bloody thing. Honestly, the amount of old toot I keep in here … Ah, here we are,' she placed a DVD, a notepad and pen on the table in front of her. 'As part of my work in Child Protection, I've been assigned Courtney Woods?' She opened the lid of the laptop and pressed the power button. Then looking between Cat and Pearson, 'As I understand it, you were the ones who interviewed Courtney in connection with the death of Michael Morris?'

'Yeah,' Pearson said, scratching at an area of neck just behind his ear lobe, 'though "interviewed" might be stretching it a bit. Not much more than a quick chat, really. Obviously, as she was sixteen, she had to have an "appropriate adult" present. And by the time we'd arranged one it was fairly late, so we didn't really get much time to talk to her. Besides, given what she'd been through . . . '

'There's no problem with your interview with Courtney,' Campbell said. Looking between Cat and Pearson again, 'if that's what you're worried about.' She ejected the DVD drawer on the laptop and fitted the disc inside, 'I'm just checking I've got my facts right, that's all. So, when you spoke with Courtney, how did you find her?'

Before Pearson could answer, Cat decided to chip in with some thoughts of her own. '*I'd* say, that her version of the events surrounding Michael's death seemed fairly

73

muddled. There was something about her account that didn't quite ring true. And when we told her that Tony Blake had coughed to Michael's murder she seemed, I don't know . . . ' Cat shrugged, 'confused?'

Fay Campbell looked to Pearson for confirmation. 'Sounds about right,' Pearson conceded.

Campbell nodded, 'Pretty much how Courtney was with us, initially. And I'd have to agree with you,' looking at Cat, 'that her story was confused. It's like she'd been told what to say . . . '

'But couldn't quite remember it properly,' Cat said.

'Exactly. Thing is, though, now we've talked to her for a bit, gained her trust, she seems less certain than ever. Anyway, you'll see for yourself,' she indicated the laptop screen. 'I'll leave you the full set of interview DVD's before I go. This is just an extract, and it's probably the only bit that will be of interest, really. And, I'll warn you in advance, interviewing these kids can be a bit like pulling teeth. But we have to take it very slowly, y'know. A single word out of place and it can put you back weeks.' Campbell nudged the DVD drawer closed . . .

The camera had clearly been set high on one wall. They looked down at a room which had been carefully furnished in an effort to put any prospective interviewee at their ease. An oatmeal carpet. The walls a muted blue. Pastel-coloured scatter cushions on an overstuffed, mid-blue sofa. An abstract painting, of the kind you might buy in the household section of a DIY store, on the adjacent wall. Fay Campbell, her back to the camera, sat at an oblong, pine table. Placed discreetly at one end, the recording equipment. Opposite the camera, and barely recognisable as the same doughy-faced goth with back-combed hair and face piercings they had first encountered behind the counter of the '*Iniquity*' sex shop, sat a fresh-faced, and very, very young-looking Courtney Woods.

'What's wrong, Courtney?' Fay asked, 'You look worried.'

'I think I might be in trouble.'

'We've explained all that, Courtney. None of it was your fault.'

'No,' Courtney said, shaking her head, looking down. 'it's not about that. It's something else.'

'Would you like to tell me about it?'

Still looking down at the table, the girl cleared her throat, 'I've been lying.'

'Okay,' Fay said, 'who have you lied to?'

'The police,' Courtney shrugged, 'everyone.'

'Okay. Maybe you had a good reason to lie?'

The girl glanced up. Momentarily hopeful. Then her expression clouded, 'Even if I *have* got a good reason, I'll still be in trouble?' Dejected, she looked back down at the table.

'Well,' Fay coaxed, 'maybe you had a good reason, and that reason will be enough so that you won't be in trouble. Why don't you just tell me about it, and then we'll see, eh?'

Still looking down. Still uncertain, Courtney nodded.

'So … what was it you lied about?' Fay asked.

The girl shrugged again, 'Everything.'

On screen, Fay Campbell shifted in her seat, suppressing her impatience, a tightness evident in her shoulders.

'Okay,' she said slowly, 'so why *did* you lie? Did you do it so you didn't get in trouble? Had you done something bad you didn't want people to know about?' Courtney frowned. Like this *might* be true, but she wasn't quite convinced.

'Or maybe you lied to stop someone else getting in trouble?' Courtney shook her head. Positive. Certain, at least, on this point.

The Fay on the screen took a deep breath, 'Or,' she said, 'maybe someone *made* you lie? Is that it?' Courtney was still shaking her head. But she was less sure, less definite this time.

'Or someone *told* you to lie?' Courtney had stopped shaking her head. But was still looking down at the table. She swallowed. Licked dry lips.

Cat saw some of the tension leave the on-screen Fay's shoulders, 'Someone *asked* you to lie for them, is that it?' At last, Courtney nodded.

'Okay,' Fay said, 'so someone asked you to lie for them. To the police. To everyone. And now you're worried about it?' Courtney nodded again.

'Okay,' Fay said, 'so are you ready to tell me who asked you to lie for them, Courtney?' Biting her bottom lip, shoulders hunched, still looking down at the table, the girl nodded. There was a long pause, then Fay asked softly, 'Who was it, Courtney? Who asked you to lie for them?'

'Tony,' the word came as little more than a whisper. Then she looked up, cleared her throat, and repeated, 'Tony.'

'Tony?' Fay asked, 'Tony Blake?' And when the girl nodded again, 'And this is the same Tony Blake who was your boyfriend?'

'*Is* my boyfriend,' the girl insisted.

'Okay,' Fay said, '*is* your boyfriend. And this is the Tony Blake who is in prison now? Because he's confessed to, not only attempted armed robbery, but also the murder of Michael Morris?'

Courtney looked up briefly. About to dispute this fact. She blinked furiously. Then, avoiding Fay's eyes, her gaze flitting around the desktop, the box of paper tissues, the tape recorder, she looked down again. This time at her hands. The fingers of the right worrying at the nails of the left. Finally, defeated, she nodded again.

'Did Tony threaten you?' Fay asked, 'Were you scared of what he might do, Courtney? Is that why you lied for him? Because he's in prison now, and he *can't* hurt you.'

The girl did look up now. Said, 'No,' shook her head again. This shake emphatic. Unequivocal, 'Tony *loves* me. Tony wouldn't hurt me.'

Fay held up a palm in a calming gesture. Said, in a soothing voice, 'Okay, Courtney. Perhaps I've got it wrong? Look, I'm a little confused. Maybe you can explain it to me? Okay? So, you tell me, how *did* Tony ask you to lie for him?'

The girl expelled a deep breath. Adopted an angry expression, in that moment looking even younger – if that were possible – her expression that of a righteously-cross toddler. 'That's the thing. Tony confessing to Michael's murder. That's the thing he asked me to lie about. Tony came up with this story – that he was going to tell the police. And he said I was to tell everyone the same thing.'

'What story?' Fay asked.

'About Michael's murder. About how it happened. Where it happened. And it's all a lie.'

13

Easing apart the dusty slats of the venetian blind in his motel room, John Hall took a sip of tepid water from the scratched and fogged plastic cup; the slight whiff of chlorine, the definite metallic after-taste not totally persuasive that it was fit for human consumption. He stared out of the window, asking himself, once again, what the hell he was doing here. He'd spent the best part of the morning gazing out of this same window. Most of the day before, looking out at the same nondescript view. The tarmacked car park. The grass verge; overgrown and in need of cutting. The unruly privet hedge. The pot-holed slip road. He might have been in any motel in any part of the country. Only the occasional dull reverberation of aeroplane engines placed him near London Southend airport. He checked the time on his phone. Still not quite afternoon, but the light would soon fade from the dismal winter sky. The amber streetlights blinked into life.

'Sorry, love, I've got to attend another seminar. Five days in Central London. No getting out of it, I'm afraid.'

Or so he'd told Jean, his wife. There *had* been a seminar. Totally optional. A seminar that he had booked himself on. But had never had any intention of attending. Instead, he had left early in the morning and driven the two hundred or so miles without a break to arrive here around lunchtime of the previous day and booked into this cheap hotel. Before leaving his home in Durham, he'd had it all fixed in his mind, had it all planned out. But now he was actually here – *so close* – all of a sudden, he wasn't so sure.

So, he said, aloud, and not for the first time that day, 'John,' shaking his head, 'man,' sighing, 'what the fuck do you think you're playing at?'

The previous afternoon, before he'd even unpacked – not that he actually had that much to unpack – he'd sat next to his suitcase on the low, sagging bed and tapped out the text message, before he'd had time to consider the ramifications. Before he'd had time to change his mind.

He and Cat Russell had met again around two months ago. In hindsight, Hall thought, Cat had taken great care selecting the venue. Somewhere out in the open, but, at the same time, private enough for their conversation not to be overheard. He had made an effort to break the ice. To bridge the gap between them. To overcome the obvious reticence, the all-too-apparent awkwardness on Cat's part. He'd resisted the urge to do anything precipitative, anything that might seem like an advance. His inaction, he hoped, acting to assuage her doubts. Force *her* to make the first move, concede the ground. Finally, she had stepped towards him. But the resulting embrace had been pitifully clumsy. Disappointingly graceless. The intimacy they had once shared now patently absent. Then he had asked if she'd been —

'Eating?' Cat had asked. Immediately cutting him off. Immediately on the defensive. Insisting that she had. Though they had both known it was a lie. It had been exactly the wrong thing to say. Both of them aware of her past, of that particular history. Even then, though, he'd not been quite ready to let the matter drop, 'You look like you've lost weight to me.'

'How would you know?' she'd asked, 'You haven't seen me in . . . God, how long has it been?'

He'd made a thing of considering the question, then looked directly into her eyes. 'Seven years, two months and three days.' Adding, 'Not that anyone's counting.'

Though he'd done just that. Searched back through his old desk diaries. Marrying up the last time he'd seen her with the cases he'd been working on at the time. Calculating, to the day, exactly how long it had been. Anticipating this very situation. Knowing that, even if the subject didn't arise naturally, he'd still be able to work it into the conversation somewhere. They had walked for a while in silence until Cat, making an effort at small talk, had asked, 'So how is everything … everyone?'

He'd affected a shrug. 'Jean's much the same. Difficult, y'know?' Although 'difficult' wasn't the half of it. As if that one word could begin to describe the state of his marriage. The state of his marriage at that time at least. The fractious relationship with his wife. The constant rows, the prolonged silences, the times he'd found an excuse to work late, the nights he hadn't bothered to go home at all. Now, of course, his marriage was over. He was out on his ear. He'd made attending the course in London the excuse not to pack his bags there and then and move out.

For a while again, he and Cat had said nothing. Looking back, the whole exchange had seemed characterised by awkward pauses and long silences. What conversation there was, stilted and self-conscious. Cat had asked about the girls. And he'd said something about Samantha, something bland, something non-committal.

'And Elizabeth?' she'd asked.

He'd felt a stab of pain. Funny how just the mention of her name could do that to him. Still did that to him. Pain, at being away from home, from her. But relief too. At not having to deal with it all for just a little while. At not having to listen every evening, as soon as he'd set foot inside the front door, to a blow-by-blow replaying of his wife's day. Not having to hear about Elizabeth's tantrums, her silences. The third-hand accounts of her unruly behaviour at school. The constant rehashing of the trouble they'd had to get Elizabeth in there in the first place. The specialists they'd seen. The hoops they'd had to jump through. The fact that autism was so much harder to diagnose in girls than it was in boys. The expense. The drain on the family finances.

Later Cat had asked, and not for the first time, 'Why are you *here*? Why have you come all this way?'

He'd hadn't told her of course. Couldn't tell her. Not the whole reason, the *real* reason. But he had hoped their meeting might have resulted in a tiny seed sown. Hoped it might result in some degree of soul searching on Cat's part. Hoped, even, for a subsequent phone call or text message asking that they might meet again. But she hadn't made any contact at all in the two months since. So yesterday he had tried again. He let the slats of the blind fall back into place, took a sip of the lukewarm water. Looked down again at the phone. How long had he spent in the last twenty-four hours with the mobile in his hand? How many times had he stared at the screen willing it to show a reply? Finally, sighing, he began to thumb in another message . . .

14

Cat Russell, standing at a desolate and windswept corner of the building that overlooked the car park, felt the buzz of an incoming text on the mobile phone in her coat pocket. But chose, for the moment, to ignore it. Leaning forward instead, to light the cigarette of Fadziso Campbell. A few minutes earlier, as the meeting in the Interview Room had wound up and they all rose from their chairs, Cat had rummaged through her handbag, found her cigarettes and lighter, and shook them at Pearson, saying, 'I'm going to nip out for a fag. I'll see Fay out.'

On the way down the stairs Campbell had asked, 'Do you mind if I cadge a fag? I *am* supposed to be giving them up, but . . . '

Cat took a drag on her cigarette, then said, 'Tough job, Child Protection. I'm not sure I could do it.'

Fay Campbell put her own cigarette to her lips. Inhaled. Or made a show of inhaling, Cat thought. Because it wasn't a proper draw. Not the proper draw of the committed smoker, at any rate.

'It can be a bit harrowing at times, I suppose,' Campbell admitted, 'but it can also be really rewarding, y'know? There's a real sense of achievement when you make an arrest.'

'Yeah,' Cat sighed, 'The trouble with my job is, that even after you've made the arrest, sometimes it's hard to work out who the real victims are.'

'With us,' Campbell said, 'you know exactly who the victims are. But sometimes the victims don't know they're victims. Or they don't *think* of themselves as victims. If that makes sense?' She looked to Cat, who nodded.

'For some of them,' Campbell went on, 'the early teens, the thirteen- and fourteen-year-olds, even some of the older ones sometimes, I suppose,' she went through the motions of smoking the cigarette again, putting it to her lips, miming taking a pull, 'they can't understand that the men that have been exploiting them have actually done anything wrong. It's like *we're* the bad guys, y'know? Sounds crazy, right? But I suppose if you've come from a bad home environment, you're neglected, or even if you just feel you've always been ignored, and then you suddenly start getting a bit of attention – especially if it's from an older, more sophisticated, man – it's easy to feel like finally someone actually cares about you, y'know? At that age, I think it's easy to mistake that sort of thing for love.'

Involuntarily, Cat's hand went to the mobile in her coat pocket. She ran her fingers over it, as if she might somehow read the text it contained. They stood for a while in silence then. Campbell's cigarette held loosely between her fingers. She wasn't even making a pretence now, Cat noted, of smoking it.

'So,' Campbell said, 'what's *his* story?'

'Who?'

'Your partner,' half-smiling, Campbell turned to face her, 'Frank, is it?'

'Pearson,' Cat said.

Campbell bit her bottom lip, raised her eyebrows. Before asking, '*Pearson*, eh?'

'What?'

'Well,' Campbell said, 'Surnames … it's almost *more* intimate than calling him by his given name in a way. Don't you think? Sort of proprietorial? Or maybe you might be deliberately trying to create a bit of distance? Which is a bit of a give-away in itself . . . '

Cat, who had been staring down at the pavement, looked up to see Fadziso Campbell smiling broadly. God, even her teeth were perfect, 'So … *are* you and him?' Campbell asked.

'Me and Pearson? God no!' Catching Campbell's look. Curious. Amused, Cat shook her head, 'Honestly. I've never thought of him in *that* way.'

'Really?' Campbell asked. Genuinely surprised, 'I'd say your Frankie was a bit of a dish.'

Frankie? Dish? Cat smiled to herself. Not a term she would have used. And certainly not in connection with Pearson.

Campbell shrugged, 'I suppose I really go for that rumpled, careworn look. He's got lovely eyes, though. Don't you think? Sort of ... kind, y'know?'

'I suppose,' Cat said, 'but I have *honestly* never thought of him in that way. I mean, don't get me wrong, he's a decent bloke and everything . . . '

Campbell shook her head, 'Don't knock it, girl. In my experience decent blokes are a rare commodity. So, what? Is he married? Divorced? Or what?'

'Separated,' Cat said, 'But, as far as I can tell, soon to be divorced.'

'Mm, interesting,' Campbell regarded her unsmoked cigarette.

'You didn't really want that, did you?' Cat asked.

Smiling again, Campbell shook her head, 'No. Not really,' and then, 'Anyway, I'd better be getting on.' She looked around her.

'There's a bucket over there with sand in it,' Cat said nodding past her shoulder, 'you can put it in there.'

When Fay Campbell finally pulled out of the car park, giving a toot on the horn and waving out of the window, Cat raised a hand in acknowledgement. Then fumbled the phone out of her coat pocket to read the message.

'Apparently,' Pearson said, in the DCI's office a few minutes later, 'Courtney Woods has also changed her tune on Layla Gilchrist's involvement in all this. At the time – '

'At the time,' Roberts interrupted, 'she told us – told *you* – ' a nod towards Pearson, 'that these "parties" she attended with Michael Morris were nothing to do with Gilchrist.'

They were sitting once again in the moulded plastic visitors' chairs. Cat in her customary place by the window. Pearson on the left-hand side. The broken chair left empty between them. No offer of a mint today, Pearson noticed. Then again, he couldn't remember the last time he'd actually seen Roberts eating a mint. Extra strong or otherwise. Maybe, having weaned himself off cigarettes, he'd finally been able to give up the mints. Pearson missed those Polos.

'To be fair, Guv,' Cat said – a look of irritation passed briefly across the DCI's face, as if he was wondering exactly what "fair" had to do with anything – 'when we interviewed her, Courtney told us that they weren't really organised parties? "*Just, like, at people's houses*". Her words. And she flat-out denied, and more than once, that they were anything to do with Gilchrist. We had no option other than to take her at face value.'

'Alright,' Roberts sighed. Relenting. Albeit reluctantly. Scratching at a cheek. considering what they had told him. Then he said, 'The upshot being, that this now seems to cast doubt on Blake's confession.'

Even at the time, Cat had harboured reservations about Tony Blake's admission of the killing of Michael Morris and the subsequent disposing of the body. Pearson had over-ridden those doubts, posing the question: 'Why confess to a murder you didn't commit?' A question for which neither of them had really had an answer. He had seen Cat repeatedly glancing over as they'd sat with Fadziso Campbell watching the video recording of Courtney's interview. As if, for her, those concerns had at last been fully justified. For Pearson though, given the same circumstances, the same *evidence*, drawing on his long years of experience, and the lack of any contradictory forensic data, he would come to the same conclusion. But he acknowledged that he could have been wrong. That that decision could come back to bite them – bite *him* in particular – on the arse. And, more importantly, that that decision could have resulted in the conviction for murder of the wrong man.

'That's about it, really,' Pearson said, 'Courtney refused to say any more until she'd spoken to Tony Blake.'

'And where are we with that?' Roberts asked.

'Blake's put in a request to be transferred to HMP Parkhurst. Child Protection requested a meeting on Courtney's behalf with Blake through Force Liaison. But Blake refused permission for the visiting order.'

'Any reason given?'

Pearson shook his head, 'No. But Blake's not interested in talking to anyone. According to the Governor he's busy keeping his head down. A "model prisoner", by all accounts.'

'Okay,' Roberts nodded slowly, 'so Woods has admitted she lied about the circumstances of Michael Morris's death. And the actual location of where it occurred, right?'

'Guv,' Pearson nodded.

'But she hasn't denied that it was Blake who dumped Michael's body on the seafront?'

'Not as such,' Pearson said.

'So, in the meantime,' Roberts said, 'as you pointed out yourself, he's still guilty of "Obstructing a Coroner" or "Preventing the Burial of a Body".'

'Plus, he's coughed to Armed Robbery,' Pearson added.

'All of which means,' Roberts said, 'that there's no real reason for him to change his story. There's nothing in it for him,' Roberts sighed, '*None* of which has moved us forward much.'

'Child Protection are going to keep talking to Courtney,' Pearson said, 'see if they can get any more out of her about exactly what happened.'

Roberts sat back, put his hands behind his head, and closed his eyes. A minute later he opened his eyes again and leant forward, 'Any connection between all this and our friend Clive Townsend?'

'Not as yet,' Pearson admitted.

'Do you think there *is* a connection?' Cat asked.

'I sincerely fucking hope so,' Roberts said, wiping a hand down his face, 'Because if there isn't, that means we've got *two* paedophile rings operating on our patch.'

15

Pearson glanced up from his computer screen and was surprised to find that there were only three other people still in the Incident Room: Cat, Gilbert, and Wendy Simpson. Even Laurence had gone home. Pearson shot a cuff and checked his watch, then leant back in his chair. Counting the cost of the late night, and a day of relative inactivity. The arse ache, having not moved from his seat for the last few hours. The stiff shoulders, having hunched forward in front of his computer screen. The sore eyes. He squeezed them shut now and massaged the bridge of his nose between finger and thumb, his mind going back to the previous evening.

'Just do your job, Detective Sergeant,' an operative of the Security Services had said, 'Wherever it may take you.'

And less than twenty-four hours later an officer from the Child Protection Unit had played them a video recording of an interview. An interview which might now cast new light on a murder investigation. A murder investigation which, up until now, *had* seemed satisfactorily closed. This was the moment, Pearson knew, where, if he were the protagonist in a work of crime fiction, he would fix his partner with a meaningful stare, and proclaim unequivocally, 'There's no such thing as a coincidence!'

Of course, in real life, coincidences happened every day. It was usually only in retrospect that connections between discrete events acquired actual significance. And for a police officer there was an inherent danger in trying to impose a connection where one didn't actually exist.

'*Apophenia*,' Cat had pronounced, on a different day, during a different conversation, 'is the tendency to mistakenly perceive connections and meaning between unrelated things. It's actually associated with the early stages of schizophrenia . . . ' before trailing off when it became obvious to her that Pearson wasn't really paying attention.

In any case, like most real coppers, Pearson wasn't a great fan of crime fiction. Especially the sort you saw on television. It was always the same old cobblers. The detectives stupid, or corrupt, or both. The plot the same trite cat-and-mouse game played with a super-intelligent yet cold-blooded psychopath. In his experience, in the experience of most working coppers, death was generally fairly prosaic. Even murder could border on the mundane. The motives all too understandable: anger, greed, jealousy. The thing that really got him about TV crime dramas, though, was the representation of mental illness. In reality those who committed crime were rarely super-intelligent psychopaths, but more often the disturbed, the schizophrenic, the vulnerable. People who shouldn't be out on the street. People who should be in a safe and secure place, being looked after. The majority of the offenders he had come across in the course of his work, rather than cold-blooded monsters, were quite often as terrified as their victims.

On the other hand, it couldn't *really* just be a coincidence, could it? He couldn't really put the meeting with Graham and the subsequent visit by Fadziso Campbell entirely down to mere serendipity. And what Graham had said, '*Just do your job, Detective Sergeant. Wherever it may take you.*' Didn't that at least suggest that there was something relating to the death of Michael Morris that was worth looking into?

'I'm going to make a move,' Cat said. Bringing Pearson back to the present, 'I'll make my own way home. I've got a few things I need to do.' When Pearson looked over, Cat was already on her feet, her coat on.

'Am I picking you up in the morning?' Pearson asked.

Cat considered his offer, then shook her head, 'No, I'm good thanks. I'll drive myself in.'

'Fair enough. See you in the morning.'

At an adjacent desk, Gilbert, running a finger around his shirt collar, a vaguely perplexed look on his face, stared intently at his computer. But Pearson had seen – a fleeting movement from the corner of his eye – Gilbert turning quickly away from his contemplation of Cat and back to his screen. Pearson glanced past the young DC and over at Wendy Simpson. There had been something not quite right about her ever since she'd returned to work. Pearson decided to take his chance. He stood up and crossed the room. As he approached, Wendy Simpson flicked a nervous glance in his direction, entered a rapid flurry of keystrokes into her keyboard, swiftly shutting down her PC. But not quite quickly enough. And this wasn't the first time since her return to work that he'd caught her doing it. Busying herself with tidying away some paperwork, Wendy Simpson tried to ignore him. But Pearson could see that her hands were trembling. Deliberately shielding her from Gilbert, Pearson leant forward on her desk. And saw her flinch. He noticed, close up, just how exhausted she looked. Noted the black rings under her eyes, the blouse with a high neck and long sleeves. Not for the first time, it crossed his mind that her low-life husband might be knocking her around.

'Wendy,' Pearson said quietly, 'I think we need to have a word, don't you?'

'I'm late, Frank,' she said. Panic flaring briefly in her eyes, 'I really should be getting home.' Getting up, she tried to brush past him. But Pearson put a hand lightly on her forearm and barred her way. Almost immediately she burst into tears. He put his arms around her and, glancing over her shoulder, he saw Gilbert looking over. Having switched off his PC, he was half on to his feet, shrugging on his jacket, holding his packet of cigarettes and disposable lighter in his hand. Pearson mouthed, '*Hormones*,' and waited until Gilbert, too, had left the room. Then he took Wendy Simpson gently by the shoulders and held her away from him. Looking down at her he asked, 'What's all this about, Wendy? Why are you back? The real reason, I mean. It's not really because you're bored at home is it? What's really going on?'

Eyes wide, tears running down her face. She produced a tissue from somewhere – how did women do that? – and dabbed at her nose. 'C'mon, Wendy,' Pearson coaxed, 'you can tell me.'

Simpson swallowed. Seemed to come to a decision. Or just gave up. 'Ronnie owes money? At least, he owed money. And he can't pay it back? He's promised he'll stop gambling, promised on the baby's life, but he's run up some big debts and what with the baby and everything . . .'

'That's not the only reason you're back, is it?' Pearson asked, 'It's not just the money?'

Simpson said nothing. She swallowed deeply again. Then cut her eyes away, 'Ronnie said that the people he owes told him the debt would be written off in return for information? He said they'd come to him and tell him what they wanted and then I just had to pass it on . . . '

'And?'

'I haven't done it, Frank.' She shook her head, 'Not yet. I just couldn't bring myself to do it. You know I love my job,' she turned to him now, appeal in her eyes, 'I don't want to do it, Frank. But I don't know what else to do . . . '

'How much does Ronnie owe?'

Simpson shook her head again, 'I don't know exactly. Eight thousand maybe?' She put the tissue to her nose again. Her eyes red, her face blotchy. Then looking down, her voice small, she asked, 'What are you going to do, Frank?'

What he *should* do, what he *wanted* to do, was to go round her house, give her good-for-fucking-nothing husband a slap. She sighed. 'I'll resign. I'm going to lose my job anyway.' She blinked. 'Oh God, I'll probably go to prison.'

'You'll do nothing of the sort,' Pearson said, 'Nothing's happened. Not yet. So, no harm done. Right?'

She looked confused. Not quite capable of taking it all in.

'Why don't you just let me sort it all out?' Pearson asked.

'I don't know if you can, Frank. It's all such a mess.'

'Well, let me give it a try, eh?'

And when Wendy Simpson nodded, he said, 'So, tell me who it is Ronnie owes the money to. And what information they've asked you to pass on.'

16

That morning, Ryan Yates had been jerked violently awake. Roused again from a dream of another, better, place by the sound of shouting. Bells being leant on by insistent thumbs. Palms slapping, fists banging on metal cell doors. To the clamour of raised voices. Persistent. Foul mouthed. Demanding. He had lain for a bit. The wing suddenly quiet. Not sure whether the noise had been part of his dream or not. Thinking that the previous day had started like this. Realising that *every* day, from now on, would start like this. Every day, from now on, would follow the same course . . .

At eight o'clock Ryan had taken his plastic plate and cup and queued for his breakfast. Given his prison number to the trustee on kitchen duty. Billy. Some old boy with shaky hands like he had the beginning of Parkinson's or something, watching as he ticked it off against the weekly order form. Almost as soon as Ryan had started to queue, Clark had fallen into step behind him. Appearing from nowhere. Standing too close. His foetid breath on Ryan's neck. Talking into his ear.

'I hear you're getting a new cell-mate today. Probably put you in with some psycho, being as what you're in for. Or some kind of kiddie-fiddler, as that's what most people have got you down as. Could be anyone, really. They don't do any vetting. As such. Be a smoker, though. They'll make sure of that. Being as you smoke. Wouldn't want to go against someone's, like, human rights, right?'

At twelve o'clock Ryan had taken his plastic plate and cup and queued for his lunch. Giving his prison number to Billy, watching as he ticked it off. Shuffling along to the serving hatch where he was given what they *insisted* was *Chilli con Carne*. Whatever you ordered, whether it was *Chilli con Carne*, or *Spaghetti Bolognese*, or Jacket Potato, or whatever, it was always best to check what it actually *was* you had been given. Because it looked, and tasted, nothing like whatever it was claiming to be. It was like it had been cooked by someone who'd never clapped eyes on the real thing. Like the only aspiration of the prison kitchen was to provide the kind of food you'd get at some deprived inner-city school. But even to achieve this modest ambition, the budget of less than two quid per prisoner per day would probably have to be doubled. Or quadrupled. Clark had been there again. Standing too close. His cock – 'I usually go commando after a few days, you've never got enough boxers, y'know? It's either that or dirty underwear' – negligently brushing his buttocks. Ryan had felt it, through two layers of trackies, and his own boxers. Clark talking again into his ear. Clark was forever-fucking-talking. He'd been talking on the day they entered the Nick. Talking when Ryan had re-entered the wing after being in the hospital. Talking at breakfast. Talking at lunch. Would be talking when they queued for their next meal at five o'clock.

Ryan had eaten alone in his cell. Washing his plastic plate and cutlery in the sink. Rinsing the knife and fork in a feeble stream of water that smelled of bleach. Jamming the plate under the set of small taps and drying it on some bog paper. Carefully pulling off a few squares. Using it sparingly because you only got one toilet roll a week.

He'd tried again to get a picture on the portable telly. But could only manage a grainy, shadowy notion of reception, and that only on the three main terrestrial channels. Finally, he'd given up and tried once again at the pharmacy for his medication. It had become a daily ritual. Turning up at the pharmacy uninvited. Standing in front of the little window. Some days, most days, he would be told by one of the people behind the counter, one of the people in red scrubs, that his name wasn't on the list. His protests ignored. Stared *through*. Like he didn't exist. Out-waited. Until … until he simply got the message and fucked off. Or until the person behind him in the queue got pissed off and shoved him out of the way. On the odd occasion he *was* asked what he wanted; he couldn't properly recall. Would stand for a while, his mind a blank. Then he would be asked, 'What's your number?' and then it would be checked against the sheet of paper on the clipboard and the response would always be, 'You're not down here. I can't give you anything if you're not down here.' And when Ryan said nothing, they would say, 'All I can do is make a note you asked for it. Okay? You need to have an assessment? By one of the Mental Health team? Have you had an assessment?' And Ryan would say he had, or thought he had; he'd talked to someone, some psychiatrist or psychologist or whatever. He'd filled in some forms. He thought. Yesterday, or the day before … And then they'd take a form from a pile in a basket on another counter and say, 'We'll need to check with your GP. You know the name and address of your GP?'

And then they'd ask more questions. No, he didn't know exactly what it was he wanted. No, he didn't know what they might be for. No, he couldn't remember when he'd last

101

taken any form of medication. Whether he'd ever taken any form of medication. And on and on . . .

And he'd stand at the counter and watch whichever one of them it was, whichever one of them it was today who was dressed in red scrubs, watch them fill in the form. Watch them put it to one side. Listen carefully, as he was told it would be passed onto the relevant people. Stand there, until finally, *They* would look through him, like he wasn't there, and wait for him to leave. And that was exactly how it had gone today. And, all the time, Clark: hovering at his shoulder, jabbering into his ear, taking an interest in his business, taking too much fucking interest in his business for Ryan's liking. Saying, as Ryan finally gave up and turned away,

'You're going to be moved after the evening meal, so I've heard.'

He'd gone to the library. Because it was the one place Clark wouldn't follow him. The one place he could get away from Clark trying to ponce a roll-up, Clark constantly asking for burn. If he was such a player, the self-styled 'Spice King' of the landing as he'd insisted on the first day, how come he never had any baccy? But then there were plenty like him inside. People who didn't mind hounding everyone for burn. So, they didn't use up their own baccy. So, they could think they'd gotten one over on someone else. Could chalk up a small victory. And Clark wasn't any kind of player. Sure, he went in and out of the Nick on a regular basis, just like he said. But he was just one of those blokes who couldn't quite hack it on the outside. One of those blokes who depended on the routine, the security of life inside. Ryan had asked at the

102

library about the books and magazines he'd ordered. Was told they weren't in yet and no, they didn't know for sure whether they were coming in, whether they had been passed as 'appropriate'. So, Ryan had left. Having to content himself with whatever he could find on the shelves. A couple of books deemed suitable for 'young adults'.

He had been lying on his bed after the evening meal, reading his book. Or trying to. He wasn't enjoying it much – something with wizards and dragons – and he wasn't really taking it In, when the cell door was unlocked.

'Yates? C'mon, you're moving to a new cell. Get your gear together.' Murray. Ryan didn't like him. Didn't trust him. Not that you could really trust any of the screws, but there was something about Murray in particular. The word was, he was bent. If you wanted anything, and that meant *anything*, Murray was the man to ask. Ryan had put his personal belongings in a pillowcase, bundled up his clothes, blankets and pillow and followed Murray along the landing. Now, Ryan stood hesitating at the threshold of his new cell. Not quite believing what he was seeing . . .

Clark sat on the upper of the two bunks rolling a cigarette. Legs swinging to a tune he was humming under his breath. Affecting an air of casual superiority. He looked up and said,

'Did a swap with your prospective cell mate. Cost me an ounce of baccy. No point in going through official channels. You know what it's like, the paperwork only gets lost. Best to just do it. Tell the screws later.' Clark gave Ryan his half-smile, 'Couldn't have my mate bunking up with some

103

nutter or nonce, could I?' He gave Ryan a conspiratorial wink, 'This is going to be *fun*, isn't it?'

17

Pearson was sitting in the back of Jack Morris's Roller. Morris had aged visibly, Pearson noted, in the short time since the funeral. He looked even more frail, the skin that much greyer, the scar on his neck even more livid, the eyes sunk deeper into the sockets. And there was a pronounced droop to the left side of his face as if he might have suffered a minor stroke.

'There's a guy owes you money . . . ' Pearson began.

'This is Ronnie Simpson, right?' Morris asked.

Pearson nodded, 'Yeah. How d'you know it was him?'

'I don't usually give credit,' Morris said, 'Apparently, this Simpson knows the manager – ex-manager now, by the way – of one of my betting shops. Soppy cunt lets him run up a huge bill. Knows he can't possibly pay it back. D'you know, of all the people I employ, there's only one of 'em I can trust. One.'

Pearson ignored him. Cleared his throat, 'What are the chances of you writing that eight grand off?'

For a second Pearson thought he saw a look of confusion pass briefly across the old man's face. But the light was poor. He couldn't be certain. Morris took a slim, gold lighter and a packet of Marlboro out of his coat. He slid out a fag and lit up. Gazing out of the window, he took a drag on his cigarette, considering. Then he turned back to Pearson, 'Why should I do that? What's this bloke to you?'

Pearson shrugged. 'Him? Nothing. But his missus is a decent woman. It's not her fault she's hooked up with a complete waster. *She* deserves better.'

'Right,' Morris said. Unimpressed. 'And who's she?'

'Works at the Nick. Team Analyst.'

Morris looked out of the window again. Sniffed, 'Goes against the grain, letting some toe rag get away with owing me money.'

'C'mon, Jack, What's eight grand to you?'

'Eight grand? Nothing,' Morris admitted, looking back at him, 'but It's a question of reputation. You know that.' Seeing the look on Pearson's face, he sighed, 'Can I at least arrange for him to get a doing?'

Pearson mulled it over for a moment. Perhaps Ronnie Simpson deserved a doing. After all, he'd seriously considered giving him a doing himself. Reluctantly, he said, 'No. It's between them two.'

Morris took a deep draw on his cigarette. And immediately had a coughing fit. While he was taking a handkerchief out of his coat pocket and dabbing his lips, Pearson pondered what Wendy Simpson had told him.

'So, the Abigail Burnett?' he asked, 'What's your interest in that?'

'The Abigail Burnett?' Morris asked, 'That's that children's home that closed down, right? All sorts of rumours about kiddie-fiddling and the like, wasn't there?'

Momentarily, Pearson was at a complete loss. Then he was pissed off, 'What the fuck's going on, Jack?'

Morris smiled. Took a final drag from his cigarette and leaned forward to grind it out in the ashtray, 'Thing is, son,' inwardly Pearson winced, 'it's not my debt anymore. I sold it on. And, for your information, it was only just over five grand Simpson owed me.'

'Why sell it on?'

'Listen,' Morris said, 'it's more trouble than it's worth, all that business. Chasing debts. Besides, since your Mum, and Mikey ... Michael . . . ' Despite himself, Pearson felt a sudden sympathy for the old man. How did you get over the loss of a child? How did you come to terms with outliving them, no matter how old they were? Especially if you lost that child as a result of murder. 'What's the point?' Morris shrugged again, 'I've had enough, Frank, that's all.'

'I'd heard you'd bought into a club in town.'

'Then you heard wrong,' Morris shook his head, 'Whoever it is, it's not me. I'm trying to sell up.'

'Okay,' Pearson said, 'so getting back to this debt.'

'Like I said, there's not a chance Ronnie Simpson's going to ever pay it back, right? So, if someone comes along

107

and offers to take it off your hands for an extra grand and a half, cash, you take it.'

'And who *was this "someone"?*'

'No idea. Never seen him before.'

'And he just turns up out of the blue and offers you six and a half grand for this debt?'

'I got a phone call,' Morris said, 'If you want to sell the debt on, we're offering six and a half grand. All you've got to do is give us a note signing it over.'

'So where did you meet?' Pearson asked, 'Not at one of your places, I take it?'

'Nah,' Morris shook his head again, 'Do you know the car park at the end of Ness Road?'

Pearson nodded. He knew that particular car park only too well.

'Okay,' Morris said, 'so it's like this … I pull up in the Roller and there's a bloke already parked up on a motorbike. He walks over and taps on the window. I lower the window; he hands in the envelope. I check the money's all there and hand over the note. And that's it.'

'Some bloke you'd never recognise again. Right?'

'I told you, he was on a motorbike. He had a crash helmet on –'

'Visor up? Or visor down?'

'Well,' Morris said, 'visor up, but it was dark. And you know how it is. You make a point of *not* looking too closely.'

'He must have said something,' Pearson said, 'Asked your name? Checked you were the right person?'

'S'pose.'

'So? Anything distinctive about his voice?'

'Like what?'

'Speech impediment, maybe? Accent?'

'He only said a couple of words –'

'Take a punt.'

Morris thought for a few seconds, 'A Jock, maybe?'

'Scottish?'

'Maybe,' Morris hedged.

'Anything else?'

Morris gazed out of the side window for a minute. Then he turned back, 'Remember I told you that I only had one decent, trustworthy geezer working for me?'

'What about it?'

'Well, he's ex-army, right? There's something about someone who's been in the Forces … a certain look … the way they hold themselves . . . ' Morris shrugged again,

'Dunno … just *something*. And this is from behind, as he's walking off? But this guy had sort of the same look about him.'

18

Daryl Crawford turned from the open wall safe and looked out towards the front of the *Double Carpet* betting shop. To where, a second or so earlier, there had been an urgent rapping on the reinforced glass door. To where a dark outline now stood silhouetted against the orange glow of the streetlamps outside. He had guessed it might come to this. Ever since that front-page article in the local newspaper; a sketchy account of the events, a few stock quotes purporting to come from an interview he'd never given, a fuzzy photograph of him in uniform under the unimaginative headline 'Army hero foils armed raider'. But he'd known for a certainty, once the story had been picked up and broadcast in a five-minute slot on a regional BBC news programme.

Daryl retrieved the two canvas bags containing the day's takings from his desk and put them into the safe. His actions slow. Calm. Deliberate. Hero. Then again, there were few enough black officers in the Army, he supposed. There was bound to be a fuss made about it. Let alone any who had actually earned the award for 'Conspicuous Gallantry'. The honour that betrayed his dishonour, the distinction that exposed him as a fraud, the decoration that bore witness to his failure. By the time he'd returned home the empathy, the patriotism initially engendered in the general public by the conflict had all but disappeared. The respectful crowds that had once lined the streets of Wootton Bassett to mark the passage of the fallen were already a distant memory. Even then, at least for him, there had been only a gradual realisation that the war had all but faded from the national consciousness. Until the commemoration of 'Armed Forces Day' in the high street. He'd returned from the excruciating and embarrassing non-event and consigned the medal, along with all his other military memorabilia, to an old shoebox that he'd then buried at the back of a high shelf in the wardrobe. The robbery, the attempted robbery, had left him badly shaken. Not because the robbery itself had been frightening. But rather because he had been shocked by his own actions. How close he had come to losing control. Having quickly wrestled the sawn-off shotgun from the robber's grasp, he had turned it on him. And had been only a split-second, a twitch of a clammy finger on a slippery trigger, from blowing the man's head off –

Daryl's thoughts were interrupted by more insistent rapping on the glass front door. This time the situation might not be so easily controlled. The man outside was more volatile, more dangerous. The course of events would be less easy to predict. The outcome less certain. Daryl took his coat down from the peg on the wall and put it on. He took one last look in the safe, at the objects inside, before shutting the door and resetting the combination lock. Only then did he make his way through the darkened shop, turn the lock on the front door, swing it open and take a step back.

'Boss,' the man, a dark outline against the street lighting, a face half in shadow, nodded a greeting. There had always been something in the cocksure quality of Danny Fraser's Glaswegian accent that was close to impertinence. Something in the one-time Lance Corporal's manner that had bordered on insubordination. But had Daryl sensed an extra hint of disrespect in that brief movement? Detected an added incivility in that single word?

'Danny,' Daryl took another step backwards, indicated with a movement of his head that he should come in, 'I was just off home.' Trying not to make it too obvious that he didn't want him here. That Danny Fraser, in fact, was probably the last person he wanted to see.

'I'm sorry, Danny,' Daryl said, 'I can't offer you a brew, mate. I'm clean out of milk.' A lie. But a reasonable enough excuse not to invite him through to the back office. Not to allow him to get too comfortable.

Fraser took in the betting shop. Lit now only by the single overhead strip light Daryl had left on in the office. The narrow, melamine counter fixed around the edge of the room. The high stools bolted into the linoleum floor. The days' runners and riders fixed behind perspex sheets on the walls. The mute slot machines. The banks of blank television monitors.

'So,' Fraser said, 'is this your place?'

Daryl shook his head, 'I'm just the manager. And I'm only *that* because the last one got the bullet for giving credit to his low-life mates. I'd been working here part-time, so the owner offered me the job. Because I'm ex-services. Or so he claimed. Probably just couldn't be arsed to interview anyone else.'

'I saw the report on the telly.' Fraser cut in, 'Looked up the newspaper article in the library.'

'Not my doing, Danny. All that war hero shit.'

'Aye, well . . . '

'I've got a partner now, Danny.' Daryl said, 'Tracy. A few years younger than me. We're expecting our first kid . . .'

For a moment, neither spoke. Daryl studied the other man properly for the first time. Outwardly, at least, he looked smart. His hair short. His clothes; the black leather coat, the loose-fitting grey crew neck jumper, the black jeans, all looked newly laundered. The Doc Marten shoes recently polished.

'So, did you go back into the building game, Danny?'

'Nah,' Fraser said. 'Had the offer. The old man died recently of stomach cancer, and my older brother – Jackie? – well,' he shrugged, 'let's just say he's never been that interested in the nine to five. So, there was the opportunity to take over the construction side of the family business. Before I joined up, I did some plumbing, a bit of bricklaying, but that's about it. Not what you would even call a proper apprenticeship. Nothing that would qualify me to be in charge of major building projects, that's for sure,' he shook his head. 'Out on some site or other with a bunch of sub-contractors who know full well I haven't got a fucking clue what I'm doing? Having them all take the piss? Over-estimating the cost of a job, booking hours they hadn't done, ripping me off for materials,' Fraser shook his head again, 'Nah. I decided it wasn't for me.'

Danny Fraser turned to him then. And the confidence, the cockiness Daryl had imagined only a few minutes ago was absent, 'Do you ever think about it, Boss?' And then, as if he had to clarify the statement. As if he might have ever meant anything else, 'The war?'

'It's ancient history now, Danny.' Daryl shook his head, 'I make a conscious effort *not* to think about it.'

'Aye,' Fraser said, 'So do I. And I've been fairly successful,' Another pause. Shorter this time, then, 'If you don't count the odd daytime flashback. The occasional panic attack caused by any sudden loud noise, the nights I've woken screaming from a nightmare . . . '

Or, Daryl thought, those unexpected and overwhelming rages that take even you by surprise. The latest of which had nearly, nearly, resulted in him blowing a man's head clean off with a sawn-off shotgun.

'But something like that . . . ' Fraser said, 'changes you, right? It's got to change you, hasn't it? It would change *anyone,* wouldn't it? Any normal person anyway.'

And there, in the almost-dark, the amber streetlights reflected in Danny's red-rimmed eyes, Daryl thought he could see the ghost of something burning; the licking of flames, plumes of black, oily smoke drifting across the dark night of the other man's pupils.

'There's people you can speak to, Danny,' Daryl said. Though he'd never spoken to any himself. Would never speak to anyone himself, 'Experts in the effects of combat stress …

Post Traumatic Stress Disorder . . . proper counsellors, y'know?'

'Aye,' Fraser nodded, 'But the thing is, Boss . . . ' He frowned. Shook his head, 'It's all of it,' and then again, 'It's all of it.' Reaching into the side pocket of his jacket and taking out a pack of menthol cigarettes and a disposable lighter, he offered the open packet to Daryl.

Crawford shook his head, 'Nah, you're alright. I've packed it in.'

'It's not just the things I've done in the past,' Fraser said. Putting a cigarette in his mouth with shaking fingers, 'All that . . . *stuff* I did when I was younger.' Sparking up. Cupping his hands around the flame. Taking a long drag on the cigarette, 'All the things I did before I joined up.' Exhaling a plume of smoke through his nostrils, 'the ... stuff that happened that meant I *had* to join up.' His eyes searching the floor between his feet, 'It's not even all the stuff that happened in Afghanistan.' Looking back up at Daryl, his brow furrowing, his fingers kneading his temples, 'All that *bad* shit . . . '

19

The view, like that through the dispassionate perspective of a camera lens, is of a footpath between mature trees. The vantage point slightly elevated. It is almost dark. The light grey. Autumnal. The path itself moistened from a recent drizzle. Here and there stones protrude through the thin covering of mud. There is a smell of rain. Earth. Rotting vegetation. Slowly, the light dims further with the onset of dusk and the slight breeze gathers speed, stirring the damp mulch, rustling the scant leaves. There is the far-off call of a bird: a crow. Then the sound of fast-approaching footsteps. Heavy, stertorous breathing. A blurring below the camera's lens. Then, from behind, the retreating form of a female jogger. She has the lithe, relaxed rhythm of an experienced runner. A loose ponytail of dark hair bobs over the hood of a grey top. A crushed, brown leaf clings to the sole of the left trainer –

There is an abrupt snap of a twig underfoot, an explosion of swirling leaves and fracturing branches as a figure suddenly materialises from the trees . . .

Time passes. The dusk fades into night. Rain falls. A gusting wind howls among the high branches of ancient oak and beech. Rattles and shakes the bare stems of denuded shrubs. Swirls and eddies in the overgrown tussocks of grass. Ruffles the edges of soggy, trampled leaves before lifting them up and urging them along a well-worn track, where they come to rest against ... a motionless figure. A girl. Lying, half-naked, among a confusion of churned mud, strewn gravel, and broken twigs. The rain intensifies, becoming a downpour, and continues for half-an-hour. An hour. Perhaps more. Then, abruptly, it stops. For a time, it is quiet. Until, from somewhere among the treetops there is the doleful 'Krah-Krah' of a crow. Then the answering far-off and equally melancholic 'Krah-Krah-KRAH' of another bird. The girl's eyelids flutter. Then open. She is alive. Though all this time, shivering, cold, petrified, she has not moved. Not dared make a sound. Has scarcely risked breathing too deeply in case that movement might have been observed. And, throughout . . . *everything* … her eyes have been squeezed tight shut. Now it is suddenly very important that she be dressed. Vital that she be covered up. So, she turns painfully on to her side. And, feeling sharp grit gouging her knees, the throbbing and tenderness in her palms, she gets agonisingly onto all-fours. Casting about for her clothing she sees her discarded underwear and tracksuit bottoms, a little way off in the damp vegetation. She struggles to her feet, hobbles over and picks them up. Realises that there is nowhere to sit down and put them on. Bending over, lifting a leg she is suddenly dizzy and reaches out for the branch of a nearby tree. But the bark is saturated, slipping and moving under her fingers – the waterlogged skin of a drowned and bloated corpse – and sloughs off from the limb beneath. Causing her to momentarily lose her balance and stumble back to her knees. She sits on the soaked ground and pulls up her rain-dampened underwear. The stinging, the soreness, the aching causing her to wince and shudder. Her track-suit bottoms have been turned inside out and she barely has the strength to turn them back the right way. Trembling, she manages to edge them up her legs and stand up. She freezes. Suddenly conscious of a sound. Faraway, it is barely audible. The piteous whimpering of a distressed and wounded animal. For a while she does not move. Does not breathe. Strains to hear. Then recognition dawns. It is her own voice. She puts her hand to her face. Finds that she has been crying. *Is* crying. That her face is wet. Snot streaming from her nostrils. Wiping at her nose with her sleeve, she flinches. With numb fingertips she gingerly explores the cut and puffy lip, the burning and stiffening cheek. After a time, padding up and down the stony path in wet and cold socks, crouching to stare into shadowy undergrowth, she finds her trainers and puts them on, then leaves the wood. As she limps home along the road it begins, again, to rain: car headlights are haloed in the drifting drizzle, tyres swish past on wet tarmac. She hunches into herself. Stares down at the pavement. She has her hood pulled up. And she holds the hood under her chin with a chill hand. To hide her face. To hide her embarrassment. To hide her shame . . .

Cat Russell came abruptly awake. Into the here and now, of a worn leather sofa. In the familiar living room of her flat. But she had brought back with her from that dream, that memory, that sense of shame, that overwhelming terror, that image of the figure that had materialised from the trees. The figure, as always, blurred and indistinct. As if a shadow or forever viewed in shadow. A figure without a face. That is, the features had been indelibly erased from her memory. Or so she had hoped . . .

But then she *had* also believed that the actual recollection of the event; the precise, jagged, visceral, fragmentary memories had been eroded over time. She had imagined that, just like the sea-glass she picked up from the beach and kept in a glass jar by her window, the constant turning over, the tumbling of one against the other, had worn their edges smooth. Had dulled their surfaces. She was only too well aware that the spaces between, the missing time, that which had been lost, that which had been intentionally unremembered, had been replaced in the intervening years by a fabrication. A fiction of her own devising. A story reconstructed from what she had been told by other people. Recreated from supposition. Remade from expediency. So that, in the end, it had become something impersonal. Something viewed from a distance. Something where the whole sequence of events might have actually happened to, and been recounted by, someone else.

But tonight, she had sat on the sofa, the television playing to itself, drinking endless bloody cups of coffee, replaying the memory over and over again in her head, lighting one cigarette after another, flicking the ash out into the ashtray on the coffee table. One of the few pieces of furniture in the room. Along with the two brown leather sofas, the flat screen TV on one wall. Despite resolving on numerous occasions to put this right. To put her own stamp on the place. To buy something to put in the fireplace; a basket of dried flowers, a pottery lighthouse, a wooden statue of a seagull. Or, at the very least, to hang some pictures on the walls. But there was still a complete lack of *anything* personal in the room. The only thing she had bought in the past few months was a standard lamp. She put this on every evening rather than the brighter overhead pendant bulb. But she had to admit that this was as much to hide the emptiness of the apartment as to ward off the darkness outside.

She leant forward, slid out a fag from the packet on the coffee table and lit up. Over the passage of time she had managed to piece together a coherent but dispassionate narrative, a solid, well-defined but entirely impersonal account that in some perverse, counter-intuitive way had become *less* substantial, more remote ... and so, for her, easier to deal with. Until the reappearance of John Hall a few months ago. Even then, the shard of memory, the most painful memory, the memory that had, in the early days, stopped her from sleeping. Or disturbed her sleep. Or dragged her from sleep panting for breath and covered in a cold sweat, had thankfully not returned. Until Hall had contacted her again. Until she had received that text message. It had been this fear of the same, recurring, terrifying dream that had tonight kept her from her bed. Cat picked up her phone. Read, for what must be the thousandth time, the brief and, on the face of it, innocuous message. One way or another, this *had* to end . . .

Reaching for the packet of menthol cigarettes and disposable lighter, cupping his hand to hide the flame, he sparked up and took in a satisfying lungful of smoke, then he dropped the cigarette packet and lighter back onto the top of the dashboard. His eyes never once leaving the view through the front windscreen. The converted Victorian semi-detached house on the second floor of which Cat Russell had an apartment. He watched for a while, smoking the cigarette, flicking the ash into the dregs of coffee in the cup on the passenger seat. Finally, the light in her living room went out. Dropping the cigarette into the polystyrene cup and turning on the car's headlamps, he started the engine . . . .

DAY THREE

20

Terry Milton leant down behind the bar and helped himself to a bottle of scotch, then picked up a clean shot glass. His club – why not? Alright, so it was barely ten o'clock in the morning. But he'd long since given up any pretence that he wasn't an alcoholic. Even to himself. He had a bottle of single malt in the bottom drawer of the desk in his office – by now almost empty – which he took out every day before lunch. Promising himself he'd only have the one. But these days? After the first, and that had been getting earlier and earlier every morning, the bottle would most likely just stay out. This morning, in particular, he felt the need of it. That comforting alcoholic haze. That opportunity to not think. The chance to blot out, even temporarily, the conviction that his pathetic life was lumbering towards its inevitable conclusion. That certainty which had been growing in him ever since the visit of Detective Inspector Sean Carragher. A proper lairy fucker. Way too full of himself. And a Scouser to boot. But there was about him also an unsettling, intimidating stillness – those dispassionate, almost colourless, grey eyes. The eyes of a psychopath – an implied threat of imminent and decisive violence. It had become obvious fairly quickly that Carragher had a pretty good idea what had been going on. He had laid out the fact as he'd known them. And hadn't been *that* far from the truth. At first Terry had thought that Carragher might just be putting the bite on him. That it was a simple case of blackmail. So, Terry had sat patiently. Heard him out. Even managed to resist having a scotch. For a little while at least. Then he'd asked: 'How much?'

125

But when Carragher had told him, Terry had known that there was no way he could find that kind of money. Not a fucking chance. He'd sat in his office for a long while then. Trying to think of a way out. A way out that wouldn't involve a phone call to the people he was already in debt to, the people who he'd agreed to let hold the parties at his club. Trying to figure out what his alternatives were. And he'd only come up with one. So desperate had he been that he'd actually contemplated whether he might be able to bash Carragher over the head and then somehow dispose of the body. But only briefly. It didn't take him long to realise that he didn't have the bottle for something like that. So, instead, he'd sat in his office. Drinking. Trying to work through things logically. The trouble was, he'd been so shocked by the conversation that he couldn't quite remember what *had* actually been said. And the more he drank, the more he convinced himself that Carragher might only have *suggested* that he knew who had approached him. That he might only have hinted at knowing who had attended the parties. That he might have simply made a few insinuations to test the water and let Terry fill in the blanks. After all, he told himself, if Carragher had really known who'd been there, he'd have reeled off a list of names, wouldn't he?

In the end, Terry had decided not to make the phone call. Later that day Pearson had rocked up. Carragher, it turned out, *was* under investigation by the Professional Standards department. After Pearson had left, Terry had mulled over this new information, had considered what implications it might have: Perhaps Carragher *was* just bent, *was* only trying to screw some money out of him. On the other hand, maybe Carragher had been a decent copper once.

126

Maybe, underneath it all, he was still a decent copper. Okay, so he was obviously a bit of a chancer, one of those coppers who overstepped the mark occasionally and fell foul of the regulations. But perhaps he'd still appreciate the opportunity to win a few brownie points. Might welcome the possibility of gaining some leverage with the impending investigation into his conduct. Would jump at the chance of information that might lead to the exposing of organised child exploitation. By the end of the night, Terry had convinced himself that there was a way out. A way to make the parties stop. A way where he might stay out of the Nick. A way where he might even be able to keep the club, make a fresh start. He would meet Carragher as arranged. But instead of giving him money, he would offer him information. Make a deal.

But the night he and Carragher were supposed to meet, he'd been held up at the club. He'd been late driving down Ness Road towards the seafront. He'd seen a car ablaze in the car park. Certain that he, or Carragher, or both, had been sussed, his bottle had gone – luckily – and he'd driven past. It was only later, through the papers and the telly, through social media, that he'd discovered what had actually happened. And he'd thought that he might have gotten away with it, that he might be off the hook . . .

And then *she* had turned up . . .

How many times now had he pulled up outside the club in the car, only for *her* to materialise out of the darkness? A white-faced apparition banging on the car roof, trying the door handle, rapping on the glass with her knuckles. A banshee pointing an accusatory finger at him and screeching, 'I know what you are!'

And how many times now had he cowered inside the car? Terrified of someone who was little more than a girl, waiting for it to stop, waiting for her to go away?

But she hadn't gone away. In fact, ever since, she'd been appearing without warning at the driver's side window of the car. Or else standing outside the club on the other side of the road. Staring. Or else not there at all. And, somehow, that was worse. The not knowing where she was. Not knowing when she might turn up again. So that now, every time he arrived to open up, every time he had to leave the club for a few minutes, every time he stood behind the curtains and took a surreptitious glance out of a front window, he half-expected to see her. Five minutes earlier, as he had backed out of the club, a black bag of rubbish in each hand, and had turned to dump them on the pavement he had caught sight of something from the corner of his eye. She was there again. Standing outside the sex shop across the road. Although it had only been shut a couple of months, the place was already showing signs of dilapidation. The door boarded up where kids had broken in and ransacked the place. The gold lettering of the name – '*Iniquity*' – beginning to flake and peel from a window sand-blasted and dirt-streaked from the recent heavy rains. The once-discreet curtaining inside now gathering dust. And there was the girl; the close-cut black hair, the deathly pale face, the heavy eyeliner, the black lipstick, that scuffed and over-sized bikers' jacket. Motionless against a backdrop of reflected thunderclouds racing across an over-bright sky. Standing. Staring. She was always staring at him. Staring *at* him. Or *behind* him. Or *into* him. And seeing him for exactly what he was. He'd turned quickly away, fleeing into the relative safety of the club. Locking the door behind him. Now, pulling out a chair, carefully placing the bottle of scotch and the glass on the table, sitting down, he felt a little better. It had just been an after-image. That was all. Like when you stare at a light for too long, so that when you look away it becomes scorched for a little while on the back of your eye. Yeah, an after-image, that was it. Because the girl had stood in the same place for so long, he just *expected* to see her.

The phone call of a few days ago had been a mistake. He knew that now. Sitting in the car. Listening to the momentary dead air on the other end of the line. Mumbling an apology. Suffering the coldness, the obvious irritation, in the other person's voice. Stammering an explanation as to the reason for the call. Justifying why this was an emergency. Receiving the curt acknowledgement. Hearing the dial tone as they hung up . . .

21

Locking the half-glazed door to his office, he took a small silver key out of his trouser pocket and sat back down behind the desk. Unlocking the bottom drawer, he took out a sheet of white butchers' paper and laid it out on the desktop. Took out a nylon washbag and placed it to the left-hand side. He unzipped the bag, took out a pair of latex gloves and snapped them on. Then, one piece at a time, he laid out the components of the cleaning kit. The soft rag. The jeweller's screwdriver. The toothbrush. The borebrush. The patchclaw. The bottles of thread locker and gun oil. He liked to apply thread locker to the screws on the grip panels of the pistol's handle. Make sure the screws didn't work loose when the gun was fired. And he preferred gun oil as a lubricant rather than WD-40. Lubricating a gun with WD-40 always seemed to leave an oily residue. In his opinion, this could easily attract dust and dirt and make the gun more likely to misbehave or jam.

Only when everything was arranged to his satisfaction did Daryl Crawford go to the wall safe in the back office of the *Double Carpet* betting shop and retrieve the Sig Sauer P226 from inside. Sitting back down he placed it squarely at the centre of the sheet of white paper. Now the medal had been consigned to the back of the wardrobe, the semi-automatic pistol was the real reminder of that final tour. The only solid 'souvenir' of his time in Sixteenth Air Assault. The illegal handgun smuggled back into the UK in the wheel rim of a Jackal armoured vehicle, the true emblem of his time in Afghanistan. He'd kept the loaded pistol in the bedside cabinet at first. But when Tracy had moved in, he'd decided it would be safer to transfer it to the wall safe. Which is where it had been on the evening of the robbery. But he had assessed the situation, evaluated the risk, and in the end had judged that the gun wouldn't be needed. In hindsight it had been the correct decision. Having wrestled the sawn-off shotgun from the robber's grasp and turned it on him he had come so, so close to pulling the trigger. How much easier might that decision have been had the weapon in his hand had the comforting familiarity of a service-issue semi-automatic pistol, a pistol he'd previously used on active service, a pistol with which he'd already killed?

For a moment, Daryl watched the shadows moving behind the frosted panel in the half-glazed door. Listened to the sporadic murmur of conversation in the betting shop beyond. Then he returned his attention to the pistol. He made an effort to regulate his breathing. To concentrate his mind fully on the task at hand. Daryl picked up the Sig, locked back the slide. Following the safety protocol. Ensuring there was no round in the chamber. The pistol hadn't been fired since his time in Afghanistan. And it had been cleaned regularly since. But he'd seen the result of carelessness. Had been present when fingers had been lost. Had learned from experience that there was no such thing as being 'too cautious'. Over the years the meticulous process of dismantling, cleaning and re-assembly of the weapon had assumed an element of the meditative. He depressed the magazine release and ejected the clip. Clicked down the slide stop, turned the take down lever round ninety degrees, and slipped the slide forward off the front of the gun. During active service the practised and familiar movements had become a method of concentrating his mind before the anticipated action to come. He took out the recoil spring rod and removed the barrel from the frame. Trying to clear his mind of unnecessary thought. With a small screwdriver he undid the screws securing the grip panels of the handle. Laying each piece in turn in its allotted place on the blank sheet of paper.

'One should never place a loaded rifle on the stage,' Danny Fraser had said, 'if it isn't going to go off.'

That night, that night where it had all gone so terribly wrong, they were in barracks. Sitting either side of a trestle table. The weapons laid out in front of them. Daryl had looked up and over at the other man.

'It's a dramatic principle,' Fraser said, 'first stated by Anton Chekhov. Every element in a story must be necessary. It's known as "Chekhov's Gun".' And then, 'You *have* heard of Anton Chekhov, right? The Russian playwright? '

That night Danny had been uncharacteristically talkative. Normally on the night of an operation – at any time – he would have been reserved, said very little. Ordinarily he would have been totally concentrated, absolutely focused. Then again, it would turn out that there would be nothing at all 'normal' about that particular operation. Nothing 'ordinary' about that night . . .

Daryl picked up the frame of the gun and the rag and began the process of cleaning . . .

Was it unavoidable, then, that this gun would go off? This was, after all, real life. But even in real life, in Daryl's experience, a pistol, once revealed, would inevitably *have* to be fired. And the reappearance of Danny Fraser only made this all the more likely. Daryl finished cleaning the individual components and began to re-assemble the gun. Dropping the barrel back into the slide, gently pushing the recoil spring guide and spring into the barrel . . .

'Did you find out what that row was about?' Daryl had asked.

Half an hour earlier, their tent had suddenly filled with smoke. Fraser had gone outside to investigate.

'Some local, burning a type of black grain or seed,' Fraser said, 'muttering something under his breath and wafting the smoke into the tent. I asked one of the more approachable interpreters what was going on. Apparently, the guy burning the seeds wasn't happy about the target tonight – ' seeing the look on Crawford's face, he said, '– Yeah, don't ask me how he'd found out. It doesn't say a lot for security does it? Anyway, he sees me talking to the interpreter and comes over and they start bickering amongst themselves, waving their arms about, y'know? Pushing and shoving each other? Obviously, he doesn't want the 'terp to tell me what he was up to.'

'And did he?'

'Nah,' Fraser said, 'they kept on shouting at each other and pushing and shoving and the argument sort of moved away, so I didn't really get to talk to the 'terp. I only caught the odd word here and there.'

Daryl clicked the grip panels into place in the pistol's handle. Applied a drop of the thread locker into the screw-holes. Tightened the screws. He lined up the machine grooves on the underside of the slide with the top side of the gun. Reattached the slide to the pistol.

'I thought you'd picked up some Pashto?' Crawford said.

'Aye. Well, when they talk slowly and clearly. And even then, half the time I have to ask them to repeat themselves. These two were talking nineteen to the dozen. Besides their regional accents are so fucking thick half the time I can't make head or tail of what they're saying,' and then, 'Then again, I have the same trouble with cockneys.'

'So, you didn't get anything of what they were saying?'

'Well, I thought I caught the word for "evil places" or 'evil spirits" or something. But I wouldn't swear to it.'

Daryl push the take-down lever back to its correct setting, moved the slide forward to its normal position, and release the

de-cock lever. Giving the gun a final wipe down with the rag
. . .

'Do you think a place *can* be evil, Boss?' Danny Fraser had asked. The pistol already cleaned, reassembled and laid out on the trestle table in front of him.

'Because bad things keep happening in the same place??' Crawford asked. Laying down his own weapon. Danny had always been that few seconds quicker. That little bit more dextrous. Had always been the better soldier, if he were honest. 'A *place* doesn't somehow attract evil, Danny. Or cause that evil to happen.' He shook his head, 'It's people that commit evil, Danny. Its people that cause evil to happen. Not a place.'

Daryl's gaze drifted involuntarily towards the ceiling. Towards the damage left by the shotgun cartridge that had yet to be repaired. For a moment he watched again the shadows moving behind the frosted panel of the office door. Then he raised the pistol. Took aim. Pulled the trigger. Heard the gratifying 'click' . . .

'I wouldn't put too much store in what the locals say, 'Daryl had said, 'It's just ignorant superstition.'

'Aye,' Fraser nodded, 'That's what I thought, Boss. But ... I don't know ... I've just got a bad feeling about this one . . . '

Daryl thumbed down the cock at the back end of the barrel. Pulled the trigger again. Nodded to himself. Satisfied. Finally, he picked up the magazine from the desk and snapped it into place.

Had there been *something* in what Danny had said? Could a place be inherently evil? Could a place somehow be able to make bad things occur? How else could you explain what had happened next? How else could you explain those twenty-three minutes? 22.

A cul-de-sac. At its entrance a single streetlamp. On each side houses sit behind large wooden fences. It is barely fifty or so yards in length. At night, this area – a break in some metal railings, a sign informing anyone requiring the Emergency Services that this was Belfairs Woods 'Entrance C' – would be in almost total darkness. It would, Cat thought, locking the car, dropping the key into the side pocket of her coat, make an excellent deposition site. It wouldn't take long to park a car here, manhandle a body out of the boot, and then dump it. In her mind the road, the bridle path and the trees beyond became the locus of a crime scene. Marked and unmarked cars haphazardly double-parked. Uniformed Constables stringing blue and white tape between lampposts. SOCO's unloading metal cases from vans. Curious onlookers gathering at garden gates to talk in hushed tones. Surely just an occupational hazard, wasn't it, thinking like this? Just the rational appraisal of an experienced copper? But Cat recognised it for what it was; distraction, deflection, procrastination. A subconscious effort to delay facing her fears.

A few paces later Cat found herself in a mature wood. The sound of the imagined car engines, slamming doors and urgently issued instructions fading away, to be replaced by ... scattered and intermittent birdsong, the murmur and rattle of wind through bare branches, the distant barking of a dog. And, beneath it all ... a low-level hum which took Cat a minute to place as the sound of traffic from the nearby A127. Nervous now, hesitant, Cat turned, looking back from where she had come. Seeking reassurance. Even the idea of a crime scene, the opportunity of falling back onto a well-rehearsed protocol and the comfort of what had become, sadly, a familiar routine now seemed more appealing than what she was about to put herself through. She took in the park entrance. And beyond, parked cars, houses, a quiet and unremarkable residential street. Then she turned back, admonishing herself for being 'so bloody silly', Cat took one of the paths leading deeper into the wood. Taking measured, deliberate strides, steady, deep breaths. And all the time reassuring herself that this was a managed area, regularly coppiced and pollarded, the footpaths frequented by dog-walkers, the bridleways by groups on horseback. But in the gloom beneath the trees – oak and chestnut – bereft of foliage at this time of year – lay churned mud, decomposing leaves, the pervasive smell of damp and decay. Then, suddenly, from somewhere near-by came the jarring 'Krah-Krah' of a crow. All at once Cat's mouth was

dry. Her stomach water. And she was back in that other wood
. . .

The stony path cold beneath her face. The jagged shards of gravel cutting into her cheek. Drawing in ragged lungfuls of air. Her palms numbed and smarting. The mud-splashed workboot appearing in front of her face. Feeling again the almost-irresistible compulsion to squeeze close her eyes. To shut down. She wants, so, so much, not to relive again that moment. But that, after all, is why she is here isn't it? Why she has driven to this wood in her lunchtime, rather than staying in the office, or going to a café? Or, better still, the pub. In the hope that somehow this might jog her memory. That somehow the faceless figure of her nightmares, the figure who came crashing repeatedly out of the undergrowth and onto the path, the monster which, up to now, she had only seen as ill-defined and out of focus, might suddenly reveal itself. Even so, she had to fight with every ounce of will power the urge to turn and run.

Last night she had texted John Hall, agreeing to his request that they meet again. But now she was having serious second thoughts. After all, wasn't it his getting back in touch with her in the first place that had brought all this back? Not only that, in the years they had been apart, her view of their past relationship had changed. She'd begun to wonder whether for him it might have just been some casual fling, whether he might have just thought of her as a 'bit on the side'. Worse still, whether he might have even capitalised on her naivety. Taken advantage of her susceptible state to manipulate her into having what now seemed with hindsight and, at best, highly questionable and, at worst, somewhat sordid affair. On the other hand, it could just be that her way of thinking had been coloured by her time in the Job, had been poisoned by her recent experiences with the sexual exploitation of vulnerable under-age teenagers at the Abigail Burnett. Still, ever since their brief meeting a few months ago there had been a definite ... *something* nagging at her. She had pored over their conversation in her mind; replaying his every gesture, reviewing his body language, searching for the truth. All of which had left her with a niggling suspicion that Hall had been lying in some way. Or if not exactly lying, then not exactly telling the truth either. Or, at the very least, holding something back –

There was a flash of lightning. A crackle of thunder. A sudden gust of wind urged a few of the drier leaves back along the path . . .

Back in the Incident Room, conscious of someone hovering at his side, Pearson looked up from his computer screen.

'No Detective Constable Russell today?' DCS Andy Curtis asked.

'Just this second left her desk, Sir.'

Pearson looked pointedly at the wall-clock, 'Lunch hour, Sir. I expect she's just popped out for something to eat.' Though where she'd actually gone, Pearson had no idea. Cat didn't usually go out for lunch. And today she hadn't said where she was going. Or even that she *was* going. She'd just picked up her handbag and coat and left. 'Is there anything I can help you with, Sir?'

Curtis hesitated, then asked, 'I understand DC Russell is Disclosure Officer this week?'

Pearson nodded, 'Sir.'

'So, she'd be working on the Clive Townsend murder case?'

'Sir,' Pearson nodded again.

'Um,' Curtis licked his lips, 'I was just interested in how it was all going?'

There was just a little too *much* interest in this case for Pearson's liking. First, whoever it was who'd bought the gambling debt from Jack Morris in order to coerce Wendy Simpson into divulging information. And now Curtis sniffing around.

'DC Russell's a very capable officer, Sir. I'm sure it's all in hand.'

Curtis nodded. But didn't leave. Pearson had the distinct impression that he might be here about something else. The previous week, Pearson had given Cat a lift home. Deciding to take the route along the seafront, they had driven past the Casino.

'Is that the wife of our DCS?' Pearson had asked, lifting an index finger from the steering wheel to point out of the front windscreen at a woman in her forties, her shoes in her hand, and obviously the worse for wear. Marion Curtis had been in the local paper. Photographed at a black-tie charity fundraiser standing between the DCS and the local MP. As they drew nearer, Pearson had realised that the grainy picture hadn't done her justice, 'Yeah,' that's definitely her,' he said. Flicking on the car's indicator and slowing down.

'Is this really a good idea?' Cat asked.

'C'mon, we can't leave her here. She's well pissed.'

Cat had sighed and muttered something under her breath that he hadn't quite caught. Though it might have been something along the lines of, 'It's not like I've actually got a fucking career.'

Pearson had pulled up to the kerb and pressed the button to lower the passenger side window, then leaned across Cat and called,

'Mrs. Curtis? D'you need a lift?'

Marion Curtis had peered blearily in at the warrant card in Pearson's hand, 'Detective Sergeant Pearson? I work with your husband?'

Even now he wasn't sure she'd actually taken in the information on the card. But, before Pearson could say any more, Marion Curtis had opened the door behind Cat and climbed in. Or, more accurately, fallen in. Pearson had glanced up at the rear-view mirror. Surprised that Curtis could have landed up with someone so attractive. Even if that night, perhaps, she wasn't at her most elegant. Judging by the state

142

she was in, she had been drinking most of the day. But she had the air of someone who was trying, just that little bit *too* hard, to look like she was having fun. Cat had climbed out and closed the rear door, and the car had suddenly been filled with the overpowering smell of gin. There was nothing Pearson hated more than the smell of gin. Except rotting bananas, maybe. He wondered if there were a cocktail made from gin and bananas. Bound to be.

When Cat got back in, he asked, 'So, where are we off to, Mrs. Curtis?' She mumbled an address in Thorpe Bay.

'Maybe you ought to put your seat belt on?' Pearson had suggested. But after a moment, during which she had neither answered nor made a move to put the belt on, he had pulled away.

Curtis looked away across the empty incident room. Frowning slightly. Licking his lips again. His wife would have told him about the lift. Would have mentioned the name of the officers involved. No surprise, then, that he was here. The only real surprise was that it had taken him so long. Then again, this might have been his first opportunity. The first time that Pearson had been on his own. He was never going to say anything in front of Cat. But he would obviously have been worrying about what might have been said. Curtis looked back now, gave a nod, then turned abruptly on his heel and left.

Marion Curtis had said little on the journey. Staring morosely instead out of the side window. But when they were only a few minutes from her home she had leant through the front seats and put her hand on Cat's forearm.

'Do you like being in the police force? Sorry, I don't know your name.'

'Cat. Catherine.'

'As a woman, I mean, Catherine? It can't leave you much time for a family. Do you have children, Catherine?'

'No,' Cat said, 'no children.'

'No,' Marion Curtis sighed, 'me either. Does your husband not want children?'

'I'm not married,' Cat said.

'Not married? And such an attractive girl. So many young, attractive girls in the police force. And you all seem to work such long hours, at least Andrew does. He's always out late on "police business", coming in in the early hours . . . ' Then, after a pause, 'As if I don't know what's really going on. All these attractive young policewomen like yourself. And him coming home late, smelling of drink. And sex.' She studied Cat's face. Then said, with the negligent cruelty of the drunk, 'Of course, Andrew generally prefers them a bit younger than you,' then, as an afterthought, 'no offence.'

Raindrops began to spot the front windscreen. He glanced up to see a sky that had noticeably darkened in the twenty minutes or so since he'd watched Cat Russell enter the wood. From this position – on the left-hand side of the street, close to the entrance to the cul-de-sac, and behind a line of other stationary vehicles, he had a clear view of the park entrance, was ideally placed to see but not *be* seen. John hall drummed fretfully on the steering wheel, needing a cigarette. Wanting that comforting ritual of smoking, craving the taste of tobacco, the nicotine hit. But, most of all, wanting reconnection with that … something … that was now lost. He found himself in a nostalgic recollection of a previous shared cigarette . . .

Half-sitting, propped up by the pillows piled against the headboard, Hall took the cigarette from his mouth and exhaled a cloud of blue smoke into the gloom of the small bedroom. In the darkness, Cat's head shifted against his chest and he reached around to put the cigarette to her mouth, felt her lips graze his fingers as she inhaled. He brushed her cheek affectionately with his thumb. Took the cigarette away, took a deep draw, relishing a filter moist with her saliva, and said,

' *"But when the melancholy fit shall fall, Sudden from heaven like a weeping cloud . . ."* '

'Keats, right? *"Ode to melancholy"*?'

'Aye,' Hall put the cigarette back to her lips, stroked her cheek once again with his thumb, 'seemed appropriate somehow.'

145

The rain came heavier now. Hall's view of the park entrance, the motionless cars, even the taillights of the car in front, suddenly obliterated by an almost impenetrable overlay of running water. He leaned forward to turn on the windscreen wipers. Then stopped, his attention caught by an ill-defined and blurry figure – Cat – coming out of the park and making a dash for it. John Hall leaned further forward in his seat. Watching as Cat unlocked the car and climbed in. He stared unblinkingly through the rapidly fogging windshield. Concealed behind the curtain of moving water. Invisible in the unremarkable dark blue four-door saloon. Confident of going unnoticed. Sure of being overlooked. Certain of being disregarded. Just as he had been when . . .

Ten years earlier. The front door opens and a younger Cat Russell steps out of the student accommodation on Gilesgate. Twisting an elastic band over her dark hair and arranging it into a loose ponytail. Staring up at the sky. Irresolute. And even this late in the day part of him, too, the better part of him, hopes that she might still change her mind. He knew her route by heart, of course. She would turn right and run up to the footbridge. Then take a left along Leazes Lane. He'd tailed her in his car as she crossed the river over Baths Bridge, turning left to follow the riverside path. Had stood out of sight behind the bandstand when she turned right onto the football ground and passed the cricket club. Had strolled unnoticed on the towpath alongside the river when she'd turned right, away from the river, and made her way around Maiden Castle

Wood. Had hidden, unobserved, among the trees as she'd crossed the road into the Great High Wood forest. Had sat behind a newspaper on a bench when she'd run through the grounds of Grey College and past the botanic gardens. Had trailed at a discrete distance in the car as she'd crossed over South Road, gone up Elvet Hill Road and back into town. Had tracked her through the zoom lens of his Nikon as she'd turned right onto the Prebends' Bridge and from there onto the island. Had been sitting in the small car park behind the bus stop as she'd crossed the footbridge back into Gilesgate. He'd sat in the Queen's Head pub at the end of the road. Ordering a pint from one of the other bar staff, then sitting out of sight in the shadows and watching her flirt with the male customers. He'd even dogged her early-morning drunken footsteps home from the many bring-a-bottle student parties she'd attended . . .

Now, John Hall watched Cat execute a three-point turn at the end of the road. Lifted his hand casually to his forehead to shield the right side of his face as she passed. Followed her taillights in his rear-view mirror, saw the left indicator come on as she re-joined the main road. Giving it a minute or so, he turned on the car's headlamps and started the engine . . . .

23

Terry Milton had never seen a gun. Not in real life. He'd seen a gun on the TV, of course, and in films. Or, what he'd always assumed was a very realistic replica of a gun. But he had never held a gun in his hand. Had never felt the cold barrel of a gun pressed against the back of his skull. But he had known right away that that was what it was. He'd been expecting it. Half-expecting it. Or something very much like it. But not at that precise moment. Not sitting at that sticky wooden table, in the dimness of a room whose only illumination came from the muted neon strip lighting along the bar, with the familiar fug of stale beer in his nostrils, and the glass of whisky in front of him. Poured, but not yet tasted . . .

Terry sat now. In the wood-panelled room behind the club. Staring down at the open bottle. Holding the empty glass in an unsteady hand. He had snatched them up from the table. Retreated to his office. And locked himself in. But too late. Way too fucking late. He poured himself a drink. His hand shaking. The bottle rattling against the rim of the glass. Usually after the first, the tremors had begun to recede. After the second, he could start to function normally. And, if he were truthful, without at least the two early-morning shots he couldn't really function at all. But this morning it didn't seem to matter how much he drank, how many he had – how many *had* he had? Three? Four? He couldn't remember – he couldn't stop the shaking. He put the glass to his lips. Then knocked it back quickly. Feeling the burn in his throat. The warming in his chest. Now it was over, now he'd said his piece, now he'd confessed, more to the point now he'd confessed and was still here, was still alive, none of it mattered. All that mattered now was the scotch. The chance to forget. Earlier, ten minutes? An hour? To be honest, he wasn't really sure how long ago it had been – of course, there had been the gun. The gun and the scotch. The scotch and the gun. But mostly the gun . . .

A Sig Sauer P226 semi-automatic pistol, he had been told. It was not an imitation; he had been assured. It *was* the real thing. Terry had harboured no doubts. He had known for a certainty. And Terry had known that voice. It was the voice on the other end of the pay-as-you-go phone he had been given. The voice that had issued him with his instructions. The voice that had told him, in no uncertain terms, that the phone was only to be used in case of an 'absolute emergency' –

The girl had come out of nowhere. He had panicked. He had made that phone call. And he had regretted it ever since. So, he *had* been expecting the visit. Just not then. Not there. But, even then, even with the semi-automatic pistol pointing at his face his first thought had been of the drink on the table in front of him. Of how quickly this might be over. Of that moment when he could pick up the glass, put it to his lips, swallow that next mouthful of scotch. So, he had licked dry lips. And spilled his guts . . .

He had told what he remembered about the night the girl had died. The girl who wasn't actually a girl. But wasn't really a boy. Something he'd only found out much later from social media –

The gun had smacked him in the temple, had given a waggle. Irritated. Impatient. Because he was rambling. Because he was scared. So, he'd started again. Concentrating on getting all the facts straight. Trying not to miss anything out. Rushing. Stumbling. Barely coherent. Because he was scared. But, most of all, because he needed that drink . . .

On the night, he'd been sitting in the office behind the club. Not really wanting to know what was going on. Having a drink, and, to be honest, making a point of *not* knowing what was going on. But there'd been something … a disturbance … a lot of noise … Follow by an abrupt silence, it had just felt like something was very wrong. So, he'd gone to see what was going on. And all of a sudden, the club was emptying. All of a sudden everyone had gone. And the girl was just … there. Lying on the floor in one corner of the club. Not moving or anything. And he'd known right away that she was dead. He'd panicked. Hadn't known what to do. Then someone had turned up. He had no idea who it was. Who'd called him. Who'd let him in the club. He realised later that one of the girls at the party must have made a phone call. So, there must have been some people still there in the club. And then the girl was gone. The situation had been dealt with. He'd simply locked up. The cleaners had come in the following morning. And it was like nothing had happened. And, finally, the gun had waggled again. He'd been allowed to have a drink. He'd picked up the scotch and downed it in one . . .

Now he wished he *had* had that bullet in the back of the head. At least then it would all be over. He knew he was only living on borrowed time. Because, sitting at that sticky table. Feeling the hard barrel of the semi-automatic pistol jammed against the back of his skull. Smelling the perfume; flowers, musk, spice, as she came around the table and sat down opposite him, he had recognised her. And he realised now that in that moment of recognition, as soon as he'd been able to put a face to that voice, he'd been as good as dead. Because now he knew *exactly* who she was; the woman he'd passed countless times in the street, the woman who, until recently, he'd seen unlocking the front doors of the sex shop opposite, the woman he knew as Layla Gilchrist.

24

She becomes dimly aware that she is lying on the ground ... her breath comes again now ... ragged ... uneven ... and a rational, reasoning part of her mind vaguely registers that *this* is a dream, that the coldness beneath her face is merely a pillow damp with the sweat of fear ... but she experiences, none the less, the sharp edges of gravel in her cheek ... feels the numbness and stinging in her fingers and the palms of her hands ... Her head swims ... there is a dull pain across her kidneys ... her right trainer is lost ... There is a stench of damp earth and mulching vegetation ... and something else. A smell fleetingly apparent but not identified and, somehow, even to her unconscious mind this has a terrifying significance ... she can hear wind rattle bare branches ... a susurration of dry leaves ... And then, footsteps ... the crunch and pop of grit beneath a heavy tread ... a mud-spattered workboot appears close to her face ... there is laboured breathing, a stream of muttered obscenities ... Rough hands turn her ... she screws her eyes tightly shut ... her resistance is minimal ... ineffectual ... and as her other running shoe is removed, her track suit bottoms and underwear yanked down ... as it begins, she hears the plaintive call of a crow and ... as if from a distance ... a piteous mewling –

Cat Russell came awake now into a tangle of bedsheets. Staring at a ceiling in the gloom of an unfamiliar bedroom. Undecided, for the moment, as to exactly where she was. Uncertain as to how she might have got here. Not sure whether she might have cried out in her sleep. Whether, in her dream, she might have kicked and thrashed in a belated, futile, illusory attempt at self-protection. It was that subconscious urge for self-preservation, she supposed, that, until now, had always managed to end this *particular* nightmare at this specific point. A state of practised, lucid dreaming which had always enabled her to drag herself into wakefulness just before . . .

She had thought that that nightmare, that *memory*, had been successfully buried. But the memory had returned or, more accurately, resurfaced with the reappearance into her life of –

'Cat?'

She was aware of the presence by her side in the bed for the first time since waking. Felt the shift in the mattress as he turned to face her.

'You okay?' John Hall whispers in the darkness, reaching out to take her hand. But still unsettled by her dream, Cat has to resist the urge to snatch her hand away.

'Bad dream?' he asks.

There is a smell in the room. Something familiar. Something disturbing. Something that has returned with her from the dream. Or was it there all along? Ignored, perhaps? Unnoticed? Was it only as she slept that her unconscious mind acknowledged its existence?

'Yeah, it's okay,' Cat whispers back. An effort at reassurance – for him? Or for herself? – and a means of stopping him initiating a conversation, 'I'm alright. Go back to sleep.'

'You sure?' he asks, squeezing her hand. The weight of his hand on hers feeling somehow repressive. The clamminess of his palm strangely repugnant.

'Yeah, yeah, I'm fine,' And as Hall rubs her forearm, Cat tries to relax. But only an effort of will, a conscious slowing of her respiration, a deliberate relaxation of her body allows her to let him put his arm across her . . .

Later, when she feels his grip slacken, his breathing slow, hears him start to gently snore, she slips quietly from the bed and leaves.

Cat was still not exactly sure why she was here. Even as she pulled the car into the car park at the end of Marine Parade. And why here of all places? She still wasn't sure. Even as she switched off the headlights. Even as she killed the engine. Even as she turned to pick up her handbag from the front passenger seat. Except that she hadn't wanted to spend another minute in that motel bedroom. Had been driving around aimlessly for the best part of the last hour because she couldn't yet face going home to that soulless apartment.

Getting out, she slammed the driver's side door and locked it, buttoned her coat, briefly scanned the sky. There was a definite dampness in the air that presaged imminent rain. The car park was deserted. The night eerily still and silent. She swung her handbag onto her shoulder, thrust her hands into her pockets and huddling into her coat, she made her way over the concrete steps and onto the seafront. Standing by the sea wall, she blindly foraged in her handbag, repeatedly cursing the 'bastard thing' before finally finding her cigarettes and lighter, lighting up and taking a long draw. She stood for a while then, listening to the sounds of the night. That low-level hum, the ubiquitous urban tinnitus, that seems to come from both nowhere and everywhere at once. The rhythmic slap of the incoming tide against the nearby Crowstone; the granite obelisk a vague grey outline in the darkness. The detective, Cat thought, rather than the murderer returning to the scene of the crime. How long would it be, she wondered, before every landmark, every *location*, would be identified in her mind with a corresponding murder case? She took another drag on her cigarette, staring out across the Estuary. At a horizon smeared and mottled by the sodium streetlights of the Isle of Grain. Then Cat's eye drifted upriver, to the memory of the intense periodic amber glow that had once illuminated the night sky. Remembering the hours spent lying in her darkened bedroom as a girl and watching the intermittent jets of flame as the excess methane was burnt off by the flare stacks of the oil refineries of Canvey Island. That feeling of not fitting in, of being constantly on edge, convinced that her family – her father in particular – were up to no good. She'd stayed on at school against her family's wishes. All the time yearning to get away. As far away as possible. A longing which had resulted in her taking a place at the University in Durham. Almost as far North as you could go before you were in Scotland. At the time even that had not seemed far enough.

And that was where she had first met John Hall . . .

'So, do I call you Catherine, Cathy or Cat?'

There had been a long pause, a suffocating silence, his calmness and composure, finally forcing her to look up from the table in the small interview room. Aware of the black eye, the bruised cheek, the stitches in her upper lip. Her shame. The pricking in her eyes. The hot tears that threatened to well over and run down her cheeks. She hadn't wanted to be there. Hadn't reported the rape after it had happened. Hadn't admitted to anyone that it *had* happened. Then one of the female student counsellors had noticed the injuries to her face. Had asked her how she had got them. Had kept on asking until Cat had eventually had to tell the truth. Even then she had had to be, at first gently persuaded, and then later more insistently cajoled into reporting it to the police. Cat had known it was hopeless but had lost the will to resist. She had showered countless times in the hours, the days since the attack. Had dumped the clothes she'd been wearing in a skip, the contents of which – it was later discovered – had been promptly incinerated. And so, had destroyed any hopes of retrieving any forensic evidence. Her eyes had scanned the face of the softly spoken Detective Sergeant. And had come to rest on the disfigured brows. The right bisected by a livid scar, '*Used to be an amateur boxer*,' Hall said in answer to her unasked question. Smiling, shaking his head, '*Never a very good one, pet. As you can see.*'

Her eyes had slid down to his. Soft. Brown. Kind. '*You look like a "Cat" to me*.' And Cat had said nothing, her eyes going, once again, to the tabletop. Her tongue wetting a

157

dry top lip. Flushing with embarrassment. He'd said, '*So, shall we go with Cat, then*?'

It had been John Hall, without a doubt, whose kindness during this time had managed to drag her back from the brink of a complete emotional breakdown. John Hall who had managed to head off the impending mental health crisis. John hall whose patience and forbearance had coaxed her out of a subsequent serious eating disorder. He had made her who she was, what she was. Had fashioned her character, shaped her worldview. Had inspired her decision to join the Police Force.

Cat took another drag on her cigarette. Nowadays the refinery was idle, the night sky dark, and all that would be seen this coming morning in the feeble light of another drizzly, grey dawn would be the dim silhouette of Canvey Island itself.

They had embarked on what he acknowledged, even then, could be a potentially destructive love affair. But Hall had been prepared to put his career in jeopardy. Had been willing to sacrifice his marriage to – or so he had claimed – the woman who had been his childhood sweetheart. Had been ready to surrender any future relationship with his two children, even though one of them was severely disabled. But Cat had not.

Cat became aware of a fine speckling of rain on the breeze. Took a last draw on the cigarette, flicking it away, watching the spiralling red glow, the trail of sparks fading into the darkness. Stared, once again, across the Estuary. To the absence on the far shore. A few months previously she'd stood in a small crowd and watched, as across the river, the chimney of the power station was demolished. She could still recall that shiver of hesitation before the tallest concrete stack in Europe fell in on itself. Toppled to one side. And was gone. Could sense the pressure wave speeding across from the other side of the Estuary. See the flocks of birds wheeling into the afternoon sky. Could hear, a second or so later, the belated echo of the explosion. Could feel, even now, the reverberation under her feet. The punch in her solar plexus . . .

So, she'd left Durham immediately after sitting her final exams, without a word to Hall. In her mind, that particular part of her life already consigned to history. Had believed, having had no contact with him in the years since, that Hall too had considered, or at least accepted, that the affair was over. That was, until she'd received the text message two months ago. She'd agreed to meet him then. Reluctantly. Because she thought that she at least owed him that much. But also, to make sure that he knew there was no hope of resurrecting their past relationship. And, although it had proved both painful and embarrassing, for both of them, she had successfully got her point across. Or so she had thought. Until Hall had contacted her again. Just when she thought the problems of the recent past were behind her . . .

It wasn't the first time her life had been wrecked by her own action. Wasn't the only occasion that she'd pressed that big, red button in her head with the words in bold, white capitals that read DO NOT PRESS. That self-destruct button that was just *too* bloody hard to resist. So, in a way, it should have been no surprise that she had weakened, that against her better judgement, she'd agreed to meet. But, even so, *how the fuck* had she ended up in bed with him?

When she stared across the river now Cat could see only the space, the vacuum, where the chimney had stood for so long. And as the fine drizzle that had been falling for the past few minutes became heavy droplets of rain, as she decided that now might be a good time to go, as she turned away and made her way back to the car, it seemed to her to symbolise all that had passed. All that had gone. Represent yet another structure that had once seemed so solid, so concrete, but had somehow collapsed and disintegrated in the past few months.

25

Standing on the observation platform by the pier, Donna Freeman turns away from the mouth of the river. From where, in just a few hours, dawn will begin to lighten the sky. And Donna gazes west. Into the darkness. In the distance she can just make out the giant, floodlit cranes of the London Gateway container port. The lights of Canvey Island. From this angle, the Crowstone is hidden from view by the casino. Though she knows it is there. In the dark. A granite obelisk half-submerged by the incoming tide. Closer, the lights of the far shore reflect in the choppy waters of the river. And to her immediate left, the Adventure Island amusement park. Beyond the glare of the halogen floodlights, the rides; the big wheel, the roller coaster, the helter-skelter, stand mute and unmoved. Lifting her white-painted face to the night sky, Donna closes her eyes. Allows the needles of freezing rain to chill her forehead. Run down her cheeks. Moisten her dry, black-painted lips. For a while, she stands and listens to its soft patter on the scuffed and oversize leather biker jacket she is wearing . . .

Back in the car Cat Russell raises the back of a hand to a stifled yawn. Cracks open the drivers' side window a few inches to allow in a little fresh air. Turns up the volume on the radio. Then swings a right out of the car park and onto the Western Esplanade. The car is buffeted by a sudden gust of wind. All at once she is aware of just how tired she is. Immediately conscious of the hypnotic downward swoop of the windscreen wipers, the monotonous, regular clunk before they start their return journey. Of the rawness in her eyes; the backlit LED display of the control panel, the sodium streetlights, the blurred glare of the wet road in the Ford's headlamps, the red taillights of the car in front . . .

Donna Freeman still hears the voices. The voices of the dead. The dead are always with her now. The dead trail her everywhere. Jostling for position. All talking at once. Clamouring for her attention. Though tonight, just for a little while, they have retreated into the background. Have become little more than an insistent whispering. But earlier the voices of the dead had urged her to follow them through the chrome gate. To clamber up onto the wall of the observation platform. To balance, one foot on the wet handrail, the other braced against the glass panel. But its bolts had somehow come loose of their moorings, and she had felt it almost immediately give way beneath the slippery tread of her boot. So that now she sways precariously over the rain-soaked paving stones seventy feet below, experiences a sudden rush of vertigo –

'Hello you.'

When Donna turns, Alicia is looking at her. Donna tries to speak. But her mouth is dry, and she can only croak, 'Hello,' and there is a constriction in her throat. Like a stone, an awkward, sharp triangular pebble covered in sand, or a petrified teardrop. So that she can manage little more than a whispered, 'you.'

'Okay, Hun?' Alicia asks, 'You frightened?'

162

Donna squeezes her eyes shut and nods her head.

'Do you want to hold hands?'

Without opening her eyes, Donna nods again.

'C'mon, Babe,' Alicia encourages.

Donna reaches out and feels the comforting warmth of Alicia's hand in hers. Opening her eyes, she looks again at her friend. Her dead friend. Part of her knows that Alicia *is* dead. Part of her, too, a small part of her, wishes Alicia wasn't here. Wishes Alicia had stayed in the mirror. Wishes the make-up, the mask, was still working. Seemingly untouched by the pelting rain, Alicia's image fades in and out. One moment so bright, so vividly luminous that it actually hurts Donna's eyes to look at her. The next so pale, so insubstantial, that the arc lights of the amusement park are clearly visible through the translucent film of her face. And yet, at that instant of transition back from the ephemeral to the corporeal Donna is sure she also glimpses something else. But something that remains just out of reach. A gentle breeze catches a strand of Alicia's long, black hair and she tucks it behind an ear, 'It's easy. Let's do it, Babe.'

Donna looks down. For a moment it all seems so simple. The rain-soaked concrete looks so inviting. Then she wavers, is not so sure. Swallows. Thinks about changing her mind. Shakes her head,

'I – I don't know . . . '

'C'mon,' Alicia says, 'let's hold hands and jump. You and me, Hun, eh? Just like it used to be?'

Donna is crying now. Staring down at the pavement. Shaking her head. 'No. I don't want to. I don't want to.' Donna feels Alicia's fingers slip from her grasp. Sees Alicia receding, becoming indistinct . . .

Shocked. Numbed. Motionless. She stares at the shattered front windscreen. The starburst of crazed glass. And, at its centre, a smear of blood, an impact point like a bullet hole. She listens to the squeal of the protesting windscreen wipers. The rain rattling across the dented bonnet and roof like shrapnel. Trying to take in what has just happened. She had seen *something flying towards her out of the dark*. Not consciously registering what it was . . .

In the car behind, Cat had slammed on the brakes. Yanked the steering wheel violently to the left. An instant and, in the circumstances, understandable reaction. But now, after the event, now she'd had time to think, it had probably not been the safest, or even the most sensible option in view of the conditions. It was not, she told herself, what she should have done. What she *would* have done . . . on any other night. Had she not been so tired. Had she not been so preoccupied. Fortunately, the car had not simply aquaplaned across the standing water on the road surface and smashed head-on into the suddenly motionless car in front. Instead, the brakes had bitten, and the car had bumped to an abrupt, jarring stop. Hurling her forward into the seatbelt. Catapulting her back into the seat. She'd been lucky, she realised. Extremely lucky. During her two years in uniform, Cat had been involved in a similar accident in the same spot. The driver of a Ford Fiesta losing control, going under the footbridge, clipping the kerb. Gouging a furrow in the metal shuttering of a shop undergoing building work. As one of the first-responders, Cat had arrived only minutes later to witness a horrific scene. The crumpled off-side wing partly imbedded in a scaffolding tower. In the faint beam of the remaining working headlight; clouds of dust, flakes of rust and bird droppings dislodged from the overhead girders still swirling in the disturbed air. Shards of shattered windscreen glass glittering across the oil stained tarmac. And, worst of all, that overwhelming odour of burnt metal, that astringent smell of leaking petrol. A scaffold pole had entered the windscreen on the driver's side. Initially the cause of death had erroneously been given in the local press as a 'decapitation'. Because the victim was female, blonde and the star of a minor TV reality show, parallels were inevitably drawn with the similarly mis-reported death of fifties movie star Jayne Mansfield. It was later established that the fatality involved in this particular RTA had been luckier. But, from what Cat had seen, not by much –

Cat shook herself free of the memory. Only now could she begin to make sense of what had just happened. To start to put the events in any kind of chronological order. The body hurtling out of the darkness. The devastating impact on the bonnet of the car in front; the startled, staring eyes of the girl, the collision of fragile bone and soft flesh with the hard, unyielding surface of the windshield, the clatter of the body being flung across the roof and coming to rest on the tarmac. Raising an unsteady hand to her forehead, leaning an elbow against the steering wheel, swallowing, massaging her temples between thumb and fingers, Cat exhaled a shaky, 'Fuck!'

165

She observes, as if from a great distance, as now, an automaton, a doppelganger, a replica of the real Cat Russell checks the rear-view mirror, flicks on the hazard lights, turns off the engine, removes the key, releases the seat belt. Then reaches across to the handbag on the front passenger seat, takes out the mobile phone and dials the emergency services.

Somehow, Cat is outside. In the filthy night. The howling wind. The rain bouncing off the road. Her blouse and trousers already stuck to her skin. Hair plastered to her skull. Her sopping jacket hanging like a lead weight from her shoulders. The mobile phone to her ear, shouting above the shrieking wind and driving rain. Trying to clearly and calmly state the facts of the situation. Then she is walking towards the driver's side door of the car in front. Pulling it open. Asking, stupidly,

'Are you alright?'

Getting an answer. Mumbled. Unintelligible. But an answer. Putting a hand to the driver's shoulder. Offering words of reassurance. Advice to stay put. That assistance was on its way. Before turning away to check the crumpled figure lying in the road. The headlights of her own car, the red taillights, the blinking amber hazard lights reflecting from the wet surface. And maybe it's just the over-sized heavy leather biker jacket. The close-cut black hair. But, even through the veil of teeming rain, the cloak of blood across the face, Cat thinks she recognises who it is. Kneeling on the wet tarmac. Gently probing the girl's blood-slick neck. Cat holds her breath. Staring through the rain, the darkness. Hoping that another car does not come up the road. Hoping that if it does, it will be able to make out the stationary vehicles in the dim illumination of the street-lighting. But most of all, hoping for even the faintest indication of a pulse beneath her frozen and slippery fingertips . . .

26

Detective Chief Inspector Martin Roberts scratched at the scalp under his thinning red hair. Wiped a hand down his face. And looking at Cat, he sighed. Made a big show of sighing. He started rolling a yellow biro across his desk. The 'bollocking pen', Cat thought. Then picking it up, he waggled it in Pearson's direction, because even Roberts had to draw the line somewhere. Because even Roberts would realise he couldn't aim his accusation directly at Cat, given what had gone on,

'What exactly is it with you?'

All the same, he let the question hang. Like it was patently obvious what he was getting at. Rather than neither of them *having a clue* what the fuck he was talking about. After a moment, a long moment, Pearson cleared his throat. Asked, tentatively,

'What d'you mean?'

'*You* . . . ,' Roberts repeated, 'two . . . ,' Roberts clarified, pointing the pen in Cat's direction, ' . . . and fucking suicides! First there was the sixteen-year-old that went off the Queensway underpass . . . '

'Alicia Goode,' Cat supplied.

'And then that … thing,' he flapped a hand at Pearson. Obviously not able to quite remember what the '*thing*' might be, ' . . . on the railway track.'

This time Cat said nothing. Resisting the urge to argue the point of whether both were actually suicides or not.

'By "the thing on the railway track", Guv' Pearson said, 'I take it you mean the Richard Lennon thing?'

Roberts gave Pearson the evils. Clearly not impressed. Then turned his attention to Cat, 'But it was you who was involved with that other thing. Right?' he said, 'The sixteen-year old that went over the edge of the Queensway underpass. The girl from the Abigail Burnett Children's Home . . . '

'Alicia Goode,' Cat repeated.

Nodding, Roberts said slowly, 'That's right. Alicia Goode. And now, this other girl falls from the observation platform by the pier. And *you*,' pointing the pen at Cat again, 'just happen to be driving along at the time. Just happen to be in the fucking car behind. Just like you,' glaring at Pearson again, 'just *happen* to be by the railway track when this Richard-Lennon-fucking-character decides to top himself.' He eyed, first Pearson, then her, speculatively across the desk. Shaking his head. As if he couldn't quite believe it. As if he suspected that something was going on to which he might not be privy. The fashioning of corn-shaft poppets or the shaping of wax effigies, perhaps. The conjuring of some kind of obscure sympathetic magic – in order to what, drum up some business? As if they didn't already have more work than they could handle. More likely, though, Roberts would believe it had all been concocted just to drag him out of his bed. Or conducted solely as a form of personal slight. Cat had found her opinion of Roberts mellowing over the past months.

Especially since she'd discovered that, at least according to Pearson, it was really only thanks to Roberts sticking his neck out that she was still in the Job. But, God, sometimes he could be *such* a prick . . .

Earlier, from her position in the back of the ambulance – shivering in her wet clothes, a blanket draped around her shoulders, having given an initial statement, having submitted to medical examination by one of the paramedics – Cat had been surprisingly glad to see, beyond the cordon of blue-and-white crime scene tape, Pearson pull up in the Mondeo. Watched as he got out. Slamming the driver's side door. Shrugging on his overcoat. Glancing towards the sky. Shooting a cuff to check his watch. Thrusting his hands into his pockets. It was a sequence of movements that was all-too-familiar. And a sequence of movements that, at that particular moment, she had found strangely comforting. A moment later, though, her heart sank as she saw Roberts stroll into view. Dressed in his habitual over-sized anorak. She'd watched the two men exchange a few words. Saw Pearson nod in her direction. Roberts glance her way and then come over. Initially, he had seemed sympathetic. Enquiring in a sensitive, even solicitous, way about how well she was coping . . .

Clearly, *that* moment had passed. And, although she was reasonably comfortable, having changed her clothes in the ladies' loo, because, being who she was, how she was, she kept a complete set of clothing in the boot of the car . . . Just in case. Along with the snow shovel, the wellies, the torch, the amber hazard lights and all the other crap which meant the

171

boot was all-but-unusable for normal everyday things … like the shopping. And although she felt at least passably like a human being, having been able to dry her hair under the hand blower, re-apply her lippy and mascara, she was about ready to drop. Barely managing to keep her eyes open. Not to mention, still a little unnerved by having witnessed a fatal accident. And, she realised, beginning to get dangerously-*bastard*-annoyed. Hoping Roberts would make his point, if he had one, before her fraying patience finally snapped and she said something –

'You,' Roberts said, shaking his head, aiming the biro at her again, '*and* you,' this time training it on Pearson, 'are a couple of fucking Jonahs. It's like bad luck trails the pair of you around.' He looked from Pearson to Cat, waited just long enough to make his point, then tossed the pen back onto the desk.

After a moment he looked up at her again, 'So? Do we have a name for the girl who went off the pier bridge? '

'Donna Freeman.'

'You're sure?'

'No official ID on her,' Cat said, 'but I recognised her. Definitely Donna Freeman.'

'The same Donna Freeman we interviewed in connection with DI Carragher's death?'

Cat nodded, 'Yes, Guv.'

'And,' Roberts said, 'the same Donna Freeman supposedly detained in a secure psychiatric facility pending an evaluation . . . ' Another look between the two of them.

Pearson cleared his throat, 'I looked into that.'

Roberts raised his eyebrows and glared at Pearson, 'So?'

'Absconded – '

'Well clearly – '

'A few weeks ago.'

'And did anyone think to inform us?' Roberts asked.

'Uniform attended but – '

'Let me guess, "Somehow the details weren't logged on the system"? Or, they're still waiting to be logged? Right?' When Pearson didn't answer, he added, 'So?'

'I spoke to one of the PC's who attended,' Pearson shrugged, 'and apparently she "just walked out" – '

' "*Walked out*?" How?'

'Well,' Pearson said, 'no one's really sure – '

'No one's owning up to it,' Roberts said.

'They're claiming staff shortages,' Pearson said, 'because of Government cuts.'

'The universal get out, these days. For anyone not doing their job. How many people does it *take* to lock a fucking door? 'And,' Roberts said, turning his attention back to Cat, 'this Donna Freeman, correct me if I'm wrong,' a warning look here, 'she's another one-time resident of the Abigail Burnett Children's Home, right?'

'Guv,' Cat conceded, 'Alicia Goode's best friend, or so Donna claimed, around the time that Alicia died – '

'And she was convinced – and sufficiently persuasive to get Carragher to look into it – that it had something to do with Clive Townsend. A senior care assistant at the Abigail Burnett and the same Clive Townsend who was recently tortured and then set on fire . . . '

'*For* which,' Pearson pointed out, 'we've already charged Ryan Yates.'

Roberts nodded slowly. Licked his lips. And looking down at the table, he sighed, 'Tell me that Ryan Yates wasn't at the Abigail Burnett?' After a moment, when Pearson hadn't answered, Roberts wiped his hand down his face. Sighed heavily, said, 'It always comes back to that fucking place.'

During the last exchange Cat's mind had wandered. Had gone back, in fact, to the moment shortly after she'd knelt beside Donna in the road . . .

She thought she might have heard a car door opening, before she'd seen the boots, the denim-clad legs, the bottom of a coat, appear in the glare of her car's headlights. But in the howling

174

wind, the teeming rain, she couldn't really be sure. Shouting to make himself understood, and half obscured by the night, he'd asked if he could be of any help and she had suggested he check on the driver.

'Any word on our witness?' Cat asked now, 'the driver who turned up a couple of minutes after the fall?' But when she looked over, Roberts and Pearson were looking back. Looking puzzled.

'What witness is this?' Pearson asked.

PART TWO

DAY FOUR

27

Cat Russell was late. Punch-drunk from lack of sleep. Still shaken from the events of the previous night. And already irritable from missing out on her morning cigarette. So, hurrying down the corridor on her way to the Incident Room, approaching the half-open door of Interview Suite 'B', she had made out the voices. But hadn't really believed – hadn't *wanted* to believe – what she was hearing. Pearson, without a doubt. Saying something she couldn't quite catch. Laughing. Sharing a joke. Another voice replying. Too low, too quiet, to hear. But the cadence, the timbre, was unmistakable. She should have left then. Simply turned on her heel and walked straight back down the corridor and out of the main entrance. And then what? Gone to her car and sat in it until the other man left? Gone home?

Standing now in the open doorway, Cat stared in disbelief. Still unable – unwilling – to quite trust her own senses. By the look of things; jackets draped across the backs of chairs, top shirt buttons unfastened, ties loosened, empty plastic coffee cups on the table between them, the two men had been talking for a while. Their shared body language had the easy manner of people who'd clearly broken the ice and already felt relaxed in each other's company. Cat dithered, undecided as to what to do next. And in that momentary hesitation the opportunity to do anything was lost. Pearson was already glancing over, pushing back his chair, getting to his feet. Ready to make the introductions. Inwardly groaning, muttering a '*Fuck!*' under her breath, carefully arranging her features into what she hoped might be an expression of friendly welcome mixed with a mild curiosity, she looked to Pearson for an explanation.

'Morning,' Pearson said amiably, 'I wasn't expecting you in,' then, indicating the man opposite, 'This is Detective Chief Inspector John Hall . . . '

John Hall was rising from his chair, a half-smile on his face, a challenge in his eyes. Cat would come to suspect later that the decision that followed, the subsequent action – or rather, the lack of a decision, the failure to act – was probably the point where everything changed. That if she had only acknowledged their past, their recent shared intimacy in the motel room, or even just a prior association, things might have been different. But, after all, couldn't Hall have done the same? Couldn't he have diffused the excruciating tension, the unbearable awkwardness, of their encounter with a simple, '*We've met*'? And wasn't the truth of the situation that he, too, simply chose not to?

Allowing Hall a brusque handshake, a curt nod, a mumbled, '*Sir,*' Cat pulled out a chair and sat down at the table. All the while making a point of not catching Pearson's eye. Hoping he hadn't picked up on her body language. Hadn't noticed the deliberate coolness of her manner.

Interview Suite 'B'. The re-designation the brainchild of DCS Andy Curtis. But it was still, essentially, the same drab, claustrophobic room containing the same moulded plastic chairs, the same scuffed wooden table in which, only a few months ago, she had been interrogated by DI Ferguson of the Professional Standards department. Cat took her time putting her handbag on her lap, taking out her notebook and placing it deliberately on the table in front of her, rummaging around in the bag for a pen.

Pearson was saying, 'John's from the Durham CID –

'

'I've spent the last few days attending a seminar in London,' Hall cut in, 'and this morning I received some information which warranted your attention. And I thought as I was in the area . . . ' He paused then. And Cat was forced to look in his direction. Out of simple common courtesy. Out of a deference to hierarchy acquired over her more-than-four-years in the Job. But mostly because she didn't want to give Pearson any reason to wonder why she hadn't.

'Not that Southend's really in the London area, of course,' Hall said, 'about an eighty-mile round trip so I'm told . . . '

Cat was instantly narked. And she wasn't sure what annoyed her the most: the deliberate parroting of the phrase she'd used at their meeting in Priory Park a few months ago, or the ghost of a smirk hovering around his lips. He's fucking enjoying this, she thought.

John Hall took a breath, reminding himself not to focus exclusively on Cat. To give the other, more senior, officer at least comparable attention. To make a conscious effort to include both of them in the conversation; to spend an equivalent time looking at each in turn, to make an equal amount of eye contact. But in his mind, he had gone back to the time, nearly ten years ago, when he and Cat had first met.

He had only recently been promoted to the rank of Detective Sergeant. But after just six months he had already recognised that any prospect of further advancement was likely to be frustrated by the indifference and apathy of his over-cautious and obstructive fellow officers. His marriage too was in trouble. Then again, when hadn't it been? He and Jean had been allocated adjacent desks on the very first day of primary school. Had been virtually inseparable ever since. When the time had come to attend secondary school, he'd persuaded his parents, against their better judgement, to allow him to give up his place at the best grammar school in the area in order to attend the same second-rate comprehensive as Jean. He'd been offered a place at university, had asked Jean to go with him, but she hadn't wanted to move away from her family. So, in the end, he hadn't gone, instead, working several menial, dead-end jobs until eventually discovering his vocation in the Police Force. And then, somehow, he found himself with a mortgage and two kids, the youngest one severely disabled.

All of which might have been bearable. Except he suddenly realised that he was profoundly and seemingly incurably … bored. The responsibilities of fatherhood, the constant battles with sceptical and bureaucratic health professionals to even get his autistic daughter diagnosed, let alone treated. Jean's constant nagging about a bigger house, a better car, expensive holidays abroad. At the same time resenting the additional hours he spent at work. Most of all, their increasingly infrequent and unadventurous love-making all conspired to drain any joy, any energy, any *hope* he might have once felt. In the next few years he had embarked on a passionate but short-lived affair with a WPC, had had any number of casual and ultimately meaningless one-night stands, and had even, on occasion, paid for squalid and unsatisfying sex with some of the sex-workers he'd come into contact with in the course of his job. But, in the end, he found the very willingness and promiscuity of the women he was sleeping with repellent.

'Like I told your DS here,' Hall said, 'I stayed overnight at a hotel in London,' Daring her to contradict the statement, the downright-fucking-lie, 'I thought, "Better check in, John, man. See what kind of shite you might be walking back into". And, my DS tells me that we've received reliable intel that a "person of interest" in a number of rapes and sexual assaults may be in this neck of the woods . . . '

Cat could not resist the glance across the table at Pearson, studying his face, gauging his reaction. Surely, he would see through this flimsy justification. Had twigged that there was something else going on? But Pearson's face was impassive, his focus, seemingly, on his notepad. Where he'd been writing something that, upside down, half-obscured by his left hand, Cat couldn't quite make out. Pearson looked up, 'Do we have a name, sir?'

'Daniel Angus Fraser,' Hall said.

28

'Daniel Angus Fraser,' Hall said, 'Born August the sixth, 1983, aged thirty-six. In 2004, Danny was the "subject of interest" in an allegation of sexual assault – '

'Subject of interest?' Pearson asked.

'The complainant changed her mind and the allegation was dropped before Danny could be interviewed . . . '

As Pearson scratched some notes on his pad Cat turned back to Hall. Who gave her a conspiratorial wink. That smirk back on his face. Like all of this was just a bit of a lark, like they might be accomplices in some jolly wheeze. Like it was merely a harmless prank at Pearson's expense. Though in the instant of turning she had caught a very different expression: anger? Betrayal? Jealousy? But it had been so fleeting, so *unexpected*, that she was already doubting herself as to whether it had actually been there at all.

'The Frasers have interests in a couple of clubs in Newcastle,' Hall went on, 'They also run "Fraser Construction Services" which, up until five years ago, was a medium-scale building firm operating in the Newcastle and Durham area. But in 2014, as part of the drive towards the outsourcing of building work to the private sector, they were awarded a substantial Government project in the north-east. Since then they have secured a number of other projects and have expanded along the east coast from Yorkshire down to East Anglia.'

'And you think that this is why this Danny Fraser might be in the area?'

'Aye,' Hall nodded.

'Okay,' Pearson said, 'Sorry, Sir, go on.'

'Until recently, the Managing Director of Fraser Construction had *been* Logan Fraser. Danny's old man.'

'Anything on him?'

'Nothing we've been able to make stick,' Hall admitted reluctantly, 'A couple of counts of possession, one of GBH. But we know he's been involved in the trafficking of class "A" and firearms. The closest we came to getting anything more serious on him was nearly twenty years ago, when we received information from a previously impeccable source, implicating Logan in the disappearance of James Gillen Robertson, who had been working behind the bar in one of the clubs in Newcastle. A severed right hand, identified through fingerprints as belonging to Robertson, was left on the doorstep of the club. We were working on the theory that Robertson had been skimming money from the drug deals in the club and this was a warning to others not to do the same thing. But there was no forensic evidence, no other body parts have yet come to light, and nothing could be traced back to the Frasers. Our source was later hospitalised in a "random" late-night hit-and-run and subsequently refused to talk to us . . .'

John Hall's gaze drifted across to Cat. Trying to reconcile the woman on the other side of the table with the awkward, unsophisticated and slightly brassy girl not long out of her teens he'd first come across a decade ago. There was no doubt that she had become a beautiful, intelligent and, at least outwardly, confident young woman. But hadn't that been mostly his doing? Hadn't he been the one to support her through, what would have been, the most sickening and traumatic experience of her life up to that point? Hadn't he been the one to nurse her through the resulting mental crisis? Hadn't he been the one who had given her an education? Had taught her about philosophy, music, literature and the classics?

"In the course of time he successfully carved an amazing skilful

statue in ivory, white as snow, an image of perfect feminine beauty –

and fell in love with his own creation."

But Cat's attention, once again, was on the older male detective.

'You said the Managing Director *had been* Logan Fraser?' Pearson asked.

'Aye,' Hall said, 'he died recently, of stomach cancer. I can't pretend he'll be missed. Word is that, Jackie, Danny's older brother, has taken over. Now Jackie, we do have something on. He's done time for rape. A particularly nasty

attack. The victim, fifteen, was left with life-changing injuries
– '

'But, as yet,' Pearson said, 'nothing against Danny Fraser himself?' Hall shook his head.

'So, getting back to this allegation of sexual assault against Danny Fraser, Sir. What exactly happened there?'

'A girl of fourteen accused Danny of attempted rape,' Hall shrugged. 'The next morning, she changes her mind and withdraws the allegation. Put it down to both of them having too much to drink, that it was partly her fault, that she might have been mistaken … the usual story.' Without looking up from his notes, Pearson nodded. 'In the two years between late 2001 and early 2004 there were a string of rapes and attempted rapes in the Durham area, and we had reason to believe that young Danny was involved.'

'But no hard evidence, I take it?' Pearson asked.

Hall shrugged again, 'Circumstantial mostly, partial descriptions of the assailant. The clothes the attacker wore; workboots, donkey jacket, jeans covered in plaster dust, a smell of paint or white spirit and the vehicle used all tallied with someone in the building trade. The assailant was said to have driven a transit van, or something similar . . . '

'But nothing that might tie it directly to Danny Fraser?'

Elbows on the table, squeezing his right fist with his left hand, Hall met Pearson's gaze. Sighed. Like he was starting to be irritated by the constant interruptions. Like he was annoyed by this contradiction of the self-evident logic of his account. Like his integrity were being brought into question.

'Danny joined the army in the January of 2001,' Hall said, 'and the assaults stopped. At least in the Durham area . . .'

'You think Fraser may have been responsible for sexual assaults somewhere else?' Pearson asked.

'During his time in the services,' Hall said, 'Danny was part of Sixteenth Air Assault, which, I'm sure you're aware, is garrisoned at Colchester. Which is another reason, by the way, that he might be in this area.'

'Because of the contacts he made while he was in the regiment?' Pearson asked.

'Aye,' Hall agreed, 'Anyway, during the time he was in Colchester, a serious sexual assault took place. No one was ever arrested or charged. But, according to the victim, her attacker was a squaddie. And the description bore a resemblance to Danny. A number of attacks have occurred in the Durham area over subsequent years, some of the dates of which directly correspond with Danny being on leave from the army – ' Pearson looked up from his notes. 'Look,' Hall said, 'even I'm not going to claim that *every* assault, attempted rape and unsolved rape in the Durham area is down to him. But the fact that *some* of them match the dates he was on leave? To my mind,' Hall paused, 'that's got to be more than a coincidence, right?'

189

'Well,' Pearson conceded, 'It's certainly something worth looking into,' and then, 'Is that it, Sir?'

'That's it.'

Pearson closed the cover of his notebook, slipped his arms into the jacket hanging on the back of his chair, rose from his seat, 'We really do appreciate your time in this matter, Sir. And we'll definitely follow it up.'

Later, back in the Incident Room. Having seen John Hall out of the building. Having brought back a couple of drinks from the vending machine for himself and Cat, his jacket once again draped over the back of his chair, tapping absent-mindedly on his open notebook with a biro, Pearson asked,

'So, what d'you make of this information from DCI Hall?' He took a sip of his coffee, 'Anything in it, d'you think?'

But looking across, Cat, who had been uncharacteristically quiet during the meeting, who had said nothing and barely looked up from the table, was staring down into her cup of coffee, lost in her own thoughts . . .

29

'Any updates on last night?' Cat asked. To move the conversation on. To forestall any further discussion on the meeting they'd just had. To stop any potential speculation on Pearson's part regarding a possible relationship between her and John Hall. But most of all because it was, after all, the reason she'd come in this morning. The only reason she'd come in. The reason she hadn't just called in justifiably, to her mind, and taken a day off sick.

'The woman in the car was released from hospital this morning. Nothing more than a few cuts and bruises really. Severely shocked, obviously.'

'And Donna Freeman?'

Pearson hesitated, 'Er ... Yeah,' he scratched behind an ear. Glanced down briefly at his desk, 'about that . . . ' Then looked her directly in the eye. An expression on his face that she didn't particularly like. An expression of regret. Of concern. Of reluctance. An expression that presaged something unpleasant. Something upsetting. Something that he would much rather not have to say, 'Sorry, Cat. Donna Freeman died of her injuries in the early hours of this morning.'

Impersonal. Factual. To the point. The recognised procedure to establish distance between a police officer and a victim. But, somehow, today it felt a touch ... brutal. Pearson was talking. Had been talking for some time, but Cat wasn't really following what he was saying. And she found that she had a pen in her hand, her notepad out and open on the desk in front of her. As if by recording the facts, by reducing everything to simple cause and effect, she might somehow be able to make sense of it all. But the pages of the A4 Major Incident notebook remained stubbornly empty. She looked up now and asked,

'Sorry, what was that?'

Pearson stopped talking. Licked his lips. Gave an almost imperceptible nod. To show he understood. Then started again, 'There's a set of gates across the pier bridge. These are usually locked at night to restrict pedestrian access. The SOCO's found evidence of them having been forced. But they couldn't find any sort of tool – a jemmy, crowbar or whatever – either on the body, the bridge, or anywhere nearby. Roberts had the road and the roadside undergrowth searched for fifty yards in both directions to rule out the possibility of it having been previously discarded or having been catapulted by the force of the collision.'

He paused. Studying her face. Gauging her reaction. Calculating whether he should continue or not.

'It's okay,' Cat said, 'Go on.'

'A partial boot print was found on a damaged glass panel on the footbridge. The tread pattern is a match for the boots that Donna Freeman was wearing. According to the measurements made by the Crime Scene Manager, from where she was standing – most likely with one foot on the handrail or brick wall – it's doubtful that she would have

ended up where she landed in the road, if she'd jumped . . . '
Pearson trailed off. Satisfied that she'd understood the
implications of what he'd just said. After a moment, when it
became clear that she hadn't, he added, 'Which means, in all
likelihood, she was pushed. In any case Roberts believes there
is sufficient doubt and opened a murder investigation this
morning.'

Cat suddenly found herself wanting to cry. And for
any number of reasons: the unexpected appearance of John
Hall at her place of work, the lack of sleep, the still fragile
state of her nerves following the events by the footbridge, the
combination of all of these. But, most of all, because of an
abrupt and overwhelming feeling of loss at the death of the
girl. But why this girl in particular? Or was Donna Freeman
emblematic of all the other girls; the dead girls, the girls who
were *still* to die, the girls she had made a personal vow to help,
the girls she had failed?

Cat looked around the Incident Room, dragging
herself away from the troubled look on Pearson's face. If she
saw that for even a moment longer, she probably would cry.
Making a conscious effort to change the subject, she said,

'I've had this feeling all morning, like something's
not, quite right?'

Across the desk, Pearson's expression moved from
worried to quizzical.

'You know,' Cat said, 'like when a piece of furniture
is suddenly missing? A picture that you've always had on the
wall, but it's been there so long you don't really see it. Then

193

one day it's not there anymore. It's like, you don't really notice it's not there, but you know something's not, quite right?'

'And?' Pearson asked.

'I've just twigged what it is,' Cat pointed across the room with her pen, 'Where's Laurence?'

At about the same time Cat had been making her way along the passage towards the Incident Room, Detective Sergeant Alan Laurence had been walking down a corridor of HMP Chelmsford. Following a prison officer. George. At least, that's how Laurence thought of him. But where he'd got that idea, where he'd heard the name, he couldn't have said. Maybe from one of the other screws. But he wouldn't have sworn to it. Weren't they always called George? George was a hard-faced Glaswegian who had a fat neck overhanging the collar of a short-sleeved blue shirt. An impressive beer-gut straining at a low-slung leather belt. A set of keys in a ziploc bag banging against a hip. Laurence gripped a leather briefcase in his left hand, his right going again to the side pocket of his jacket. Feeling the lack of weight. The absence of his phone. How many times had he reached for it during the walk along this corridor? How many times since he'd handed it over at reception? Where, predictably, he'd been held up for ages while they checked the paperwork. Because apparently nobody at the prison was actually expecting his visit. Despite what Roberts had said nearly two hours earlier . . .

I've already passed it to Prison Liaison at Force Intelligence to make the appropriate arrangements,' Roberts said. Laurence had stood for the previous few minutes trying to come up with a reason why he couldn't go. Why he wasn't the right person for the job. That he was too busy with other things. He'd had a bad feeling ever since he'd glanced up from his computer in the Incident Room to see Roberts standing at the open door, scanning the assembled officers, his gaze settling briefly on Laurence before moving on. He'd thought he'd gotten away with it, had turned his attention back to his screen, when half a minute later he'd heard his name being called. And looked up to see that sour, unimpressed look on Roberts's face. And the dreaded crooking finger. When he'd entered Roberts's office the DCI had barely settled himself back in his chair before he'd picked up a sheet of paper from his desk and shook it at him.

'There's been a "death in custody" at HMP Chelmsford. They need an officer over there right away. Something to do with a "vulnerable prisoner". Probably another suicide. As per-fucking-usual the details are all-but-non-existent . . . ' Sensing Laurence's reluctance he'd added, 'Look, everyone else is tied up, and I've got a prior engagement with the Chief Constable, or I'd go myself.' And when Laurence had still not moved, he'd flapped the piece of paper irritably at him, 'Go on then, get a move on. You're expected . . . '

Murray. The prison officer's name suddenly came to Laurence now as they stopped at a room and he selected one of the keys he was carrying and unlocked the door. Pushed it open and flicked on the light.

'I'm afraid this is the only room we have spare at the moment.'

Laurence entered the room, glancing at the clock on the wall, pulled out a chair, sat down and placed his briefcase on the table.

Earlier, he'd interviewed Irene Fairbridge, one of the psychologists attached to the prison. Middle-aged, bespectacled, plump, she wore a black Adidas tracksuit over a red sweatshirt and pink trainers. An effort, he supposed, to put her patients at their ease. Though Laurence wondered if they, like him, would have preferred her to wear a suit. To at least give the impression of being business-like. Of appearing halfway competent. The effect wasn't helped by not wearing make-up, not having bothered to brush her hair. Though this was probably a deliberate statement rather than an oversight. But, even in the short time they'd spent together, Fairbridge had struck him, in common with so many in her profession, in his *own* profession, as jaded, disinterested and almost completely demotivated. The initial eager enthusiasm having obviously been worn down, not only by the years of repeated and over-intimate contact with the very worst that human nature had to offer, but also the effort of trying to put yourself in their place, to think as they did.

Laurence opened the briefcase, took out the manila folder containing the transcript of the mental health assessment of Ryan Yates. And, catching *himself* sighing now, he opened the folder and began to read . . .

196

30

For a while, Cat had been able to submerge herself in mindless routine. Had, for once, been grateful for the countless statutory procedures, the endless administrative processes the job involved. Had been able to stop herself thinking about the death she had witnessed the previous evening. Had been able to stop herself thinking of anything at all. She checked the time on her phone. Pearson, she reflected, was the only person she knew who still wore a watch. The beaten-up old Timex. The watch obviously held some kind of sentimental value for him. But, she realised, that in all the time they'd worked together she'd never thought to ask him about it. She was surprised now to find that nearly two hours had passed. Two hours in which she managed to delay the inevitable and necessary examination of the previous night's events. Why had the death of this particular girl had such a profound effect on her? It was right to think of her in that way. A girl. Because she was – had been – so slight of frame that, whatever her age, it was almost impossible to think of her as anything else. Why her? Wasn't she just … another dead girl? Another dead girl. It seemed that lately that particular phrase had become her personal mantra. No, she had intentionally *made* it her mantra. Another dead girl. But had the words been repeated so often in her mind that they had lost all significance, all context, all meaning? Was it now nothing more than an empty phrase?

Why had she felt such a deep connection with Donna Freeman? And had the girl felt it too? In the interview room, when they had questioned her following the death of Sean, the girl had looked up, studying Cat's face. Looking, not *at* Cat, exactly. But sort of through her. Or around her. As if Cat was obscuring something of more interest.

But, later, when Cat had asked, 'So what were you doing in the car park with Sean?' Donna had said,

'*He was one of the policemen who came and spoke to us when Alicia died.*' And she had studied Cat closely again. As if trying to work out where she knew Cat from, as if she thought Cat might have been there too . . .

Finally, hesitantly, tentatively, Cat allowed her mind to return once more to the events of the previous night. To the crumpled figure lying in the road. The headlights of her own car, the red taillights, the blinking amber hazard lights reflecting from the wet surface . . .

Cat kneels on the road. Gently probing the girl's bloody neck. Staring down at the over-sized heavy leather biker jacket. The close-cut black hair. The cloak of blood across the strangely incongruous make-up. The white face. The black lips. And even as Cat hopes desperately to find just the faintest indication of a pulse, she recognises ... Pierrot.

Now, in the cold light of day, in the, for her at least, prosaic and familiar surroundings of the Incident Room, she wonders what possible significance the sad-faced clown of the *Commedia Dell'arte* could have had for Donna Freeman. Cat herself only had a vague recollection of the story. Or, at least, the version of the story in the English *Harlequinade*. How did it go? The shy and awkward Pierrot is hopelessly in love with the beautiful Columbine. Columbine spurns Pierrot for the sly and mercurial Harlequin. If Donna Freeman had cast herself as Pierrot, who was her Columbine? Cat supposed, given the evident obsession she had with solving what had been the apparently accidental death of her best friend, that this was Alicia Goode. But who then played the role of Alicia Goode's Harlequin? And would Donna even have been familiar with this story? Cat doubted it. In more recent times Pierrot had come to represent the alter-ego of the alienated artist. Wasn't there something about the artist having to initially take advantage of the creative, irrational subconscious in order to conceptualise their art? And only later connect with the logical, rational conscious part of the brain in order to police these ideas? Or perhaps Cat had made this all up. In any case, this was just reaching. Trying to force a connection between her and the girl that just didn't exist. She doubted that any of this would have the slightest relevance to the girl. More than likely the character of Pierrot itself had no significance for Donna at all. Perhaps it was simply an image she'd seen on TV. Maybe the sad face held the appeal. And the actual application of the mask was the object. Hadn't Cat herself worn a mask of sorts since the attack on her ten years ago? And, after a time, didn't the distinction between the mask and the wearer of the mask become less and less easy to determine. Couldn't Donna Freeman have also adopted that particular mask as a way of keeping something out? Or, perhaps, keeping something *in*?

Cat noticed a cup of cold coffee sitting on her desk. Pearson obviously having brought it back from the vending machine and placed it there without saying anything. Or if he had said something, she hadn't heard him. Cat felt drained. Slow-witted. She had only had a few hours' sleep. What sleep she'd had, had been disturbed. The hours lying awake spent replaying the incident over and over in her mind. And, if anything, this had only succeeded in making her memory of the events less clear-cut, less certain. Now, she wasn't at all sure of what had actually happened next. Did she remember the sound of an engine? The swish of tyres on wet tarmac? The sharp application of brakes? A car door opening? Or had she just imagined it all? She had definitely seen boots appear in the glare of her headlights. Had seen the pair of legs, the bottom of a coat. But the rest of the figure had been obscured by the night. She had heard him ask, '*Can I help?*' And she had asked him to check on the driver. At the time, in the pelting rain, the howling wind, she hadn't been able to make out the man's voice. Not properly. Now, though, she had a suspicion that it might have been John Hall. Except, she had left him asleep in that motel room. To be at the scene of the accident, he would have had to have been awake. Or awoken soon after. He would have had to have followed her without her knowledge. If it *had* been John, surely, he would have announced himself at the scene, wouldn't he? Would have hung around to help? To give a statement to the police officers who later investigated what had happened? Instead, the witness, whoever it was, had seemingly just disappeared. No, it was ridiculous. Pure paranoia. His unexpected appearance at her place of work had simply unsettled her. Hadn't it?

But, in Roberts's office, Cat had asked, 'Any word on our witness?'

And when she had looked over, Roberts and Pearson were looking back. Looking puzzled. And Pearson had said –

'Daniel Angus Fraser.'

'Cat looked across the desk now towards Pearson, 'Pardon?'

'Daniel Angus Fraser?' Pearson said, 'The guy DCI Hall spoke to us about a few hours ago?'

'What about him?'

'Hall said Fraser had served in the army. Remember?'

'Yeah. So what?'

'So, he served in Afghanistan in Sixteenth Air Assault. Which just happens to be the —'

'The same unit as Daryl Crawford.'

'Daryl Crawford being – '

'The manager of the *Double Carpet* betting shop that Tony Blake attempted to rob.'

Pearson shot a cuff and checked his watch. 'It should still be open now. I think it'd be worth us going and having a word. I can drop you off afterward. I don't think it's a good idea, you driving. Leave your car here tonight. It'll be safe enough. I can pick you up in the morning.'

31

Detective Sergeant Alan Laurence opened the manila folder containing the mental health assessment. He paused. Taking a moment. Attempting, as was his habit, to connect with the person he was to investigate. Trying to put himself in the place of Ryan Yates. Then he began to read . . .

'So how are you feeling today?' the woman had asked. She had introduced herself as Irene Fairbridge, 'Call me Irene'. But she hadn't actually explained what she was, why she was here, what it was she wanted from him. Had not looked up again since that brief introduction as he'd entered the room. Writing, instead, in a manila folder she had open on the table.

Ryan Yates had marked the ponderous advance of the minute hand around the face of the wall-clock while she leafed backwards and forwards through several sheets of A4 paper. Ticked off boxes. Nodded. Murmured under her breath. Made the occasional note. At one point she had taken a packet of Werther's Originals out of her tracksuit pocket, unwrapped one of the sweets and popped it in her mouth. But had not offered the packet to him. She wasn't even looking at him now. Now she had finally acknowledged his presence. Now she'd actually asked him a question.

Ryan Yates didn't know how he felt, not exactly, and even if he did know how he felt he wouldn't be able to explain it, not properly, not in a way this woman might understand.

Not that she *really* wanted to know. It was just a question they asked. They *had* all asked. The *first* question they all asked; the teachers, the social workers, the psychologists, the psychiatrists, the police officers, the solicitors … all of them. But they didn't *really* want to know –

'I'd like to ask you a few questions,' the woman – Irene – was saying now, 'Is that okay?'

They always asked that, too. Like you had any choice. Like they wouldn't just ask their questions anyway, 'And, Ryan, they might not seem, at first, that they're at all relevant, but it really would be helpful if you could try to answer them for me. Okay?'

And this was what they all said as well. It was something he'd heard hundreds of times. From any number of people with official-sounding titles. Before they'd asked him hundreds of other stupid questions and ticked hundreds of stupid boxes on hundreds of stupid forms. They must still have all those forms. They *must still have* all his answers. So why did she have to ask the same questions all over again?

Instead of saying that he would *try* and answer *her* questions, which is what he usually did, Ryan asked a question of his own, 'When can I get some medication? I think I know what it is I need.'

He'd managed to talk to a few of the people queueing up at the pharmacy. Ask them what they were taking. What they thought he should be taking. They all seemed to agree that he should have an anti-depressant. Something like *Fluoxetine*. They always started you on *Fluoxetine*, they said.

204

They couldn't make a fuss about *Fluoxetine*. Then maybe an anti-psychotic. Something that would make him feel … better, sort of … less anxious. Something like *Risperidone*. But the trouble with *Risperidone*, they said, was that it had side effects; if you were on it for a long time you could grow breasts. Or you put on a lot of weight. He couldn't quite remember. But it definitely raised your blood sugar levels, so there was a risk of diabetes. Chances were, they wouldn't let him have that. Best just ask for *Fluoxetine* to start off with –

'All in good time, Ryan. But first I really would like you to try and answer a few questions for me. Okay?'

Ryan looked around the room. At the bare bulb hanging from a single pendant. At the paint peeling from the discoloured ceiling. At the sliver of leaden sky visible through the semi-circular barred window set high in one of the whitewashed brick walls. Hoping that Donna had been right. Hoping, somehow, that the room – the whitewashed brick walls, the scuffed linoleum floor. The scratched, grey Formica table beneath his restless fingers might only be some kind of facade. That behind it all, might be 'something else'. Something better.

Ryan decided to ask another question. It was a question he had asked before. Asked, in that first interview room, of the police officer. Asked, in the room under the court, of the woman appointed as his solicitor. And had got no answer. But this woman was a psychiatrist, or a psychologist, or at least some kind of mental health professional, so she would know best, wouldn't she?

So, not looking up from the table. Rubbing, instead, at its scarred surface with a thumb, Ryan asked his question, 'Do you think you can catch madness?'

'*Catch?*' Fairbridge asked, 'Like a disease? You think "madness" might be a kind of virus? Or a bacteriological infection?'

Ryan wondered if the psychologist had deliberately misunderstood the question. Or just had him down as some kind of thicko. The expression on her face of ... smug amusement. The barely hidden sarcasm in her voice. Belittling him. Because he wasn't articulate. Because he didn't have the right education, the correct vocabulary to get across what was in his head.

'What about, like, the witch trials in Salem – '

'Well, one theory is that that was caused by – '

'Ergot poisoning, yeah,' Ryan nodded, 'I've read all that. A fungus that grows on rye. That's what they say *now*. That's the logical, rational, scientific theory *now*. What about mob hysteria? Like football hooliganism? Or what about . . . ' Ryan searched for another example, 'what about the Nazis? What about the people who worked as guards in the death camps?'

'I really don't think – '

'What about someone like Charles Manson? You know about Charles Manson and his "*family*", right? What they did? What he *got* them to do? What about someone who can make other people do vile unspeakable things? What

206

about if that someone isn't actually like that themselves? Isn't, like, an evil person, like Manson? What if that person is like ... mentally ill or something?'

For a time neither spoke. Fairbridge waited, wondering, believing that Ryan Yates still had more to say. Then, finally, Ryan glanced up from the table.

'What about if you, like, do something but you're not aware of what the consequences might be?' Then looked quickly down again, 'There's this thing ... *mens rea*? You've heard of that, right? In common law, for a person to be found "guilty" by the court there must be both *actus reus*, a "guilty act", and *mens rea*, a "guilty mind". So ... you've got to, like, actually know what you're doing is wrong?'

Laurence stopped reading for a moment and did exactly what he suspected the psychologist might have done at this point: he flicked back through the folder to check what books and periodicals Yates had checked out of, and requested from, the prison library. Wondering whether Ryan Yates might be trying to retrospectively construct a persuasive, or at least plausible, defence for the appalling, violent murder he'd committed. Finding the piece of paper and running his finger down the list, Laurence noticed that it did indeed contain quite a few law books and psychiatric journals. All of which had been requested ... but, as yet, not received. On the other hand, by all accounts, Ryan Yates was very intelligent, so maybe, Laurence thought, he'd simply come across the terms during his journey through the criminal justice system. Nevertheless, he made a note of it on his pad, then went back to reading the transcript . . .

'In terms of *mens rea*,' the psychologist said, 'It used to be the case that you had to prove the intention to commit a crime. It's not that straightforward these days. There are what is termed "modes of culpability". In your case they – that is, prosecuting counsel – might argue "oblique intention", that is that the result was a virtual certainty of your actions and that you would have appreciated that was so. Or they might argue that you knew, or should have known, that such a result would occur. They might even argue "recklessness" on your part . . . ' Fairbridge trailed off when it became apparent Ryan was no longer listening.

'Do you think,' Ryan looked up now, holding the psychologist in a steady gaze, 'that evil – badness, wickedness … sin, whatever you want to call it – could exist independently outside of us? Or is it inside *all* of us? Or just some people? Can some people, good people, or people who thought they were good, be made to do bad things by someone else?'

32

At the knock on the open half-glazed door, Daryl Crawford looked up from the desktop: the pad, the calculator, the pile of betting slips, the computation of a complicated multi-combination accumulator. Even before they said anything, even before they introduced themselves, he knew. The man: middle-aged, a crumpled grey suit, the top button of his shirt undone, the tie slightly askew. And in his left hand a leather slip case. The woman: late twenties or early thirties, her dark brown hair in a loose ponytail. A black trouser suit over a white blouse. Now she, she could maybe get away with being an estate agent or a solicitor. But him, he couldn't be anything other than a copper.

'Mister Crawford?' the man asked.

'Yep,' Daryl said, 'that's me,' then, standing up, 'How can I help?'

The man slipped a warrant card from the inside pocket of his jacket and held it out for Daryl to read.

'I'm Detective Sergeant Frank Pearson,' he waved the card in the direction of the woman, 'this is Detective Constable Catherine Russell.'

Daryl shook their hands. Then he pointed past the male detective – Pearson – to a stack of moulded, plastic chairs in the corner of the room,

'D'you want to grab somewhere to sit?'

Then he nodded past the woman – Russell – and asked, 'Could you close the door, please? Pearson separated a couple of chairs from the pile and placed them in front of the desk. Russell turned her back to close the door. And Daryl couldn't resist stealing a glance at the wall safe.

Pearson looked up at the ceiling, 'Blimey, he made a right old mess of that, didn't he?'

'Yeah. the owner keeps promising me he's going to get it repaired.'

'Jack?' Pearson asked. Looking back at him, 'Yeah, good luck with *that*.'

'Do you know him?' Daryl asked.

'Know *of* him,' Pearson said, 'Tight-arse. By all accounts.'

As they all took their seats, Daryl asked, 'Is that why you're here? The robbery?'

'No,' Pearson shook his head, 'we're here about another matter.' He flipped open the leather slip case and read from his notes, 'Daniel Angus Fraser? As I understand it, you served together in Afghanistan?' A quick glance up and Daryl, not sure, at this point, what to say. Not sure how *much* he wanted to say, how much he could get away without saying. Settled on a single nod of confirmation. 'You were part of Sixteenth Air Assault? Is that correct?'

210

'Well,' Daryl said, 'Pathfinder Platoon. Which is, technically, a part of Sixteenth Air Assault, but sort of a specialist division, what's known as a Reconnaissance Unit.'

'Which means,' Pearson asked flipping over a clean page in his pad, 'what exactly?' Taking out a silver pen from his inside pocket and clicking the top.

'Pathfinder is dropped in, in advance of Sixteenth Air Assault, to perform reconnaissance operations, mark out DZ's and HLS –' Pearson looked up from his notes and gave Daryl a quizzical look. 'Sorry,' Daryl said, 'Drop zones and helicopter landing sites.'

'So, we're talking about parachuting in behind enemy lines? That sort of thing? Pathfinder's like a sort of SAS?'

Daryl shrugged, 'I suppose you could think of it like that, yeah.'

Pearson nodded, made a face, like he was impressed. Then, looking down at his notes again, he asked, 'And what was *your* role?'

And Daryl wondered then whether he'd already said too much. Asked, 'Is all this relevant?' Decided he didn't like the direction in which these questions were heading, 'Only I'm not sure I'm at liberty to discuss matters pertaining to operational issues.' Then he opted for a more conciliatory, 'I'm sorry, I'm not trying to be obstructive or anything. It's just . . . '

'Fair enough,' Pearson conceded, 'I'm just trying to get some background on Mister Fraser. Would it be fair, then, to say you were his Commanding Officer?'

'Well,' Daryl said, 'again, technically, yes.' Daryl decided to give the copper a little. And at the same time distance himself from whatever it was that Danny Fraser might have been up to. 'But Pathfinder operations are usually carried out by small, compact units. They rely on flexibility, on the members of each unit being able to think on their feet, to react to a given situation. Rather than just blindly following orders.'

'So how many, typically, would be in each unit?'

'Typically? Six? Eight? It depends on the specific operation.'

'So … half-a-dozen blokes … all dependant on one another … everyone having to put their complete trust in everyone else? You must end up being pretty close?'

'I suppose,' Daryl hedged.

'So, you'd say you got to know Mister Fraser – Danny – pretty well?'

'As well as you *can* get to know someone like Danny, yeah.' As soon as he'd said it, Daryl regretted it. As Pearson wrote something down on his notepad his gaze drifted towards the female detective who, up until now, had said nothing . . .

Cat Russell sat on the uncomfortable plastic chair, idly toying with the strap of the handbag on her lap. Looking at the man on the other side of the desk. Daryl Crawford, the ex-Special Forces soldier, the decorated war hero, the man who had recently foiled an attempted armed robbery, the man now relegated to a grotty back office in a tatty betting shop run by a dodgy small-time businessman. But not really seeing him. Deliberately not taking in the conversation. Trying to blot out any hint of the man who might very well have raped her and left her for dead a decade ago. And feeling an overpowering sense of not wanting to be here. Experiencing, once again, that almost overwhelming urge to run . . .

Daryl realised the male detective was saying something. He turned to face him.

'Why do you say that?'

For a moment, Daryl didn't answer, couldn't answer, couldn't remember what it was exactly that he had just said.

'Why "*as well as you can know someone like Danny*"?' Pearson prompted.

Daryl took a deep breath, took a moment to collect his thoughts. Then, affecting an ease he didn't really feel, he said,

'Danny wasn't much of a talker, that's all. Some blokes ... they never stop yakking; you'll pretty much get their whole life story within the first ten minutes of meeting them. With Danny ... you'd be lucky to get more than a few words. Not that he was stand-offish, or he thought he was better than anyone else,' Daryl shrugged, 'he just didn't say much.'

'That sort of environment, though,' the Detective pressed, 'between ops, leading up to an op, blokes talk, right? You must have learned *something* about him.'

'I suppose,' Daryl said again.

Pearson looked at him. Patient. Waiting. After a while, when Daryl had still not said anything, he asked, 'What about his time *before* the army? Did you ever speak about that?'

Daryl watched the shadows beyond the frosted glass of the door. Glanced down at the pile of winning bets on the desk he'd yet to calculate. Figured he'd have to give these two something or they'd never go. Daryl sighed, scratched at a cheek,

'I suppose Danny's story was fairly typical of most of the blokes you come across in the Army. Your home life's crap and the services – anything – seems a better option. From what I could gather his family were a bunch of toe-rags. And he didn't fancy getting dragged into whatever it was they were up to.'

'But he didn't say what that was?'

Daryl shook his head, 'No. But I got the impression that some of it might have been pretty heavy?'

'But, as far as you knew, he wasn't personally involved?'

Daryl shrugged again, 'Who knows. Most of the blokes who join the army are not exactly what you might call model citizens. And the Services is not a vocation or a career choice, just better than the alternative.'

'Okay,' Pearson said, 'so how would you characterise Danny? On a purely personal level?'

'Probably the best soldier I've ever come across?'

A knock on the door. A shadow moving behind the frosted glass. A turning of the door handle. A hurried, *sotto voce* conversation carried on with someone else. And, whoever it was, changed their mind and moved away.

'Look,' Daryl said, 'can I ask what all this is about? Only, if I don't get these sorted,' he indicated the pile of betting slips on the desk, 'the punters out there are likely to start kicking off.'

'Fair enough,' Pearson said, 'Mister Fraser's name has come up in connection with a number of serious sexual assaults –'

'Danny?' And when Pearson said nothing, 'When?'

'Have you seen Mister Fraser recently?'

'No.' Almost before Daryl knew it, the lie was out. And before he could stop himself, he compounded it even further, 'I haven't seen Danny since the Army. Are these assaults supposed to have taken place recently?'

'No,' Pearson said, 'these assaults are from a few years back. Around the time Sixteenth Air Assault were garrisoned at Colchester.'

'And you think Danny –'

'Like I said, Mister Fraser's name has come up. Knowing Danny as you do, even to the limited extent you claim, do you think he might be capable of something like that?'

Daryl shook his head, 'Danny?' Emphatic, 'Sexual assault?' Convinced, 'No.'

'Why so sure?'

'He just never seemed interested. In women, I mean.'

'Could he have been gay?'

'Maybe. But it was more like he . . . Danny was all about honour, integrity, the "way of the warrior" and all that sh – ' he glanced briefly at Russell, 'Danny liked to read. If the rest of the lads went out on the lash, you'd more than likely find Danny in barracks with a book.'

'So,' Pearson said, 'not really interested in either men or women?'

'I wouldn't exactly say that,' Daryl said, 'like I said, he wasn't much of a talker. But I got the impression that before he'd joined up there'd been a ... relationship, and, for whatever reason it hadn't worked out. It was like after that, Danny wasn't interested in anyone else.'

Embarrassed, Daryl looked across at the female detective – Russell – hoping that *she* might be more empathetic. Hoping that *she* might understand . . .

After the two detectives had left, Daryl picked up the betting slip he'd been working on. A Union Jack patent. Nine horses. Fifty-six bets: eight trebles, twenty-four doubles, twenty-four singles. Looked at the calculations he'd begun on his pad. And realised that he would have to start all over again. He ripped off the top sheet, scrunched it into a ball and pitched it at the wastepaper basket. Looking up, his attention was snagged on the wall safe. And Daryl Crawford's mind flashed back to Afghanistan. To those twenty-three minutes where it had all gone so horribly, horribly wrong. To the shocked and stunned silence of the aftermath. The buzzing of flies. The smell of blood and human flesh. The sticky mess starting to coagulate on the dirt floor. To retrieving the spare jerry-cans from the armoured vehicle they had been driving. Dousing the building in petrol and setting it on fire. To standing, mute, not daring to catch each other's eye, as they watched the building burn. Later, they had raked through the ashes, only to realise that the fire had not quite done its job. So, they had taken shovels then, and buried the truth of that twenty-three minutes forever in the incurious sand of the desert. Or so he had thought . . .

33

'Are you saying you didn't act alone?' Irene Fairbridge asked, 'Only the police have found no forensic evidence, Ryan.' The psychologist paused. Allowing Ryan Yates time to take in the significance of this statement, 'There is no forensic evidence at all that might suggest that there was anyone else in the room apart from you and Mister Townsend.'

Then, when Ryan said nothing. After she had left it a while and it was obvious Ryan didn't want to add anything more,

'People – even very intelligent people – *have been* persuaded to do things that they might have thought, previously, they wouldn't. Are you saying that *you've* done something against your will? That *you've* been persuaded to do something that previously you didn't think yourself capable of? We're talking here about the murder of Clive Townsend, Ryan?'

Ryan Yates nodded, 'Yeah.'

'So, *are* you saying that you didn't act alone?' Fairbridge asked again. And when Ryan once more said nothing, she added, 'This is *your* chance, Ryan. Your chance to put your side of the story, to say exactly what happened. Wouldn't you like to do that, Ryan? Wouldn't you like to tell me what happened?'

Ryan hesitated. Looking down at the table. Running his fingers across the surface. Tracing old scarring. Mapping the evidence of previous abuse. Finally, he nodded.

'Good,' Fairbridge said, 'So, tell me what happened, Ryan. Start at the very beginning . . . '

'I went to see Donna – '

'Donna?'

Ryan nodded, 'Donna Freeman. She was ... we were at the Abigail Burnett together ... at the same time, I mean.'

'Okay,' the psychologist said slowly, 'and Donna was where?'

'Some kind of hospital,' Ryan thought for a moment, 'Like a residential mental health facility?'

'Okay. Sorry,' the psychologist said, 'rude of me to interrupt. It's just Donna is someone new, okay? I don't have anything about her in my notes here. So ... you were at the hospital with Donna . . . '

'Yeah,' Ryan said. Shaking his head, like he was beginning to remember, but still couldn't quite believe it, 'When I got there ... Donna was already in the visitor's room ... sitting at a table ... She was ... kind of, like ... I dunno, worked up, y'know? Excited about something? Like she couldn't wait to tell me whatever it was. Even before I sat down, she was talking . . . ' And now that Ryan had started talking himself. Talking to the table. As if no one else were in the room, he found that, just like Donna, he couldn't stop talking. 'She was, like, fidgeting, y'know? It was like she *couldn't* sit still, like she was all sort of agitated and that . . .

And then, suddenly, he was back in that cold, empty room. A room not that dissimilar to this one. Except there were more tables, more chairs. But the chairs were still the same orange moulded plastic. The tables the same scarred and scuffed wood . . .

Donna Freeman sat at the scratched wooden table, dressed in an oversized black tee-shirt. Her dark hair slicked back. Her skin deathly pale. Her eyes over-large in her gaunt face, thick bandaging from her wrists to her elbows. And heavy bruising on the inside of her thin upper arms. Like she'd been viciously and repeatedly pinched by someone. Or, Ryan realised, had been pinching herself.

Her yellow, feverish eyes had traced his progress across the room. Watched him pull out the chair. Place the plastic carrier bag containing sweets and magazines he had brought with him on the floor. Slowly take off his jacket, sit down – all the time she had been keeping up a running commentary. Mumbling something under her breath, talking to herself. Donna looked in the direction of the orderly who, having shown Ryan in, was now sitting at a chair a few tables away, engrossed in something on his smartphone, before turning back and leaning forward,

'They tried to put me on medication,' a furtive glance towards the orderly, 'but so far I've managed not to take it,' Her speech was rushed, her tone urgent, her voice barely above a whisper, 'One of the other girls showed me? You sort of put it in your mouth and pretend to swallow, but you can, like, hide it under your tongue? Then later, when no one's watching, you can spit it out into a tissue or something and then flush it down the bog? But they,' another brief look in the direction of the orderly, 'like, hide it in your food and that? That's why I'm not eating anything, and they won't listen to what you say, they won't believe you, they pretend they're listening, they sort of, like, make notes and that? But they're not actually listening, not really. They won't believe me, Malc. You've got to get me out of here – '

'Malc?' The psychologist asked, 'as in Malcolm?'

'Yeah,' Ryan nodded.

'Who's Malcolm?'

'He . . . ' Ryan began. Then he seemed to change his mind, 'I'm not sure, I dunno.'

'But it was definitely "Malc"?'

'Yeah,' Ryan shrugged, 'I s'pose.'

Laurence huffed an exasperated sigh. As if, at that moment, he might be in the room with them. As if he might be sitting at the same table. As if he could have looked across at the psychologist and shook his head to indicate that she shouldn't keep interrupting. He looked up briefly from the transcript.

Wishing she would just let Ryan Yates talk. Let him tell his story. Go back later to pick up on any queries . . .

Obviously, the psychologist didn't have a clue who 'Malcolm' might be. But, for Laurence at least, the name rang a definite bell. Malcolm Mitchell. Present, along with Donna, at the scene of DI Sean Carragher's death, he had been charged with murder and was now on remand awaiting trial. Though, for the life of him, he couldn't quite see the significance of the reference here. Perhaps Donna Freeman had just been confused. But he wrote the name down on his pad anyway. Added a question mark. Underlined it three times. He'd need to follow that up later. Just to be certain. Then he went back to his reading . . .

'Sorry, Ryan,' Fairbridge said, 'I've interrupted you again. It's just … *all* these names. What did Donna mean "*They won't believe me*"?'

'What do you mean they won't believe you?' Ryan asked, 'Believe you about what?'

'About *him*,' Donna said, 'About Clive Townsend –
'

'Mister Townsend? From the Abigail Burnett?'

'*Mister* Townsend? Yeah, Mister Townsend. Him,' Donna said, 'they won't believe me. About what he's done. What he is.'

223

'All that … stuff,' Ryan said, 'All the things that were supposed to have happened at the Abigail Burnett – '

'*Did* happen. *Did* happen.'

'Okay. Did happen. All that, was, like, after I'd left? Or, if it happened while I was there, I never knew about it.'

So, Donna told him. Told him about Clive Townsend. That he paid the girls for sex. That he arranged for them to have sex with other men for money. That it was his fault that Alicia Goode had died. And all the time Ryan was staring into those fevered eyes. The sickness burning in them. Burning behind them. All the time listening to the intense, hypnotic quality of her voice. Donna telling him that she had *tried* to kill Clive Townsend. Tried so very, very hard. But couldn't. Couldn't because she had been so scared, so terrified, of what she'd seen in that car. Something evil, something inhuman, something bestial –

And all at once Ryan had been eight years old again. Watching a documentary about a slaughterhouse on a knackered portable TV; the grainy picture, the colours all wrong, the red saturation too high, the volume too loud, the clattering of hooves on a wooden gangplank, the bellowing of terrified animals . . .

Donna was crying now. Her face properly wet, was saying, over and over again, 'He knows, Malc. He fucking knows. We've got to make him tell us, Malc. We've got to – '

'Tell us what?' Ryan asked. To make her stop saying that name. To make her stop saying that same thing over and over again. Just to make her fucking *stop*.

'Everything. Everything *he* knows. We've got to find out who else is involved. Who's behind it all. You've got to help me get out. You've got to.'

'How?' Ryan asked. And it was him now who looked over at the orderly. To see if he was paying attention. To see if he'd heard.

'Go to my room,' Donna said, 'If anyone asks, you can say you're dropping off that stuff,' she nodded at the carrier bag. 'Get my jacket. It's hanging in the wardrobe, it's black leather, like a biker's jacket with zips and badges? The wardrobe's locked. They won't let me have it because it's like a safety hazard or something, like they think I might try to cut myself on the metal zips or something? Pick up some clothes, anything of my other stuff you can carry. They won't watch you. Wait outside. In ten minutes, I'll come out – '

'What about – '

Donna was shaking her head, 'They don't check. They don't. Just go to my room and get my jacket. Please … Ryan. Please?'

Laurence looked up from the transcript and at the wall-clock. Calculating his return journey. Gauging where he was in the investigation. He'd spoken to the psychologist. Had the mental health assessment. He'd interviewed the relevant 'eyewitnesses'. For what that was worth. Prisoners who had seen and heard a sum total of precisely nothing. On the other hand, he had still to talk to the prison officers who had been present on the landing. Was still awaiting the results of the forensic examination of the scene which would not be available until, at the earliest, the next morning . . .

Laurence closed the folder, dropped it into the briefcase and shut the lid, snapping shut the catches. Stood up and shrugged on his jacket. He'd have to leave now if he wanted to miss the traffic . . .

34

Pearson pulled the Mondeo to a halt. For a while, neither moved. Both reluctant to finally call it a day. To judge by the look on his face, Pearson had something on his mind. And, for her part, Cat was in no hurry to return to her miserable, sterile flat. She barely had the will to eat, let alone cook, would no doubt end up scrabbling around in the fridge in the hope of finding a few leftovers from which she might construct something resembling a meal. Could not yet face the prospect of another night spent in front of the telly watching yet another trite and far-fetched police drama serial in which the cops were either stupid, or corrupt, or both. Or else, the latest in a seemingly, never-ending series of banal reality shows in which some so-called 'celebrities' who she'd never heard of competed against each other to complete a task she had absolutely no interest in. So, instead, Cat stared blankly out through the front windscreen. When she *was* alone, of course, her thoughts would inevitably turn to the events of the day. The death of Donna Freeman. And the unexpected appearance of John Hall . . .

Cat's gaze drifted up towards the darkened windows of her flat. Momentarily, she experienced a feeling of separation, of dislocation. A brief but powerful sense of disconnection with her immediate surroundings. Like she was observing the house of a stranger. Like she was the participant in some type of bizarre stakeout –

God, she needed a fag right now. And it was that, that craving, that overwhelming *need*, that anchoring dependency, that brought her back to the present. 'Stakeout'. Having been on a few herself, that phrase, Cat thought, certainly belied the true reality of the situation. Gave it a weight, a thrill of excitement, a sense of danger, it really didn't deserve. All it actually amounted to in truth was, basically, sitting for hours on end and staring at a chosen property, a particular window, a specific entrance or exit point until your eyes ached. At least if you were in a house you could take a comfort break every now and then. Or nip out into the back garden for the occasional cigarette. But if you were in a car . . .

Sitting now in the passenger seat of the Mondeo, lifting the back of a hand to her mouth to hide a stifled yawn, Cat found herself surreptitiously studying Pearson's profile. Found herself, albeit reluctantly, agreeing with Fadziso Campbell, the DC from Child Protection. Up to a point anyway. Although Cat wouldn't have said he was exactly what you might have called 'handsome', at least not in the conventional sense, Pearson wasn't actually *that* bad looking. He had reached that age where someone's face generally reflected their character. In Pearson's case that meant kind, considerate, decent. And, as Fay Campbell had pointed, out he did have sort of nice eyes. But he had that edge, too, that meant you knew if the need arose, he could look after himself. Or you. Cat had always thought of herself as a strong, independent woman. She *was* a strong, independent woman. All the same, it would be nice if sometimes, just sometimes, someone else would look after her for just a *little* while –

'Did you know,' Pearson broke the silence. Not looking round, his elbow resting on the door sill, his fingers drumming absent-mindedly on the top of the steering wheel 'that there is a bigger time difference between a Stegosaurus and a Tyrannosaurus Rex than there is between a T. Rex and Man?'

Then, 'Or that a nanosecond is to a second, what a second is to thirty-two years?'

Cat left it a beat, two, but then just couldn't help herself.

'Or,' she said acidly, 'that sometimes just a few minutes in *some* people's company can actually feel like a week.'

Pearson refused to bite. Instead, staying calm, humouring her. Which was all the more infuriating. Sometimes, she had the suspicion that this was exactly why he did it. After another silence, Pearson cleared his throat. It was a clearing of the throat that told you that *he was finally ready to say what had so obviously been on his mind.* A clearing of the throat that told you it was something that he regarded as a little delicate. Something that he found a bit embarrassing. Something that he didn't *really* want to broach. Or that he didn't know quite how to.

'I'm not going to ask what it's all about,' Pearson began. By now Cat already had her seatbelt unbuckled, her fingers on the door handle, but she turned to see Pearson staring fixedly out of the front windscreen. Pointedly not making eye contact, 'but there's obviously something going on between you and DCI Hall, right?' When she didn't answer he went on, 'Or something has gone on in the past?'

And when Cat still said nothing, 'All I'm going to say is,' Pearson ploughed on, 'If he's bothering you in some way … you could always have a word with Roberts. *Whatever* it is. You know,' he scratched an earlobe, 'as an officer of equal rank? Another DCI, whatever needs to be said … it might be better coming from him . . . '

'Get Roberts to warn him off you mean.'

'If you like.'

'Because,' Cat said sarcastically, 'Roberts is "*a big fan of mine*", right?'

'Look, I know you don't believe me. But you really have got the wrong idea about him.'

'You're doing that thing again.'

'What thing is that?'

'That *thing*,' Cat said, 'where you try to be all cryptic? But I haven't got a fucking clue what you're on about. Then we go all round the houses for a bit. And in the end, you have to spell it out. Look, it's getting late, I'm tired. And, yes, I'll admit it, I may even be in danger of appearing a little … offhand – '

'I'll take *that* as an apology,' Pearson said, 'as it's probably the nearest to one I'll get – '

'So . . . ' Cat said, 'it's probably better if you just tell me . . . '

Pearson looked down at the steering wheel. Running his fingers absently around the rim. Finally, he said, 'It's just, that he of all people, might know how you feel.'

' "*He of all people*"? What does *that* mean?'

'He's the sort of person . . . ' Faltering, Pearson leant his hand on the top of the steering wheel, lightly drummed his fingers. Started again, 'He's different at work . . . to what he is out of it?'

'Oh well,' Cat said, 'that explains everything.' And then, 'So, what? Are you going to tell me that he's a family man? That he loves his wife? That he dotes on his grandchildren?'

When Pearson didn't reply, Cat suddenly had a horrible feeling that there might be a tragedy in the family. That perhaps a toddler had been lost to a fatal childhood disease, leukaemia or a brain tumour, perhaps –

'No,' Pearson said reasonably, 'I'm not going to tell you that he's a family man.'

'What then?' Maybe it was Roberts. Maybe he was ill. Had terminal cancer or something. All of a sudden Cat wanted to know. Wanted to know that she hadn't got it all horribly wrong. That she wasn't a complete bitch –

'Not a family man in the way you're thinking, anyway,' Pearson cleared his throat. Again. Choosing his words, 'No wife. No children, no. But a long-term partner.'

After a moment Cat asked stupidly, 'Roberts is gay?'

Pearson turned now to look at her. Gave it a moment or two for the meaning to sink in. Then he nodded slowly, 'Roberts is gay. His partner's name is Tim. They've been together . . . ' he shrugged, ' . . . well, forever. For as long as I've known him, anyway. Tim's a lecturer at the Guildhall School of Music. Classical piano. Though, as I understand it, there's a bit of trouble at home at the moment . . . '

Cat's mind went back to standing outside Roberts's office, surprised at the sound of classical piano she'd heard from inside, her knuckles hovering over the window in the half-glazed door. The DCI's recent, even more than usually, disagreeable mood. Now it all made sense.

'But keep it to yourself, eh?' Pearson sighed. Shook his head, 'Roberts wouldn't thank me for telling *you*.'

'Why?'

'Well for one thing, as Roberts has told me on more than one occasion,' Pearson adopted a west Country accent, ' "*It's no-fucking-body's business, but mine.*" ' When Cat looked unconvinced, Pearson went on, 'Look, you've got to understand, Roberts is from a different era. People just didn't come out in those days. Back in the eighties?' He shrugged again, 'What with all the AIDS hysteria. And it would have been career suicide, apart from anything else. Attitudes weren't the same then. Especially in the Job.'

'Attitudes haven't changed that much,' Cat pointed out, 'Not in the Job.'

232

'Which,' Pearson said, 'is why you need all the friends you can get.'

'Okay,' Cat conceded, 'I'll give some thought to talking to Roberts.'

But a minute later, standing in the street outside her flat, rootling through her handbag for her front-door keys, a lit cigarette in her mouth, Cat was already thumbing out a text message on her mobile phone . . .

DAY FIVE

35

Detective Sergeant Alan Laurence was back at HMP Chelmsford. Back in the same room where he'd spent most of the previous day. Back in the same room where, he imagined, Irene Fairbridge, the prison psychologist, had carried out her mental health assessment of Ryan Yates. Laurence was waiting, and had been waiting for some time, for Murray to bring back his final interviewee. So, when he heard the soft knock at the door, he felt sure it was the prison officer. He experienced the fleeting certainty that all of this would be quickly wrapped up so that he could be on his way. Only for that hope to be immediately dashed when he opened the door to find the senior Scene-of-Crime-Officer. They had a brief, hushed conversation about the preliminary results of the forensic examination of the crime scene. Then Laurence shut the door, retook his seat, and quickly jotted down on the A4 notepad a précis of what he'd been told. Convinced now that he was dealing with a murder.

Laurence glanced at the wall-clock, anticipating – hoping – that Murray wouldn't be *that* much longer. Then he returned to his review of the psychologist's report . . .

'Donna had this plastic bag,' Ryan Yates said, 'like a supermarket carrier bag or something? She went out one night and came back with this bag with all ... like, Sellotape or something round it?

I mean like tons of it, it took her ages to pick the stuff off …
but when she finally opened it there's all her old stuff inside?
Her phone and charger … a pair of clippers – y'know, the
ones you use to do your hair? Make-up?' Ryan shrugged,
'There might have been some other stuff, I don't remember.'
As he talked his index finger traced and retraced an arcane
motif on the surface of the grey Formica, 'I saw her slip
something out of the bag and into the pocket of her leather
jacket. But I couldn't see what it was,' Ryan looked up then.
'I only found out *later* that it was the knife … '

'Can you tell me what happened, Ryan,' the
psychologist said, 'the night Mister Townsend died?'

And Laurence pictured her making notes in the folder.
Deliberately not looking up now. Fearing that even the
briefest, the most negligible eye contact might cause Ryan to
lose his nerve and stop talking. Imagined her making an effort
to keep her tone casual. So that it might appear that they were
talking about something very ordinary. Something *completely*
normal. And not the callous and brutal murder of a human
being …

'I can't remember,' Ryan said, 'not properly … and that's the
truth … it's all, like, jumbled … all mixed up in my mind …
I can't make any sense of it; I can't explain it … what
happened. I can't explain it … '

238

Laurence checked the wall-clock. Again. Sighed deeply. Again. Then went back to his reading . . .

'Why don't you just give it a try, Ryan. This is your chance to talk. To get it all off your chest. Just take your time. You'll feel better if you tell me about it. This is your chance to say what happened in that room, Ryan. To find an explanation, if only for yourself, for why you're in here?'

There was a long pause. As if Ryan wasn't going to say anything. And then, in his faltering, his confused, his disconnected way, he began;

'I don't know how Donna found out the address ... I mean, I don't remember her phoning anyone or anything ... maybe she spoke to someone? Like, on the night she went out to get that bag. I don't know . . . ' Frowning, Ryan worked his fingers into the corner of an eye, 'it's all, like, muddled in my mind ... I can't remember the order of things ... what happened first? What happened second?'

'It's okay, Ryan. Take your time. Why don't you tell me what happened once you got to Mr. Townsend's flat?'

'So, we went to Mister Townsend's place – it was like, y'know, one of those bedsits in a big house? I don't think anyone even knew we were there ... no one ever looks at anyone else in those places. As we turned up, someone else was coming out ... so we just sort of held the door open for them and walked in. We went up the stairs, and I knocked on the door. Donna was sort of standing off to one side. Before we left, she'd, like, clippered the sides of her hair? But it was sort of mad, y'know? She'd cut it so short you could see all

239

her head through it ... and she'd hacked at the top with a pair of scissors and then ran a load of gel through it. Like she was trying to spike it up or something? But it was a real mess, y'know? And she'd put on this white make-up? And, like thick eyeliner and black lipstick? Like a clown? But sad? Like a sad clown? *"Warpaint"* she called It. Her "disguise". But it looked weird, m*ad*, kind of ... scary, y'know?' Ryan took a breath. Shook his head. As if just the memory could still put him on edge, 'And all the way over there, she'd been talking, getting into my head, y'know?'

And Ryan was back outside that bedsit again. And it was like they were outside that bedsit with him. Donna off to one side, Ryan standing in front of the door, Laurence and the psychologist right behind him.

'When the door opened,' Ryan said, 'he was wearing some kind of bathrobe – Mister Townsend? – like he'd just had a shower or something, or maybe that's just what he wore when he was at home? Like, maybe, when he was at home, he didn't bother getting dressed ... And, all the time, Donna was talking? Just talking, talking, talking ... getting into my head, y'know?'

Ryan was outside the bedsit. And, at the same time, he was eight years old again. Sitting too close to that knackered portable TV. The misfiring cathode ray tube tracing a grainy picture in blurry lines across the screen. The colours awry. The red saturation set way too high. The volume turned up too loud . . .

But he could still hear Donna's voice. Above the underlying buzz of that remembered television set. Above the clattering of hooves on a wooden gangplank. Could hear her voice above the shifting of heavily muscled, powerful bodies. Hear her voice above the bellowing of terrified animals. And all at once he had a hammer in his hand. And he could hear her voice, even as he swung it. Could hear her voice above the sound of the metal bolt slamming home into the cow's skull . . .

And then they were all in the bedroom. Ryan staring down at the bed. Laurence and the psychologist peering over his shoulder . . .

The man on the bed, naked. A black sock in his mouth serving as a makeshift gag. His arms stretched above his head. And secured to the metal rails of the headboard by a pair of handcuffs. The whole scene was so ridiculous, so absurd, so unexpected, that, at first, Ryan had had the almost irresistible urge to laugh. He had no idea how the man had got there, where the handcuffs had come from, whether they had found them in one of the drawers in the bedroom, or whether Donna might have brought them with her. They were the sort of handcuffs you could buy in any sex shop. Those handcuffs covered in sort of pink feathers. Pretend handcuffs. The man on the bed looked dazed. But at the same time, like he thought it was all a bit of a joke. Like he thought Ryan and Donna weren't going to do anything, weren't capable of doing anything to him.

Ryan had asked Donna then, 'So, what is it you want to know?'

'Everything,' she said. And Donna had had it all worked out, 'Everything h*e* knows about the parties,' she said,

241

'Where they were held. Who arranged them? Who went to them? Who else is involved – '

'Okay, okay,' Ryan said softly. Making a calming motion with his palms. Though he *didn't feel* calm. Didn't feel calm at all.

'So, the first thing we need to do,' Ryan said, 'is take that sock out of his mouth, okay?'

And Donna was *still* talking. And it was like back in that hospital waiting room. Those fevered eyes. That voice. Getting into his head. Then Donna was pressing the knife into *his* hand. And Ryan could feel her hot, sticky fingers – 'He knows, and he's going to fucking tell us,' – could feel the sweaty metal handle of the knife, – 'everything.' And he couldn't tear his gaze from that unearthly white face. 'He's going to tell us everything.' Those eyes. 'Make him, Malc. Make him tell us. Make him tell us, Malc,' she repeated. Like some kind of deranged chant. Some lunatic refrain. Over and over and over again, 'Make him tell us. Make him tell us, Malc . . . '

And then, somehow, it was all different. Somehow, everything had changed. Somehow in that ordinary, dingy bedroom, the single bare light bulb swinging crazily on its pendant, the faint glint of metal from the blade of the knife he held in his hand, somehow, for a short while, he *was* Donna. And he could smell what she smelled. Could hear what she heard. Could see what she saw. Could *see* the beast, the thing with horns; the bull, the ox, the whatever-the-fuck-it-was, lying on the bed, thrashing against its bonds. Its red eyes rolling wildly into the top of its head, a crescent of white flashing beneath. Its wet nostrils flaring. A foamy lather smeared across the threadbare suede of its chest and abdomen . . .

'I can't remember what happened next,' Ryan said, 'I don't know. Maybe I blacked out or something and then came to, sometime later?' He looked at the psychologist, 'Do you think that's possible? Do you think I could have blacked out? Do you think, like, you could do something, something really bad, and have no memory of doing it?'

And then Ryan was back in that ordinary bedroom. The bloody knife in his hand. Surrounded by the reek of the abattoir. The musk of bestial fear. The smell of blood. The stink of animal faeces. Looking down at the man, the man, the *man*, on the bed. The man streaked with sweat. The man smeared with shit. The man covered in blood. The man bleeding out. The man dying. Looking down at the blood pumping out of the severed femoral artery –

Laurence was startled by a hard rap on the door. Almost immediately, Murray entered, escorting a prisoner. He left him by the table before going to the far wall, perching awkwardly on a stool, and unfolding a tabloid newspaper acquired somewhere en-route.

Laurence had left his own paper in the car. A copy of *The Racing Post* he bought religiously every day. Though he rarely, actually, had a bet. But he liked to pick out the horses and follow his selections, check the result of his imaginary wager. Just to see how it would have done if he *had* actually

243

put the money on. It was a mental exercise. And that was all. A distraction. On the very rare occasion he did have a punt, he wouldn't ever stake more than a few quid. A fiver his upper limit. But he'd heard the whispers back at the Nick. The rumours that he was some inveterate gambler. That the phone calls were to his bookie, the text messages he made was him tapping in a bet, those he received an alert from some online gambling app.

Laurence shut the manila folder and dropped it into the briefcase, watching the man opposite scrape the chair across the floor and slump into it. Noting the smirk as his own left hand slid along the tabletop, closing around the spectre of a non-existent phone, and he stared stupidly down at the space where his mobile should have been. He observed the man assessing him. This middle-aged, balding copper wearing a cheap dark suit. Tired-looking. His skin sallow and unhealthy, his eyes pouched, the lower lids red-rimmed where he was constantly rubbing at them. Since the death, as long as it was under investigation, and until the investigation was closed satisfactorily, he was, and would be, in a cell on his own. So, there was no incentive, no real advantage, for him to co-operate. No reason at all to say what had really gone on . . .

Laurence saw him glance across at the screw. Murray was studying the racing pages of the newspaper, marking out his selections with a blue biro. Or pretending to. Acting like none of this was of any interest. But, no doubt, taking it all in. Laurence looked back at the man seated on the other side of the grey Formica table, sliding his warrant card from his inside jacket pocket. Holding it out for him to see.

'My name is Detective Sergeant Alan Laurence.' Putting the card away. Taking a deep breath and, feeling obliged to stand up at this point, he cleared his throat, 'Gary Clark, I am arresting you on suspicion of the murder of Ryan Jordan Yates. You do not have to say anything, but it may harm your defense if you do not mention when questioned something which you later rely on in court. Anything you do say may be given in evidence. Do you understand?'

'Yeah,' Clark said, and he shot a glance in Murray's direction. Then he giggled, 'Course.'

36

Laurence gathered together the sheets of A4 containing the results of his investigation. The psychologist's notes on the mental health assessment of Ryan Yates. The findings of the SOCO who had examined the crime scene. The laboriously set down longhand record of the eyewitness accounts of the prisoners in the vicinity; predictably enough amounting to the seeing and hearing of absolutely fuck-all. The equally unrevealing interview with the closest prison officer to the incident; who just happened to be Murray. He tucked them inside the manila folder, dropped them in the leather briefcase and snapped the catches shut. Looking over, he saw the prison officer miming boredom. Openly yawning and casting glances at his watch. Looking more-than-ready to go back onto the prison's landing.

Laurence detected in him an underlying irritation. The hoped-for hour or so of skiving before the end of his shift well and truly scuppered. Laurence checked the wall-clock. Yesterday he had been lucky: leaving before rush-hour, it had taken less than an hour to get back to Southend. He would have to get back to the Reception, retrieve his mobile and other belongings, sign out the appropriate paperwork and leave the Nick in say, the next fifteen or twenty minutes to have any chance of missing the rush hour today. Sighing, he clicked the top of his biro and opened his jacket, slipping his pen into the inside pocket. Not a chance of that now. Not now he'd arrested Clark for murder. Clark had to be taken officially into police custody. Which meant he had to be transported to the police station in order to be interviewed. They had the tape machines, the video cameras, could provide a duty solicitor if Clark had none of his own. Protocol – and courtesy – demanded that the Prison Governor be informed. Something that he maybe should have done before the arrest. Maybe. He had considered, and quickly rejected, the idea. Weighing up the implications of showing his hand before he'd asked Murray to produce the prisoner. Concerned that Murray might claim that it was close to Clark's mealtime and to deny him food would be a breach of his human rights. Or that maybe, because it was nearing the end of Murray's shift, he would want to knock off rather than get involved with the hassle of a handover. That Murry would simply not reappear and that he would have to chase down another prison officer to do the official hand over.

Now the arrest had been made, he felt reluctant to allow any further interaction between Murray and the prisoner. Had the sense that something else was going on here that he couldn't quite put his finger on. Had the suspicion that, despite the prison officer's attitude of casual indifference – the yawning behind a hand, the absent scratching of the neck, the feigned interest in the folded tabloid and the marked selections in the racing pages – Murray was paying particular attention to what was being said. Besides, Murray had wasted enough of his time as it was. He couldn't afford any more delays. Much better to present the arrest as a fait accompli. Take the consequences later. Most likely this would amount to a phone call from an irritated Prison Governor that would result in a bollocking from Roberts. As it was, arrangements would have to be made through Force Prison Liaison for the transportation of Clark. And, as usual, endless bloody paperwork would have to be filled out . . .

And so, it was more than an hour later that Laurence pressed the electronic fob to deactivate the central locking system of his car, opened the driver's side door and slung the leather briefcase onto the passenger seat. The sleet that had been falling on his journey into Chelmsford had turned to snow in the hours he'd been inside the prison, a quarter of an inch already settling on the roof. He undid the top button of his shirt, loosened his tie and pressed the power button on his phone. Hesitating momentarily before entering his pass code, dreading what he would find. Almost immediately the mobile came alive in his hand with the repeated Ping! Ping! Ping! of received messages. Even before he tapped the messages icon, he knew what it would contain. At first, the messages would have been sent every eight to ten minutes. When no answer was forthcoming, the frequency would increase, coming every four or five minutes. Until finally they would come almost every minute. Each succeeding message more frantic, more panicked than the last. Then they would abruptly stop as the person sending them started to call . . .

Laurence was sitting in his car on the road out of Chelmsford. Had been sitting for quite a while now. Staring through the front windscreen at snow falling from a weirdly orange late afternoon sky. The traffic at a standstill. The Army and Navy roundabout was a nightmare at the best of times. Despite the flyover operating a contra-flow system during the morning and evening rush hours; into Chelmsford in the morning, out of Chelmsford in the evening, there were still daily traffic jams. Today was even worse. The flyover closed again due to on-going engineering works: yet more chunks of concrete and rusty metal having fallen from its crumbling superstructure. Since leaving the prison, he had been alternately calling "Christine mobile" or "Home" through the car's Bluetooth phone system. Repeatedly getting the recorded message that the mobile was turned off, then listening to the landline ring out. He made an effort to switch his mind into neutral. Cease all conscious thought. Staunch all emotions. To set his face into a well-practised mask of outward affability. For years now this had been his coping strategy. Just lately, though, he had begun to feel a tightness in his facial muscles. Was aware too that the expression the rictus smile, had somehow come to resemble the embodiment of most people's idea of a village idiot. This was his method, the only way, to cling onto some vestige of sanity. But there was another Alan Laurence. Locked deep inside. Banging bloodied fists on metal walls in a box no bigger than himself. Screaming. In desperation. In panic. In terror. And he knew that *that* Alan Laurence must never get out . . .

37

Cat Russell swings a left off the main road and into the Ness
Road car park. The car's headlights briefly illuminate the oil-
stained asphalt before strafing the low, white sea wall at its
perimeter. She pulls to a halt. Applies the handbrake. Stares
out for a moment through the front windshield. She'd always
thought of this place as a car park, but in reality, it was little
more than an extended tarmac apron next to the concrete
slipway.

In the past few days she had, she realised, been
moving backwards through time. Retracing her history, re-
living the significant events of her recent past. Revisiting the
Crowstone. The deposition site of a body. And the start of an
investigation which she had thought, at the time, had marked
the beginning of her recovery. The rehabilitation, in part at
least, of her reputation within the Force. Then returning here,
the place, where a few months earlier, DI Sean Carragher had
been burnt to death in his Audi A8. The place where, if it had
not all *begun*, it had surely, for her at least, all begun to
unravel again; professionally, emotionally and most of all,
psychologically. And now? Now she was … well, she wasn't
quite sure what she was about to do. Or what she thought all
of this might actually achieve . . .

Cat climbed out of the car and slammed the door. She
needed to kill a few minutes. As usual she was way too early.
Stretch her legs. A few steps later she stopped dead. Christ,
Laurence was right, she *had* been working with Pearson too
long. It was a sequence of movements she'd seen Pearson

execute on countless occasions. The shrugging on of the overcoat. The glance towards the sky. The thrusting of the hands into the pockets. Now she'd just caught herself doing the self-same things. But it wasn't just the movements themselves. It was the near-perfect unconscious mimicry of him; the set of his shoulders, the tilt of his head, the expression on his face. Swearing softly to herself, she started walking again. Fossicking in her handbag for her fags and disposable lighter. Stopping by the sea wall she lit up and took a long draw on her cigarette, shaking her head, musing out loud. '*Gay?*' Still not quite sure how she had managed to miss it for all of this time.

But surely the real question wasn't how she'd contrived to overlook all of the signals, but rather: how the fuck could Tim, could *anyone,* put up with Roberts for more than *twenty* years?

Then again, who was she to talk? Her judgement hadn't exactly proved that sound lately, had it? Lately? Ever. It had got to the point now where she couldn't be sure of *anything* anymore. Which was exactly the reason why she was standing here, right now, wasn't it?

As the headlights of another car swung into the parking area, Cat's nerve immediately failed her. Maybe this wasn't such a good idea after all. Maybe she *should* have just talked to Roberts as Pearson had suggested. She made her way back to her car. Asking herself why she'd sent the text. Why she'd arranged this meeting. And why here? Why here of all places? She'd deliberately positioned the car in the middle of the parking area in order to leave plenty of space on all sides.

But, standing by the driver's side door, she was uncertain now as to whether this really was the best spot. Maybe she should have parked closer to the entrance. So, she could keep the car between them. Carry out the conversation across the roof. Leave the driver's side door open. Just in case. Too fucking late now. Instead, she put her hands into the deep pockets of her coat. Fingered the pepper spray in the left. And in the right, partly concealed in her sleeve, the comforting solidity of the telescopic carbon fibre baton. Just in case . . .

The engine of the other car died. The headlights went out. The driver's side door slammed and the man she had arranged to meet walked around the back of the car –

'I'd rather you stay where you are, John.'

John Hall looked momentarily confused. Then awkward, then embarrassed, he folded his arms and leant back on the car.

'I've been thinking about yesterday's meeting,' Cat said.

Hall chanced a smile, 'We both had the opportunity to admit we'd met before.'

'Yeah, okay, but that's not what I'm talking about.'

'So, what then?' Hall asked, his smile fading.

'The stuff about Danny Fraser? The workboots, the plaster dust, the smell of paint and white spirit . . . '

'So what?'

'*So what*? It was straight out of the statement I gave you after the attack, that's "*so what*".'

'And the statements of four other victims.'

'The point is,' Cat said, 'that you never mentioned you might have had a suspect. Let alone a name. Not in the time we were together. Not in all the time since.'

Hall said nothing. Cat took a breath. Shifted from one foot to the other. Felt again the pepper spray in her left hand.

'So, I'm wondering now, where exactly *is* the lie? Maybe you never did have a suspect. Maybe there *was* nothing to keep from me. Maybe you just made all that stuff up in the meeting. On the other hand, maybe you *have* suspected this Danny Fraser all along. Maybe you didn't tell me. Because, maybe you thought you had good reason not to?'

For a while neither spoke. Cat watched Hall's breath freeze on the night air. Finally, he asked, 'What's all this really about, Cat? This meeting? Why did you ask me to meet you here? What is it that you want?'

'I want the truth, John. Because now it's got me thinking … ever since you came back, I've had the feeling that you've been hiding something. It's got to the point where I'm starting to doubt everything – '

'About what?'

'Everything. You. Your motives. About the circumstances surrounding our first meeting.'

Suddenly realisation dawned. 'Christ! Is that it?' Hall asked, shaking his head in disbelief, 'Is that what all this is about? You think it was *me*? You think I raped you, don't you?' He kneaded his temples with his fingertips. 'Let me get this straight,' staring past her for a moment, frowning, he exhaled a long breath, 'You think I raped you.' He ran his hands through his hair, then turned back to face her, 'And then, what? I befriended you, as what, some sick kind of joke or something? And the rest of it? The time we spent together, what was that?'

'So,' Cat asked flatly, 'why don't you prove me wrong?'

38

TEN YEARS EARLIER

Cupping his hand to hide the flame, a callow, a newly promoted, a highly ambitious, Detective Sergeant John Hall sparks up and takes in a satisfying lungful of smoke, then drops the cigarette packet and lighter back onto the top of the dashboard. His eyes never once leaving the view through the passenger side window. The bedsit in the student accommodation on Gilesgate. The bedsit which, he is convinced, is home to the next victim. Almost convinced. Because although the female occupant fits the general physical profile of the other women who have been assaulted, at least in terms of build, hair colour and facial features, and there is a similarity in lifestyle; a single female, living away from home, who is gregarious and out-going and works evening shifts at a local pub, it is merely an approximate physical likeness, only an imprecise equivalence of lifestyles. And in the end, as his DCI had pointed out, it amounts to little more than a hunch. A hunch the Durham CID do not have the manpower to follow up. And as a result, it is a theory which only he fully believes in. A line of enquiry he alone is working on . . .

Hall sits for a while then; impatiently drawing on the cigarette, nervously tapping the ash into an ashtray already brim-full of dog-ends. He ducks down over the steering wheel to risk a glance through the front windscreen. A low sun is setting in a darkening sky. Streetlights blinking into life as dusk falls. A gust of wind riffles the sparse foliage of the nearby trees, briefly stirs sodden leaves from wet pavements. The drizzle of the day has abated. For now. But cumulonimbus tumble and bank on the horizon, black and pregnant with rain, signalling the imminent arrival of a torrential downpour. He has left the Nick early, claiming a prior engagement. Has taken his usual place in the parking area behind the bus stop. A position that affords the best view of the buildings opposite. Hall is acting on 'information received'. He has handed over a substantial amount of his own money. In exchange he has been given a name. Danny Fraser.

At this point in time little is known about the man Hall is seeking. The attacker has committed a number of as-yet-unsuccessful attempts at rape. Each more violent in nature than the last. He has his own transport which, judging by the statements given by the four women he is known to have attacked, suggests he might be in the building trade. A vehicle *'like one of those white delivery vans, but dark blue ... or black maybe'*, which *'might have a sign or logo on the side that someone's painted over'*. The sketchy descriptions of the assailant would also seem to bear this out; *'work boots with steel toe-caps,'* a *'heavy coat, something like a donkey jacket'*, *'tatty and faded jeans caked with plaster dust'* and the possible *'smell of paint and white spirit'*. Fraser has no criminal record, but Hall's source is normally reliable. Danny Fraser is, after all, a builder and, word is, has a history of minor assaults against women.

Hall has sat here many, many times before, observing the self-same ritual. The front door opening. A younger Cat

Russell stepping out onto the street, twisting an elastic band over her dark hair and arranging it into a loose ponytail. Apprehensively scanning the sky. Zipping up her top, repositioning the hood. Kneeling to re-tie the laces on one trainer, then the other, taking the opportunity to gently flex her hamstrings. Putting headphones into her ears, selecting the music on her *iPod Nano* and slipping it into the pocket of her hoodie. He knows her route by heart. Has sat in his living room at home, charting it on a map. Timed her journey on a stopwatch. Made a note of the locations where an attack would be most likely to occur. He has stood out of sight behind the bandstand as she turned right onto the football ground and ran past the cricket club. Has strolled unnoticed on the towpath alongside the river when she has turned right, away from the river and around Maiden Castle Wood. Has hidden, unobserved, among the trees as she has crossed the road into the Great High Wood forest. He has sat, concealed behind a newspaper, as she has run through the grounds of Grey College and past the botanic gardens. Has posed as a tourist, pretending to take photos of the cathedral and castle on top of the hill as she has turned right onto the Prebends' Bridge and from there onto the island, tracking her through the zoom lens of his Nikon D40X. He has dogged her early-morning return home from student parties. He has lied to his wife about having to work late, in order to spend many tedious hours in the Queen's Head pub at the end of the road. Sitting through Cat's evening shifts behind the bar, nursing a pint out of sight in the shadows, watching her flirt with the male customers, trying to spot which one might be a potential attacker . . .

Detective Sergeant John Hall lifts a cuff now and checks his watch by the dull orange light of the adjacent streetlamp. Tonight, he and Jean have a meeting at Elizabeth's school. And he daren't be late. So tonight, he will only follow again in the car. Cat will run up to the footbridge that crosses the main road and he will tail her – *can* only tail her – as far as Pelaw Leazes Lane. Will, at best, catch a distant glimpse of her crossing the River over Baths Bridge as he drives across the New Elvet road bridge. All the time searching the traffic for any van that might be used by a builder. Running his eye over the faces of the passing pedestrians. Continuing onto Hallgarth Street he will turn right at the roundabout onto Stockton Road then left onto South Road. Pulling into the kerb he will put on the hazard lights, check the stopwatch, wait anxiously … until he catches sight of her coming out of the botanic gardens. Until he can trail her at a discreet distance in the car as she crosses over South Road, goes up Elvet Hill Road and back into town on Potters Bank. He will leave her as she turns left at the roundabout along Quarryhead Lane. Will sit fretting, once again, over his stopwatch back in the small car park behind the bus stop until she crosses the footbridge into Gilesgate.

Now, Hall watches the younger Cat Russell disappear along the street and turn right. Tonight, something will happen that will change – *has changed* – *both* their lives – forever. Giving it a minute or so, grinding out his cigarette in the ashtray and turning on the car's headlamps, he starts the engine. But tonight, the road is extra busy on the way up to the roundabout, the traffic lights are against him. Tonight, it takes that little bit longer to navigate his way around the roundabout and back onto Leazes Road. So that, rather than

260

being halfway across, Cat is already coming off the other side of the footbridge as he approaches. Tonight, because he is late, because he has an appointment at Elizabeth's school that he dare not miss, because he really shouldn't even be here, because he is not paying proper attention, he does not see the car on his inside as the two lanes merge into one by the footbridge . . .

There is an ear-splitting grinding, an ear-piercing screech and a deafening bang as the two cars collide, the off-side wing crumples and the front bumper is torn off. Behind him Hall hears the screech of brakes, the blaring of car horns as he watches through the front windscreen the retreating form of an oblivious Cat Russell disappear along the path next to the road. He checks his rear-view mirror, opens the driver's side door and steps out. The other driver is already out of his car, assessing the damage. As Hall approaches, he turns.

'You fucking maniac! Couldn't you see me on the inside, man? You could have had us both killed?'

Hall slips his warrant card from his inside pocket.

The other driver looks away, shaking his head, 'Oh, fucking great! I can just see how this is going to go down . . . '

39

'Christine?'

Laurence *said* his wife's name. Deliberately not calling out. Not shouting. Not raising his voice much above the level of normal conversation. Adopting a tone that was studiedly casual. Consciously nonchalant. He hoped. Seemingly unconcerned. Like this might be enough to communicate the utter normality of the situation. Like *this* might be a day just like any other. Like there hadn't been the agonising wait for the processing of his murder suspect to be completed at the prison, the excruciating delay at the Army and Navy roundabout, the desperate and panic-stricken forty-five-minute drive to Southend. The ten minutes spent outside in the car, gripping the steering wheel and taking in deep and calming breaths, staring at the front door, loathe to take that final step, dreading what he might find inside. As if he hadn't snatched up his leather briefcase from the front passenger seat and flung open the driver's side door before he'd had time to change his mind . . .

Now, having let himself in as quietly as he could, Laurence stood in the darkened hallway. Straining to hear a reply. Not daring to move. Not daring to breathe. For fear of missing anything. The signifiers of a hoped-for commonplace routine; the clatter of pots and pans, the radio playing quietly, the humming accompaniment to a song. Any intimation, in fact, that might yet mean everything was actually going to be okay – There it was … not quite a sound, but the merest indication of movement from further inside the house.

'Evening,' Laurence said, sauntering into the kitchen, 'everything alright?'

He could tell right away that it wasn't. His wife stood at the worktop next to the hob. Pointedly turned away. A premeditated and wilful blanking of him. A tension evident in the set of her shoulders. Her movements urgent and energetic, her head bowed, seemingly focused on whatever task it was she was performing.

'I've been trying to ring you,' Laurence said. Striving for breezy. Attempting to inject some levity into his tone. As if, perhaps, the battery might just have gone flat, 'Your phone must be off.' As if this might only be an oversight on her part. As if she might have simply switched it off for some reason then forgotten about it. As if it wasn't a calculated act of petty revenge. Wasn't something consciously planned in order to make him worry.

'I'm sorry, love,' Laurence said, changing tack, 'I had to go to Chelmsford Nick. I did try and get out of it again. But as I was the one who'd done the initial investigation, there wasn't really a lot I could do.' On entering the kitchen, Laurence had immediately caught the whiff of something … something familiar, 'Like I said yesterday, you're not allowed mobiles in there. Remember? You have to hand them in at the gate?' Familiar, yet out-of-place. 'And when you do get out you can't get any bloody reception. They have this device for blocking the signal. Not that it actually works inside the Nick. Otherwise, why would they go to the trouble of smuggling phones in . . . ' Something very definitely out-of-place in this ordinary domestic setting, 'Then I got held up at the Army and Navy flyover. Stuck in a bloody traffic jam for nearly an hour. Some kind of accident.' Laurence edged as casually as he could around his wife's back. Trying to get a look over her shoulder to see what exactly it was she was up to. 'As it is, it's a bloody nightmare in and out of Chelmsford.' On the worktop he caught a glimpse of potato peelings. A *lot* of potato peelings. Way *too* many potato peelings for a meal being prepared for just two people. The glint of the overhead fluorescent light reflected by a metal blade. How many times had he told her about using the potato peeler? 'Let alone at rush hour,' he said, 'Southend, too, come to that. I know I should've told you, but I thought I'd only be at the Nick a couple of hours. Three at the very most.'

At the exact moment he finally placed the smell – that coppery tang of blood – Laurence, who had managed to edge slowly up to his wife's side during the one-sided conversation, got his first proper look at what she was doing. As he'd expected, peeled potatoes filled a metal saucepan. But the potatoes were a peculiar blotchy and livid pink. Red streaks and swirls now clouded the surface of the once-clear water. Daubed the wooden handle. Smeared the length of the marble worktop. Spotted the white, porcelain surface of the gas hob to her left.

Christine Laurence held a black-handled paring knife in her right hand. A partly-peeled potato in her left. Blood streaming from her lacerated fingertips, her gouged and slashed palm. Saturating the cuff and sleeve of her white cotton blouse.

'Blimey!' Laurence said, 'How many potatoes are you doing?'

It had all been explained to him. That last time. By the hospital psychiatrist. The psychiatrist young enough to be his daughter. In that sparsely furnished and utilitarian room set aside for the fretful or newly bereaved family members just off the emergency department. Had it explained. Succinctly. In layman's terms. But, not unkindly, with a compassion, an understanding, he had recognised, and been able to appreciate, even at the time.

'Christine is experiencing what is called "perimenopause". This is the period before the actual menopause begins. It typically lasts between five or ten years. During this time there is a decline in the levels of oestrogen and hormones in the body. Hormones are messengers which regulate the body's chemical and physical functions. Progesterone and oestrogen are the key hormones which control fertility and the reproductive system in women. A decrease in, or fluctuation of oestrogen levels can interact with the brain's chemistry which, in turn, can give rise to, for instance, aggression, irritability, confusion or depression. Or, any combination of them. Many women who have a pre-existing mental health condition, such as bipolar disorder, as in Christine's case, can find that this condition is triggered or exacerbated by the fluctuation in oestrogen levels.'

But having it explained, knowing what it was, understanding it, being understanding *of* it, still didn't make it any easier to bear.

266

'Why don't you let me wash that knife up for you?' Laurence asked, holding out his hand, 'You've done enough spuds. More than en – '

'You promised me!' She wheeled on him. Brandishing the blade. The half-peeled, forgotten, wet potato still clutched in her left hand, 'You promised yesterday you wouldn't leave the police station again. That you'd stay at your desk, where you're safe.'

'I know I did,' Laurence said. Aiming now for reassuring, 'I'm sorry, love,' trying to keep eye contact, 'I always do my best to – '

'You know I don't like it when you're out of touch. You know I start to worry.'

Laurence knew. He'd had this explained to him too. *'Co-morbid conditions . . .* ' the psychiatrist had said. A different psychiatrist. On a different occasion. In some other featureless, institutional office, ' . . . are conditions which can occur alongside the main disorder. With bipolar disorder, these can include various anxiety disorders. In Christine's case, these are Obsessive Compulsive Disorder, or OCD, Panic Disorder and Separation Disorder.'

Try as he might, Laurence's gaze drifted unavoidably towards the knife in his wife's hand. Because, he'd been stabbed before. He'd not reported it of course. Had gone to the hospital simply claiming a stupid and thoughtless accident on his part.

'It won't happen again,' Laurence said, 'I won't go out next time. Not if it means switching off my phone.'

She turned away. But Laurence wasn't convinced she'd accepted his apology. His eyes stayed on the knife, more worried about her harming herself than him, 'Anything I can do to help?' he asked.

She ignored him. He stared down at the knife she'd placed on the worktop. At the tarnished blade. At the congealing blood clotted on the sticky handle. Momentarily, Laurence stood frozen with indecision. Would he be able to move quickly enough to snatch up the knife and slip it into his pocket before she had time to react?

What happens next will be relived many, many times in the months and years to come. The sequence of events pored over, each movement recalled in agonising and precise detail, every action scrutinised and dissected in turn in a vain effort to see what might have been done to prevent what, even in hindsight, would seem the almost inevitable result. By contrast, the one-and-only recounting of, what will later be referred to only as '*the accident*', to someone, to anyone, *by* anyone, will occur only a few hours afterwards in a bleak and cheerless hospital waiting room . . .

Christine Laurence picks up a box of matches in her bleeding and mutilated left hand. She takes a step to her left and turns on the front right ring of the gas hob. She opens the box and takes out a match. There is the rasp of a matchhead being drawn along the striker, a wisp of smoke, the match bursts into life, and the gas jet catches with a soft whoompf! . . .

40

'Stay where you are!' Cat warned. Having reluctantly released her grasp on the pepper spray in her pocket to raise a cautionary finger. While he'd been talking, telling his story, Hall had leant against the wing of the car. Hands in pockets. Legs crossed at the ankle. A studiedly relaxed pose, she guessed, he'd adopted to appear non-threatening. But almost as soon as he'd finished, he'd taken a step towards her, taking his hands out of his pockets to hold them apart in a gesture of modest appeal. As if, Cat thought, as far as he was concerned, everything had been explained. As if, now, they could just … what? Move on? Hug? Hall stopped dead in his tracks, his arms flopping miserably to is sides. Clearly confused. As if, now he'd said his piece, he couldn't quite believe that everything wasn't suddenly somehow okay.

'Just,' Cat said, wagging the same admonitory finger, still trying to take it all in, repeating, but less emphatically, less certainly, 'stay where you are, okay?'

A fine snow began to fall. The vanguard of the forecast blizzard moving down from the north of Essex. A gust of biting wind caught the collar of her coat and slapped it painfully against her cheek. And Cat was suddenly aware of just how far the temperature had fallen in the minutes since Hall's arrival. Registered, all at once, the chill that had crept up through the thin leather soles of her boots, oozed into her stiffening muscles, seeped into her aching joints. She slipped her hand back into her pocket, fingering again the comforting solidity of the pepper spray, as an icy realisation slowly crawled into her guts and settled there,

'You *knew* me?' she asked. Asked of herself more than anything. To put her chaotic thoughts in some kind of order. To say it out loud. To make it real, 'You knew me. even before that first interview . . . '

'*So, do I call you Catherine, Cathy or Cat?*'

That Catherine Russell had looked up at the question. The Catherine Russell of ten years ago. The Catherine Russell not yet out of her teens. The Catherine Russell who was living away from home for the first time in her life, who was acutely aware of his proximity in the small interview room. '*You look like a "Cat" to me.*' The Catherine Russell who was conscious of her black eye, her bruised cheek, the stitches in her upper lip. Her shame., '*So, shall we go with Cat?*' Conscious, too, of his eyes. Soft. Brown. Kind . . .

'It's all been just one big fucking lie. Hasn't it?' Cat asked now.

'What d'you – '

'Everything. You, me, us. Us! That's a fucking joke. There is no *us*, is there? There never has been.'

'Cat, c'mon . . . ' Hall said, spreading his hands again. An appeal to reason. Making a tentative move forward. An offer towards reconciliation, 'This is stu – '

'Stay where you are, I said.'

Hall retreated. Putting his hands back in his pockets. Leaning back again on the car.

'Christ,' Cat said, 'Right from the very start … there's been no *us*, has there? Not what I thought of as *us* anyway. All the time I was just . . . ' and it came to her then just exactly what she was, what she had been to him, 'just fucking *bait*! That's the truth of it. I was only ever just bait in some stupid fucking macho game of yours.'

'I had a *suspicion* . . . ' he said. Slowly shaking his head. The tone of voice mollifying. Conciliatory. Infuriating. ' . . . That you might be the next victim. Just a suspicion, that's all. No evidence. No proof. Just a suspicion. A hunch. No more.'

'A "suspicion",' Cat said, 'that you decided to keep to yourself.'

'I *thought*,' Hall said, 'that I'd be able to keep you safe.'

'But you didn't,' Cat said, shaking *her* head now, 'did you, John? You didn't keep me safe.'

'I told you – '

'Yeah. You were involved in a car accident. You said. But the thing is, John. You didn't tell *me*, did you? You didn't warn *me* that I might be in danger!'

'I was watching you, Cat. All the time. It was sheer bad luck that on that particular day I happened to be involved in an accident. That's all. Just sheer bad luck. If it hadn't been for that – '

'If it hadn't been for that, what?' Cat asked. Making little effort to keep the sarcasm, the bitterness, out of her voice, 'What *exactly* were you going to do?'

Shamed, embarrassed, Hall studied the ground for a minute or two.

'When you turned up at that first interview . . . ' Cat said, 'Fuck. I thought you were *so* kind. So, understanding. And all the time . . . ' Briefly her anger left her. Subsiding into something ... something like hurt, something like regret. Cat took a deep breath, then asked, 'Did I *ever* mean anything to you, John?'

'I loved you, Cat. Surely you know that. I love –'

'You spent all that time with me, after ... after I was raped. All that ... *stuff* ... that I thought was you being considerate, you being understanding ... and all it was ... was fucking guilt. Because you knew that you should have done more, you should have said something, you should have protected me.'

Hall looked away for a few seconds. When he looked back, he nodded his head, 'You're right. I should have done more – '

'The thing is, John' Cat said. Cutting him off. Not wanting any apologies. Unable to bear any feeble attempt at self-justification. It was *way* too late for that, 'The thing is, that now I'm not sure of anything anymore. Our whole relationship is built on a lie. So, everything that happened after, just seems like more lies. Like it was pure manipulation on your part. Like you took advantage of my naivety, my vulnerability, to get exactly what you wanted. Which was to get me into bed.'

Hall shook his head again, 'It was never like that.'

'So, what *was* it like?'

Hall looked away for a moment. Considering. Choosing his words. Or just choosing the lie, 'I'd been assigned a sexual assault case; these days you'd have had a specialised female officer, more convivial surroundings … Y'know,' he shrugged, 'ten years ago, things were different. Anyway, you know what these things can be like, everything last minute. You get a load of papers shoved into your hand, nobody knows the details, or if a preliminary statement *has* been taken it's not passed on to you . . . ' he paused. Then turned back to look at her, 'Look, the bottom line is … I didn't know it was you until I walked into that room. And that's the truth. The car had been out of action for a few days following the crash, so I hadn't been round to your place, I had no idea what had happened. When I saw the state of you … your face … I was shocked. Horrified. I knew I'd messed up. And badly. So, yeah, I felt guilty. Like maybe it was partly my fault,' he held up a palm to forestall any protest, 'It *was* my fault, okay? And, yeah, as a consequence maybe I put that little bit of extra effort into your case, to making sure you were okay, that you got over it as far as was possible – '

'No. The bottom line *is*, John, that I was a teenage girl living away from home. A teenage girl that had gone through a terrible, traumatic experience. And, whatever way you look at it, you took advantage of that fact. You were a serving police officer. You got involved with a witness – a *victim* – in a rape case. You were married, for fuck's sake! Although, of course, you didn't tell me that either, at the start, did you? All that came out later. And as if that wasn't enough you had – *have* – a severely disabled daughter who is dependent on you . . .'

'Look,' Hall wiped a hand across his mouth, 'it's not something I'm proud of. But I didn't mean for it to happen, any of it. It just did. At first, okay, there was an element of guilt, of shame, on my part. At first. But the more time we spent together, the more I got to know you . . . ' Hall shrugged. Heaved a sigh, 'I fell in love, Cat. All the rest … it just didn't seem to matter.'

They were quiet for a time, before Cat said, 'And so we come back to what you said in yesterday's meeting. That's *why* you're back in the area. Isn't it? To track down this Danny Fraser. That's why you got back into contact in the first place. You'd heard he was in the area. And you thought I'd be able to tip you off as to where he might be. It's nothing to do with me at all, is it? It never was,' Cat laughed bitterly,

274

'Jesus Christ! And all the time … all the fucking time I kidded myself that it was because of me. What a fucking idiot.' She took her hand out of her pocket now, releasing again her grip on the pepper spray. Rubbed at her temples, 'I even ended up in bed with you. Again!' Then she shook her head. Sighed, 'What a fucking idiot.'

'No. Cat, I love you.'

Cat laughed, 'Love?'

'Okay, look, part of what you said is true. Maybe I did get back in contact with you because I thought you might be able to help me locate Fraser. But after we met, I realised I still had feelings for you. I hoped we might be able to have some kind of … relationship again.'

Cat was shaking her head, 'Not … a … fucking … chance!'

The tone of Hall's voice changes to … resentment? Indignation? 'So, what, is it that partner of yours?'

'Pearson?' Cat asked. Confused by the abrupt change of tack.

'Aye, Pearson,' he replied contemptuously, 'Is that why you're not interested? Because you two have got a thing going?'

Cat sighed, 'John,' shook her head again, 'For fuck's sake. Just go, will you?'

For a time, neither moved. Neither spoke. Then the silence was broken by the sound, from the main road to her right, of a decelerating car engine. The approaching headlamps sweeping across the back bumper of Hall's car, the rear wing against which he was leaning, the back windscreen and, finally, Hall's face. And Cat wasn't sure she liked what she saw there. By the time the car had turned, and the parking area was once again in semi-darkness, Hall's driver side door was slamming, and he was reversing at speed into a skidding three-point turn. The red brake lights briefly illuminating, the tyres struggled to gain purchase on the slippery tarmac before the car exited onto the main road without indicating.

Fifteen minutes later, back inside her own car, and despite the heating being on, the windows rolled up, the central locking engaged, Cat was still shaking. With anger. With frustration. With the reaction to the adrenaline that was now draining from her system. Feeling, and not for the first time, embarrassed at just how fucking stupid she'd been. Not just because she'd arranged to meet a man she'd, less than an hour ago, suspected – or half-suspected – might have been the man who raped her ten years earlier. Arranged to meet in an ill-lit car park hidden from casual view. Not just because she'd let him back into her life – been to bed with him, for god's sake – when he'd been out of her life for so long. Not even because she'd allowed herself to think – because she'd been flattered, because it had fed her ego and made her feel good about herself, even if she had had in her mind to turn him down – that they might be able to rekindle their old relationship. No, in the end, it was because she'd finally seen John Hall for

276

exactly what he was. Dishonest. Manipulative. Weak. Pathetic. This was the man who, in the most impressionable period of her life, had influenced her taste in literature and music. Had guided her study of politics and philosophy. Had helped to form her very worldview. The man who – up to now – she had believed had made her who she was. So, if it had all been based on a misconception, if her idea of their relationship had just been a fallacy, if the whole-*bloody*-thing had just been a lie … where exactly did that leave her now? And that's when the tears came . . .

41

Pearson's hand hovered uncertainly for a moment an inch above the material of the other man's jacket. Then he laid his palm sympathetically on the shoulder beneath, giving a brief squeeze before moving past and taking a seat in the dismal hospital waiting area. For a time, Pearson, not knowing what to say, said nothing. Instead, he watched Laurence. Sitting in the chair opposite. Head bowed, staring at the floor, leaning his elbows on the leather briefcase in his lap, wringing, something like a cardboard tube, between his hands.

'Shall I take that?' Pearson asked.

Laurence looked up at Pearson's outstretched hand. Then down at the manila folder in his own. Like he was surprised to find it there.

'That the notes from today?' Pearson asked. And when Laurence looked puzzled, 'The investigation into Ryan Yate's death?

'Yeah,' Unrolling it, laying it on the briefcase, Laurence made a desultory attempt to flatten it beneath his palm, 'I was going to read it while . . . ' He flapped a hand hopelessly in the general direction, Pearson could only presume, of where he imagined the operating theatre might be located.

'It's alright,' Pearson said, gesturing at the folder, 'I'll take it. What's in the briefcase?'

Laurence shrugged, 'Nothing.'

'Why don't I take that too, then'

Laurence put the folder in the briefcase, shut the lid and passed it across. Pearson placed it on the empty seat next to him. Then leant back. Time passed. Pearson folding and unfolding his arms. Surreptitiously puffing out his cheeks. Trying, without much success, not to fidget too much in the uncomfortable plastic chair. Trying to ignore the ticking of the clock. The sluggish progress of the red second hand across its face. Trying to focus on a distant radio, playing a song he could not quite place. His attention broken every now and then by a far-off intermittent, wracking cough. But he became slowly aware of the sound of skin rasping against skin. Laurence staring at the floor, his hands moving absently across each other, as if, now he'd given up the folder, they might be at a loss as to what to do with themselves. Finally, unable to bear it any longer, Pearson unfolded his arms, cleared his throat, and asked, 'Fancy a coffee?'

Laurence didn't reply. Pearson got up anyway and went to the vending machine in the corner of the room, fishing in his trouser pocket for change, then feeding coins into the slot. He brought the coffees over and stood next to Laurence. When the other man made no move to take it, he placed the cup between Laurence's feet and retook his seat. Pearson took a sip of his coffee, still at a loss as to what to say. His gaze drifting around the waiting area. Looking for inspiration. Finding nothing among the ubiquitous moulded orange plastic chairs, the worn brown carpet tiles, the neglected and faded public health posters on the dreary olive-green walls, then returned to Laurence; sitting hunch-shouldered, his suit crumpled and shiny, his hair dishevelled. It was even thinner than Pearson had realised, the skull beneath slightly misshapen and lumpy, the scalp freckled and shiny. Laurence stirred. Picking up the coffee cup from between his feet. Cupping it in both hands. Staring down into the murky brown liquid. Then, with the contrition of the guilty, the air of the penitent, and in the hushed and serious tone reserved for the confessional, Laurence began to speak.

'She's got this condition – Christine? – Bi-polar Disorder. She doesn't like me to leave the Nick, she gets sort of, nervous, if she can't contact me. So, she likes to be able to text and get a reply . . . ' shaking his head at the floor, ' . . . and I still let Roberts send me out. I should've just said "No" and taken the consequences. Rather than . . . ' Laurence took a gulp of his coffee, sighed, 'She relies on me, Frank. And I let her down.'

Pearson began to wonder whether he might have misjudged the man opposite. Question whether he and Laurence might have more in common than he'd care to admit. He suspected that Laurence might even be the better man. Ruth, of course, didn't need – or at least claimed she didn't need – looking after anymore. But, even in her darkest times, could he honestly say he'd acted as selflessly, as considerately, as Laurence? Christ, all those texts, those personal phone calls, the reluctance to leave the Nick, and all the shit he'd got about it. All for the love of his wife. He'd sacrificed his reputation, his professional standing, in order that she felt safe. More than that, he'd taken the grumbling,

281

the moaning, the piss-taking of his colleagues and not said a word. All out of respect, out of loyalty.

Laurence shook his head again, 'She's been alright for a fair while now. I honestly thought we'd got past all that . . . ' The next word was delivered reluctantly. After blinking rapidly. After glancing to one side, even though he'd still not properly met Pearson's eye, ' . . . business.' He paused momentarily, though it was obvious that he wasn't going to – didn't want to – elaborate as to what "all that business," might have been. He took another sip of the coffee. Swallowing noisily. Forcing it down. Saying again, 'She just likes to be able to text. Y'know? Know that I'm there?' He lapsed into silence again. Staring morosely into his cup.

'What's happening about this animal rescue thing?' Pearson asked. After another pause. A pause long enough to make it clear that Laurence had no immediate intention to say more, 'Didn't you tell me you and Christine had plans to open a donkey sanctuary or something?'

Laurence didn't reply. Didn't look up. But Pearson thought he might have detected the faintest of nods. So, ploughed on regardless. Now Laurence had said something, had at least acknowledged the presence of someone else in the room, Pearson figured it imperative to keep him talking, 'You can't have that long left till you retire. What is it, a couple of months? I'm sure you'll still be able to do that, y'know when ... when things get back to normal.' *If*, thought Pearson. *If* things ever get back to normal.

Laurence, looking at him now, was shaking his head again, 'Nah, it's never going to happen. I mean, yeah, that was the idea. But Christine's . . . ' Laurence licked his lips, ' . . . she's like, got this thing about cleanliness, right? Like she's forever washing her hands and stuff. Obsessive Compulsive Disorder. Anyway, the other weekend, she's feeling a bit low. So, I say to her, "*Lets' go and have a look at a donkey sanctuary*", right? To see what it's all about. To get an idea of what it might actually entail. So, anyway, I drove for miles – somewhere up in Lincolnshire it was – thing is, when we got there, when she actually like gets in amongst the animals … she doesn't like it. They're "dirty", they're "smelly" … I mean . . . ' Laurence made a noise. Something like a laugh, though without a lot of humour in it, ' . . . what did she expect?' Realising his slip. His criticism and suddenly embarrassed, he cleared his throat. 'Anyway . . . ' he finished the remainder of his coffee, 'It's all off.'

Pearson, sensing the time was right – or, at least, realising there would probably never be a better time – which amounted to about the same thing, asked, 'So . . .what happened, Alan? Tonight, I mean.'

Laurence stared for an uncomfortably long time into his empty coffee cup. And, later: after the surgeon had arrived to give an update on Christine Laurence's condition, Laurence asking if he might be allowed to see her and getting unsteadily to his feet and following the surgeon out of the waiting room, Pearson understandably forgotten and making his way out of the hospital; later, when he'd replayed in his mind what Laurence had told him on the drive home, it was the oddly detached nature of the recounting, the almost robotic tone of Laurence's voice, that had propelled him into the very centre of the shocking events of that evening . . .

Christine Laurence picks up a box of matches in her bleeding and mutilated left hand. A yellow rectangular box divided in to two squares of red and green. The stylised picture of a white bird and the words 'Swan Vesta' smeared scarlet. She takes a step to her left and turns on the front right ring of the gas hob. Opens the box of matches and takes out a match. The rasp of the matchhead being drawn along the striker is almost deafening. The head of the match leaves a trail of grey-white residue along the length of the rough, pink strip. A wisp of smoke and the match bursts into life igniting with a white flare. There is an area of intense, invisible heat at its centre surrounded by a blue flame. The matchstick glows red. Writhing and twisting it draws into itself. Briefly glowing, then blackening and shrivelling in the hissing gas jet. Before, finally, it catches with a soft whoompf! . . .

Laurence leans casually on the worktop, his hand a foot or so away from the bloody paring knife, as she turns on him again, 'You promised me. You promised me you'd stay where I know you're safe.'

'I know, love,' Laurence replies, 'I'm sorry. It won't happen again,' All the while inching his fingers along the worktop towards the knife's black handle.

'You said that yesterday.'

'I *know*, love. I'm sorry.' His fingers close around the knife, 'Look, the investigation's closed. I won't have to go out again.' And all the time holding her gaze, 'I won't do anything you don't want me to,' he palms the knife, 'In a few months, I'll be retired. I won't even have to leave the house. Not if you don't want me to,' and then slips it into the side pocket of his jacket.

'You always say that. What exactly have I *got* to do to keep you in the Nick?' she asks, 'How far do I have to go in order to keep you safe?'

He looks at her properly now for the first time in maybe ten minutes. Her face is set. She is staring at him. Blinking rapidly. Her face flushed. Beads of sweat stand out on her forehead. So intent has he been on getting the knife, putting it out of harm's way, that he has not noticed … that smell. The odour of the barbecue. The reek of burning human flesh –

He moves as if in slow motion. Shouting something. Something animal. Something primordial and unintelligible. Lunging desperately towards the arm that is by now totally engulfed in flame, the hand that rests, blistered and blackened, in the roaring blue petals of the gas hob.

THE LAST DAY

42

Terry Milton sat in his kitchen under the stark illumination of a single bare bulb. He had been sitting here for the best part of the night. At a round, wooden table that he'd wrestled up the narrow staircase a few days ago. He hadn't been downstairs since. There didn't seem to be any point. The club basically ran itself nowadays. And no one had bothered to come up and check on him. He picked up the bottle of scotch – an expensive single malt he had been saving for a special occasion – filled the shot glass and took his first real sip of the whisky. Only then did he permit himself to consider the open bottle of sleeping tablets on the table in front of him. He downed the remainder of the glass. Only then did he allow his mind to return to the events of three days earlier . . .

Terry had never seen a gun. Had never felt the cold barrel of a gun pressed against the back of his skull. But he had known right away that that was what it was. And, he had closed his eyes. Expecting the trigger to be pulled. Hoping, just for a moment, for the gunshot that, in all likelihood, he would never hear. Wanting, most of all, for all of this to be over.

'What you can feel at the back of your head is a Sig Sauer P226 semi-automatic pistol,' the voice behind the gun had said. Male. Not local. Though, at that precise moment, Terry couldn't quite place the accent.

'In case you are not familiar with guns,' said another voice. And this voice at least Terry *had* been able to identify. It was the voice on the other end of the pay-as-you-go phone he had been given. Female. Educated. The voice that had, from the outset, delivered the arrangements that he was to follow 'to the letter' on the nights of the parties, 'I can assure you that It is not an imitation.' she came around from behind him and sat down on the other side of the table. 'It *is* the real thing.'

'I'm not about to bore you with technical specifications,' Layla Gilchrist said, 'I have no idea what sort of ammunition the thing uses, or how many bullets it fires per second, or whatever. I really have no interest in all that,' she wrinkled her nose, '"boy's toys" stuff. In any case I'm sure you appreciate the seriousness of your situation. Much as I hate to lapse into the melodramatic, we are rather pushed for time, so I think in the circumstances it *is* probably the easiest way to get my point across … So, Terry, you have a number of options. Your first option is a bullet in your spine. Which would render you paralysed from the neck down.

Gilchrist paused theatrically, allowing the words to sink in, 'Your second option is a bullet through the skull. This would be quicker, and for you at least, less bothersome. But it would result in an awful lot of mess for the bar-staff and cleaners to deal with. And we,' she nodded over Terry's shoulder, to the man Terry couldn't see, the man Terry had made a deliberate point of not seeing, the man pressing the gun barrel into the back of Terry's head, 'are, after all, here to clear up a mess, rather than make another one.'

The man had moved to his side then. And now he could see the gun, could see *only* the gun, Terry had changed his mind. Had decided he didn't want to die after all. Had decided he would do anything *not* to die. Almost anything. But, even then, even with the semi-automatic pistol pointing at his face. Even with the threat of imminent death – or worse – his first thought was still of having a drink. And his eyes had drifted to the glass of scotch in front of him on the table. And he had wondered, just for a second, whether he could safely make a move for it. But, instead, Terry had swallowed.

'Do I,' had cleared his throat, 'have any other options? I thought you were here about the phone call.'

'Ah, yes, the little girl who's been bothering you,' Gilchrist shook her head. Disappointed. It wasn't the first time someone had been disappointed in him. Wasn't the first time he'd felt an abject failure. Wasn't the first time he'd experienced complete and utter shame, 'We'll get to that. But first of all, I need a little information.'

Terry cleared his throat again, 'About what?'

'The parties, Terry. I want to know about the parties – '

'But you – '

'Specifically, Terry, I want to know what *you* know about the parties. Things will go better for you if you at least *try* to be completely honest. And it will save a bit of time if you just assume that I know nothing … and simply start at the beginning.'

291

So … he had started at the beginning. He had been in debt, he told Gilchrist. So, he had torched the club. Claimed the insurance. But, even after that, the club still wasn't making money. Not enough money. All the other clubs were part of a national chain. Could offer more: better lighting, better sound systems, could run special events featuring reality TV stars, could undercut him on the price of drinks. So, he had decided to torch the club again. Only, somehow, he had fucked up the insurance. He'd gone on-line, filled out all the forms, but he hadn't clicked the right button or something. And then he hadn't followed it up to make certain he actually was insured.

Then he had been approached, been made a proposition, been asked to do 'a little favour'. Been offered enough money to do up the club, to pay off his debts. He had been approached by a man who he had later seen in the local papers and on the telly. A man who had been found tortured and burned to death in a bedsit not far from here. And Terry had faltered then. Suddenly aware that this man had been Gilchrist's partner. That Gilchrist might have had some part in his death. And Terry had started to cry. Because he felt humiliated. Because he was ashamed. Had started to plead. Because he was scared. Because he didn't want to die after all. He hadn't wanted to host the parties. He regretted ever agreeing to it. It wasn't right, the things that went on –

The gun barrel had struck him in the temple. Not hard enough to knock him off his seat. Not hard enough to draw blood. Not even hard enough, really, to break the skin. Just a little rap to refocus his mind. To show that the gun was bored. To remind him that the gun was still there … Then the gun had waggled for Terry to move on. So … Terry had moved on.

Moved on to the visit of Detective Inspector Sean Carragher. A copper under investigation by his own Professional Standards department. Carragher had known exactly what had been going on at the club, he told Gilchrist. Or had hinted as much. Terry had thought that it was just blackmail. That Carragher was after some cash. Cash he simply didn't have. But he had hoped that Carragher might do a deal. Might allow Terry to trade information about the people who attended the parties, for an exemption from prosecution. Or, at the very least, a reduction in the severity of the charges he might face. All the time, Terry had been aware of the gun. Had wondered if telling the absolute truth would be something that might count in his favour. Or if he was just digging a bigger hole for himself.

When he had finished, Gilchrist had nodded thoughtfully, 'The pity is, Terry, that for you, that *would* have been your way out. If it hadn't been for DI Carragher's murder – '

Terry was conscious of a movement by his side. Out of the corner of his eye he saw the hand holding the gun lift a cuff and show the face of a wristwatch. Gilchrist nodded her understanding. 'Now, Terry, perhaps you can tell me what you remember about the night Michael Morris died.'

When Terry had finished, and for only the second time since they had entered the club, the man spoke again, 'We need to get going.'

And now, sitting at the table in his kitchen, and though he might be the first to admit that he was no expert on dialectic variations, Terry finally identified the accent. A jock. Glaswegian. Probably.

'Alright, Terry,' Gilchrist had said, 'I think you can have that drink now.'

And, as much to please the gun as anything else, or at least that's what he'd told himself since, Terry had picked up the glass and downed the scotch in one. Gilchrist was leaning down, picking up her handbag from the floor, putting it on her lap, rummaging inside. Now he'd had a drink Terry felt brave enough to look past the gun. And at the man. Had he recognised that face? Was it a face he might have seen at the parties? A face he'd had a fleeting glimpse of in the gloom of the darkened club. Even now he couldn't be sure.

'We're going to leave you now, Terry. I fear we may have been here too long already,' Gilchrist was pushing something across the table towards him. 'This really is the easiest for you, Terry. For everybody . . . '

Automatically Terry reached a hand to take the thing off of her. Then stopped. There was something weird about her hand. The colour ... the lack of definition ... the absence of fingernails. With a jolt he realised she was wearing latex gloves. She nudged the bottle of sleeping pills with a finger, 'Go on. Take them, Terry, it really is the best way. The *only* way . . . '

And Gilchrist had been right. It *was* the best way, the only way, to end all of this. Except it wasn't exactly the easiest way. He hadn't appreciated until he had the first half dozen tablets in his mouth just how hard they were to swallow. Hadn't realised until he'd tried crushing them that they would stick to his teeth, cling to the roof of his mouth, coat his tongue. His original idea had been to wash them down with the scotch, but he hadn't reckoned with them tasting so bitter. So bitter, in fact, that he couldn't enjoy the scotch at all.

They *had* got around to the girl. Just before Gilchrist had pushed the sleeping tablets across the table at him. Donna Freeman. Gilchrist had supplied the name. He had told her how the girl kept appearing suddenly out of the dark. How she kept rapping on the car window. How she kept trying the door handle. How she *must* know what had been going on. But he hadn't wanted anything to happen to her. He hadn't. He had just wanted it to stop.

Now, the girl was dead. He'd seen her face on the telly. Read her name in the papers. Seen all the stuff across social media. Donna Freeman was dead. And it was his fault. He would mix the crushed tablets with milk. Fuck the ulcer. What did that matter now? He'd crush all the tablets and force them down with a pint of milk. Later. First, though, he'd enjoy a drink. He deserved that much, didn't he? One last drink? He'd paid a lot of money for this particular bottle of single malt. Had been saving it for a special occasion. Well, this *was* a special occasion, wasn't it?

43

'Are you *sure* you don't want a solicitor, Mister Clark?' Cat asked. Not for the first time. Because – Clark's decision or not – the lack of legal representation would result in a bollocking later from Roberts, 'If you don't have a solicitor of your own, we *can* always provide you with one.'

But Gary Clark was staring past her, 'Is that thing on?'

Turning in her seat, Cat looked up at the camera mounted on the wall of the interview room, 'See that little light under the lens?' she asked, pointing it out with her pen, 'When the camera is in use, that light comes on.'

Gary Clark's PNC profile put him at thirty-four. But the grey in his mousy hair, the effects of long-term addiction; the characteristic stripping away of subcutaneous fat, the jaundiced sclera, the bad complexion, the loss of most of his teeth, made him look much older. Squinting, his head bobbing from side to side, Clark eyed the camera for a few seconds more. Then his gaze swept the room. He frowned. Still not quite persuaded. As if he *might* be being tricked but couldn't quite work out how. He cast a last doubtful glance up at the camera, then he nodded at the twin tape deck, 'Can't we do this without that?'

Pearson, who was unwrapping the cellophane from a DAT cassette, shook his head. 'Er . . . no ... I don't think that's a good idea, Mister Clark. Best follow procedure, eh?'

And looking up, 'We don't want you claiming later that we put you under some sort of duress, do we?'

Squirming. Sniffing loudly. Working his right hand up the sleeve of his grey sweatshirt to rub at the inside of his left elbow, Clark leaned forward and whispered, 'Just for a minute.' He flicked a glance at the door, 'I want to ask you something.'

Pearson took the tape out of its case. Wrote on the label. Snapped it into place in the machine, said, 'You've got until I unwrap the other tape and put it into the deck.'

Clark indicated the door with his chin, 'Is anyone out there?' And when Pearson made no move to check, 'Look,' Clark said, 'I'm not about to try anything, am I? That thing,' he nodded at the metal strip running at waist height around the room, 'is an alarm, right? I try anything. You hit the alarm. And thirty seconds later a dozen coppers are in here kicking the shit out of me. Right?'

Pearson stared him down.

Clark appealed to Cat, 'Can't you just have a look and see if there's anyone out there? Please?'

Pearson looked across at her. Smiled. Raised his eyebrows. She glared back. Puffed out an exasperated breath. Shook her head. But she rose from her seat – albeit scraping her chair noisily across the linoleum floor in the process – went to the door, opened it and popped her head outside. When she came back and retook her seat she said, 'No one out there. Satisfied?'

'I want to make a deal,' Clark began.

'Well,' Pearson said, starting to unwrap the other tape, 'of *course* you do. Of course you do.'

'Look, I can't go back to that Nick,' Clark said, 'I just can't. it's not safe for me there. So, I'm not going to tell you anything. Not unless I get a transfer somewhere. If I go back there, I won't last five minutes,' Clark's right hand disappeared inside his left sleeve again. Scratching this time, 'And don't tell me you'll keep me safe, because you won't. You can't. It's not even safe in segregation, some nonce will shank me just so his life is a bit easier. So *he* doesn't get a kicking every day, so he doesn't get shit put in his dinner . . . '

After a moment, Pearson said, 'This is not America, Mr. Clark. No deals. No promises.' But, Cat noticed, Pearson hadn't loaded the tape into the machine. Not yet. 'You say what you've got to say, and we'll see what we can do. And that's the best I can offer. Okay?'

Clark looked torn. His gaze skittering around the room. As if the solution to this particular riddle might be hiding in one of its corners.

'Look,' Pearson said, 'if you do feel you *are genuinely* under threat, then we might – *might* – be able to arrange for you to be moved. At least temporarily. But,' he shook the tape at Clark, 'it's all going to have to be on the record. Okay?'

Reluctantly, Clark nodded. Pearson removed the second tape from its case, wrote on the label and snapped it into the machine. As Pearson pressed the 'record' button he looked across the table at Cat. Unimpressed. Doing everything, in fact, but rolling his eyes. It was a look that told her Pearson regarded Clark's assertion as 'complete and utter bollocks'.

Almost as soon as the preliminaries were over – introducing themselves for the tape, reading out the charges, Cat asking Clark again if he was sure he wanted to waive his right to a solicitor, just in case – Clark started talking . . .

'Look, I want it on record that I'm in danger, right? I'm not safe. And I want a transfer to another prison.'

'Alright, Mister Clark,' Pearson said. Bored. World-weary, 'It's on the record.'

'D'you know where all the stuff comes from inside?' Clark asked. And it was immediately apparent to Cat that this was the beginning of something well-rehearsed. Something recounted on numerous occasions to countless other people. To anyone, in fact, who would listen, 'D'you know where it comes from? The drugs ... the phones ... the baccy ... the, like, I dunno,' he shrugged, 'all of it. Anything you can't get hold of inside is valuable, right? So, d'you know where that all comes from? D'you think it's smuggled in by new prisoners? Well, it's not that easy; these days most nicks have got BOSS chairs – the Body Orifice Security Scanner, you've heard of that, right? – D'you think visitors bring it in? You've been through security at prison reception . . . '

Cat watched Clark scratch the back of his head. Watched as he continued to scratch. His chewed, dirty fingernails raking at his scalp.

''Course,' Clark said, 'to read the *Daily Mail* you'd think you could just ring up and order a drone delivery. Am I right?' He looked between them. Then he wiped his hand across his face, 'So where d'you think it all *really* comes from?'

Pearson sighed, 'Why don't you enlighten us, Mister Clark?'

'The screws, of course. You've just got to find the right one, that's all. And there's always at *least* one. You've just got to ask around the Nick, that's all. Someone will know which one of them is bent, tell you who to speak to if you want anything. You ask any screw, right? He'll tell you there's not one of them has been searched on the way into work since they started in the prison service – '

'Are you making an allegation of corruption against a specific prison officer, Mister Clark,' Cat asked. Just to stop him talking for a minute. To prevent any further scalp-gouging. She didn't think her nerves could stand it. All that fidgeting, the scratching, the face-rubbing … it was like watching Roberts on fast-forward. 'Are you able to provide us with the name of this prison officer? Or any solid evidence to substantiate your claim? Presumably the prison officer in question is not paid directly? So, he, or she, must be working together with someone on the outside, right? So, are you able to provide us with the names of these individuals? The details of the bank accounts used?'

'Have you ever been in a prison van?' Clark asked, 'You're sort of locked in a little metal box? There's, like, rows of metal boxes with a gangway in between? So, all the way here I'm in this little box, and this screw's standing right outside, in my earhole all the time about what he can have done to me, about how easy it would be . . . '

'You're claiming intimidation by a prison officer?' Cat asked. For the tape. For the benefit of the jury in any future court proceedings.

'I'm not "claiming" intimidation. I'm not "claiming" anything. I'm saying that's what he did. It's a fact.'

'And why would this prison officer be threatening you?' Cat asked.

'Because of this Ryan Yates thing,' Clark said. In a tone that suggested it should have been patently obvious.

'This Ryan Yates *thing*,' Cat said, 'His *murder* you mean?'

'Well, yeah,' Clark said. Not picking up on the sarcasm in Cat's reply. The annoyance in her question. Assuming, instead, that she might just be slow on the uptake, 'This murder that I'm *supposed* to have committed. And, I know what it looks like. On the face of it, yeah, I look guilty. My DNA's all over the shop. But it's bound to be, isn't it? I mean, we were cellmates, weren't we? My DNA's bound to be everywhere. Look, the truth is, I was meant to do it. I was shown how to do it. Make it look like a suicide. Shown how I could get away with it. But ... when it came down to it . . . '

Clark shook his head, ' . . . I just couldn't do it! Look, I'm just some sad junkie. That's all. Thieving, selling hooky gear, that's my limit. I'm no killer. And I didn't kill Ryan Yates.'

'Well,' Pearson said, 'Detective Sergeant Laurence seems to think you did. Detective Sergeant Laurence thought he had enough evidence to charge you.'

And all at once Pearson realised that *he* didn't. That the notes Laurence had made the previous day were in the manila cardboard folder. Inside the black leather briefcase. Which, right at this moment, was at home, on his kitchen table.

'Yeah,' Clark giggled, 'I know.'

'We *are* talking about a murder here, Mister Clark,' Cat said coldly, 'I have no idea why you should find *that* funny.'

'I don't,' Clark shook his head. Put his hand to his mouth, 'I don't,' he pressed his lips shut with his fingers. Because, Cat realised, this was the only way to stop the inappropriate laughter bubbling out, 'Sorry.'

At that moment Cat stared into Gary Clark's past. And saw the many opportunities that had been missed to maybe move his life in another direction. The shifty fourteen-year-old after his first arrest. Being interviewed by an irritable and unsympathetic copper. The requirements of PACE that an 'appropriate adult' be present – overlooked. Feeling threatened. Intimidated. Cowed. The twitchy and agitated ten-year-old in the headmaster's office at his primary school. Not quite sure why it was only him that was in trouble again. The grubby and fidgety toddler standing in front of the latest in a long line of his Mum's short-lived 'boyfriends'. Waiting for the slap. The punches. The kicking. All the times in his life he'd been unable to meet the other person's gaze. All the times he'd been unable to resist that involuntary and uncontrollable compulsion to laugh.

'Look,' Clark said, 'I was supposed to kill Yates. But, like I said, I couldn't do it. That's why this screw was on at me in the van. Because I *didn't* do it. And that's why I can't go back to that Nick. I'm no grass, but I don't want to do time for murder. I'll be put in with all the proper nutters. The lifers. The ones who have got no chance of ever getting out. All they care about is their reputations. Who's top dog on the wing. Someone like me. I'm not going to last five minutes, am I?'

Clark turned to Cat, 'Look, you're right, there *is* a bank account we're supposed to use. But I'm not good with numbers. I've got it on a piece of paper back at the Nick. You get me a transfer and I'll tell you where it is, and you can go and get it. Then you can check it out yourselves. No point in asking a screw, more than likely it'll just disappear. So, you arrange for someone to make a payment into this account and this screw'll get you what you want. And I'm talking *anything* you want: heroin, weed, spice … obviously nothing that's going to make you lairy. So, no speed or coke, right? But he'll get you anything for a price. Any mobile, and we're talking anything from an *iPhone* to a cheap model that just has calls and texts – '

'So,' Pearson said, 'If you didn't kill Ryan Yates. Who did?'

'The screw that brought me in the van. Murray. George Murray.'

'And I take it that George Murray is also the prison officer you are making an allegation of corruption against?'

'Yeah.'

'And the prison officer you are claiming issued threats against you in the prison van on the way here?'

'Yeah.'

'And what reason would this George Murray have for killing Ryan Yates?'

'You've got no fucking idea, have you?' Clark shook his head. A pitying expression on his face, 'You think I'm just some sad bitty, don't you? Just some paranoid junkie? Asking about the camera? The tape? Getting you to check if there was anyone outside? You just don't get it. George Murray works for the Fraser family. You've heard of the Frasers, right? So,' a look to Cat, 'the Frasers are the people on the outside. The ones providing all the stuff,' back to Pearson, 'but it's not *just* them. It's everyone: screws, solicitors, politicians, police officers – and I'm talking about high-ranking police officers, right? – they're all in on it. So, you step out of line, and it'll get back to them. Right? That's what I'm saying, you're not even safe inside. Look at Ryan Yates. He knew something. Something the Frasers didn't want getting out.'

'The Frasers,' Pearson repeated. The tone of voice making it obvious that he didn't believe him.

'Yeah,' Clark nodded, 'Or these other people the Frasers are involved with.'

44

Daryl Crawford had woken that morning from a dream of heat, of white-hot sky, of sweat and stinging sand. A dream of blood and buzzing flies, of fire and roasting human flesh. Had woken, sweat-slick, in a confusion of bedsheets in the almost-light of the hour before dawn. Had woken ... into the ordinary. The everyday. He had stared up at a cracked artex ceiling in dire need of a coat of paint. Had become slowly aware of the faint stirring of net curtains in a listless breeze. Had turned his head to see the framed photo of the twelve-week baby scan on top of the white Ikea bedside cabinet. The digital clock-radio blinking 10.34 p.m. He had reached across and pressed the reset button. Then he'd picked up his watch to check the actual time. The hands of the fake Rolex showed ten past six. And, for the first time in weeks, Daryl had felt the need for a cigarette. He'd smoked since the age of thirteen. And had given up as soon as Tracy had discovered she was pregnant. He'd managed pretty well, apart from the odd craving. But that need, that desperate hunger, had returned, had stayed with him ever since . . .

Danny Fraser had reached into the side pocket of his jacket, taken out a disposable lighter and menthol cigarettes and offered him the open packet.

'It's *all* of it,' Fraser had said, sparking up, cupping his hands around the flame and taking a long drag on his cigarette. Exhaling a plume of smoke from his nostrils. His eyes searching the unswept floor of the betting shop. An abacomancer divining the future in the dust. 'It's not even all the stuff that happened in Afghanistan.' Looking back up at Daryl, his brow furrowing, his fingers kneading his temples, 'All that *bad* shit … it's all of it, Boss. And worst of all, it's what I'm doing now.'

In the gloom of the betting shop, Danny Fraser had studied the glowing ember of the cigarette for a few seconds, before putting the filter between his lips and taking a long draw. Then looking back at Daryl, one eye closed against the smoke, he'd said,

'D'you remember when we were approached by someone offering private security work?'

'Yeah,' Daryl nodded, 'Not long before we came home. We went for an interview. And we thought the whole set-up looked dodgy. So, we decided to give it a miss. Don't tell me you're working for *them*?'

'Aye,' Fraser admitted, 'that's right.'

'So, what changed?'

'I came home,' Fraser said, 'signed on. After six months, the best offer I'd had was as a security guard in a shopping mall.'

'I don't suppose there's a lot of work for people with our sort of skill-set. So, what exactly is this "private security work"?'

'To start off with, it was personal protection. American diplomats. Oil executives. Bankers. Money men. Anyone who wanted safe passage into and around Afghanistan. Once the big deals had been done, though, the protection work started to dry up. They were happy enough with what I'd done. Said that they might have other jobs coming up ... that they . . . ' Fraser rubbed the bridge of his nose between thumb and forefinger, ' . . . had some sort of contract-work for the British Government.'

'All sounds a bit . . . '

'Vague? Aye, that's *exactly* what it is. Vague. Secretive. Shadowy. However you want to put it. Dodgy, basically. The sort of work an organisation wants doing but wants kept at an arms-length.'

'"Plausible deniability" right?'

'Aye,' Fraser shook his head, 'But some things ... s*ome* things are just *wrong*, Boss.'

'Such as?'

'Such as,' Danny Fraser had taken a final drag on his cigarette, dropped it onto the floor and ground it out with his heel, 'the deliberate concealment of systematic child abuse?'

Next to him in the bed; half-turned away, half-propped up on pillows – because even this early in the pregnancy the baby had already started to make sleeping through the night difficult – Tracy had stirred in her sleep. Daryl had laid a reassuring hand on her hip. And, after a minute Tracy had settled again. Then a sudden draught had flapped the net curtains at the half-open window. Bringing with it the merest notion of a perfume. It was an impression he had experienced a thousand times since his return. And, regardless of his attempts at rationalisation, despite telling himself that it was just an olfactory hallucination, it always took him instantly back to that night. He'd googled it, of course. Once he'd got home. Those clouds of fragrant smoke which had filled the tent. The burning of Esfand seeds. An ancient Zoroastrian rite to ward off the evil eye. But who, exactly, had been being protected from whom?

Now, in the almost-dark of the back office of the locked and empty betting shop, and even if he squeezed his eyes tight shut, Daryl Crawford could still see the amber streetlights, the ghost of something burning reflected in Danny Fraser's red-rimmed eyes. Could still here him asking, '*Do you ever think about it, Boss? The war?*'

The truth was, since Danny Fraser's return, he'd thought about little else. Afghanistan. Those twenty-three minutes. Those twenty-three minutes which, until now, he had successfully managed to obliterate from his memory. That inexplicable loss of control. That absolute, unmitigated insanity . . .

The two figures kneeling on the dusty stone floor. Their hands on their heads. Sweat streaking dusty bodies stripped to the waist. Tears wet on dirty cheeks and the soft down of nascent beards. The sound of sobbing and the drawing of a steel blade from a sheath –

Daryl forced his eyes open. When it came down to it … they weren't really soldiers … they were little more than children. And, whatever way you looked at it, it was still torture. It was still murder. Daryl pushed himself up from his chair. Even as they had doused the place in petrol, even as they had set it ablaze, even as they had taken those shovels and buried the bodies of those kids in the desert, Daryl had known that the whole stinking, rotten, shameful truth of it was bound to come out eventually.

And now, that past had returned, in the form of Danny Fraser. Worse, a damaged and unpredictable Danny Fraser. Daryl had spent the time since Danny's reappearance, and the later visit of the two detectives, carefully weighing up his options. He opened the wall safe. It was obvious that he couldn't just do nothing. He stared down at the pistol. He just had too much to lose. Daryl picked up the gun and slipped it into the inside pocket of his jacket.

45

Daryl Crawford pulled down the metal shutter on the front of the *Double Carpet* betting shop, snapped the padlock into place and gave it a little jiggle to make certain it was secure. Then he stood up and turned … to stare down the barrel of a gun.

'You're getting soft, Boss,' Danny Fraser said, 'Time was, I'd never have been able to creep up on you like that.'

It was, in fact, the second time in as many months that Daryl had had a firearm pointed at his face. And, to be honest, he was getting a bit tired of it.

'I could pull this trigger now,' Fraser said, 'and be away and out of sight in less than thirty seconds.'

'If you really wanted to kill me, you would've pulled the trigger already,' Daryl replied coolly. Hoping that it was true. Trusting that that was just the hint of a smile he could see on the other man's face.

'Maybe I wanted to look in your eyes while I put a bullet in your head.'

Daryl's conviction that this was Danny's idea of a joke began to falter.

'Pass me the Sig,' Fraser said. And when Daryl didn't move, he added, 'Inside left pocket of your jacket,' The tone weary. As if he might already be bored with the whole thing, 'Reach in slowly and pass it over to me. Butt first.'

Daryl did as he was told.

His own gun in his left hand, Fraser weighed Daryl's pistol in his right, 'Chekhov's Gun, Boss? D'you remember?'

' *"One should never place a loaded rifle on the stage,'* Daryl quoted, *'if it isn't going to go off."* Right?'

'Aye. And the thing is, Boss, you wouldn't be carrying this, unless you intended to use it. Right? Fraser slipped it into the side pocket of his leather coat. Then transferred his own pistol to his right hand, 'Think of this as saving you from yourself.'

'Isn't there something about *"If you save a life, from that point on you're responsible for that life"*?'

'Aye, well,' Fraser said, 'you see that? That's not really a thing. People think that that idea comes from an ancient Chinese tradition. When it's actually just a trope of action movies. Like I said, I'm here to save you from yourself. And I reckon that the best way to save your life, to start off with, is to stop you trying to take mine.'

They stood for a moment, staring at each other, saying nothing, then Fraser put his hand inside his coat. The pistol disappeared, to be replaced by a packet of menthol cigarettes and a disposable lighter. He indicated a nearby metal bench, 'Shall we sit down?'

Danny Fraser opened the pack of cigarettes and offered it to Daryl. He'd told Tracy he'd given up. Promised. Then again, Tracy wasn't here, was she? Daryl took one and Fraser lit both of the cigarettes.

'D'you know why I came here, Boss? A few days ago, I mean.'

'I had wondered.'

'I wanted to know that at least one of us could come back and live something like an ordinary life. All the other blokes in our unit … they're either alkies, or living on the streets. That's the ones who haven't topped themselves. The truth is, I envy you,' he indicated the closed metal shutter of the betting shop, 'your job. Your life. Your relationship: Tracy, isn't it?' Daryl nodded. 'And a kiddie on the way? Soon enough you'll be a regular little family.'

'So, what about you?'

Danny Fraser drew on his cigarette, looking away up the street, 'I joined the army to get away from my family,' Fraser turned to Daryl, 'I suppose I never said much about my family, did I?'

'*You* never said much about anything.'

'Aye,' Fraser gave a wry smile, 'True enough,' he flicked ash onto the ground, 'I think I told you I got offered a job in the family construction business? The thing is, "Fraser Construction Services" is just a front – at least it was, up until a couple of years ago – the main business of the Fraser family is class A drugs. I tried to steer clear of that side of things, did some plumbing, a bit of bricklaying … all of which suited my old man. I never did fit in. My brother, Jackie was always his favourite, so even early on it was obvious he would be the one to take over.'

Daryl drew on his own cigarette and waited for Danny to go on.

'I think I also told you that Logan, my old man, died recently of stomach cancer? So . . . ' he shrugged, 'I went back for the funeral. More for Maggie's sake than anything. Maggie, that's my mother? Never really been keen on "Mum" and "Dad", my parents. First names, ever since I was a kid,' he took a drag on the cigarette. 'Anyway, let's just say,' he expelled smoke through his nostrils, 'that there weren't a lot of tears shed at the funeral. So, straight after the service, before we'd even got out of the chapel, my brother, Jackie, comes over. Says he'd like a word, and can we go for a little walk. He's like, I know you and the old man didn't get on, but now he's gone things are going to change. He says he's got no interest in the construction business. Says he'd like me to take it over. No hard feelings. Even if am not really family. So, I'm like, *What're you talking about?* So he looks at me and says, *Don't tell me you didn't know? Didn't you think it was strange that you don't look like any of the rest of the family? You're not the old man's, Danny. Why do you think he hated you so much?* And I'm just looking at him. Stunned, y'know? So, he says, *If you don't believe me, go and ask Maggie.*'

Fraser took a draw on his cigarette, shrugged his shoulders, 'Anyway, turns out, it's true. My real father is –

was – a man called James Gallen Robertson. Uncle Jimmy. When I was really little we used to go to the park, me, Maggie and Uncle Jimmy,' he shook his head, 'and I still didn't fucking work it out. Jimmy used to work behind the bar at one of the clubs. So, Jimmy disappears, right? At the time, the story was that he'd been dealing for my old man. He'd got greedy and started skimming off some of the profits, so the old man had topped him to teach everyone else a lesson,' he dropped his cigarette onto the pavement and ground it out. 'In reality, my old man had found out about him and Maggie. So, you know what he did? He had Jimmy's dismembered hand delivered to the flat where Maggie was staying. Complete with the gold ring she'd given him as a present.'

'Jesus Christ,' Daryl said, 'what a fucking family!' He finished his own cigarette and dropped it on the floor, 'It's no wonder you decided to join up?'

Danny offered the open packet of fags to Daryl. This time he shook his head.

'I had to get away,' Danny said, 'An allegation of rape had been made against me,' he put another cigarette in his mouth, cupped his hands around it and sparked up, 'an "allegation". Because it wasn't true. Jackie's a … monster. What I think they call nowadays a "*sexual sadist*"? And he has a particular preference for under-age girls,' he flicked the ash from the end of his cigarette. 'I was out of the area doing some building work. Jackie was using my van. Telling everyone his name was "Danny". He'd already done time for rape, so I suppose he thought it'd be safer. Plus, he probably thought it'd be funny. He's not right in the head, my brother.

A fucking psycho, if you ask me. Anyway, this particular girl, he raped her. Beat her up pretty badly. Her family persuaded her to report it. By the morning, she'd changed her mind. Dropped the charges. Either Jackie or Logan had gone round to the family and put the frighteners on. But Jackie let me know about it anyway. His idea of teaching me a lesson, right? The little brother who thought he was too good for the family business. A way to show me that they could just as easily dump me in it, as get me out of it. Jackie's way of sending me a message "*Toe the line ... or else*". So, t*hat's* when I decided it was time to get out . . . '

All the time he had been talking, Danny Fraser had been smoking, and staring into the middle-distance. Now, he turned back to Daryl, 'The irony is, that, after all the trouble I went to, to get away from my family, all that effort to do the right thing, here I am back involved with the sexual abuse of minors. And who d'you think it is that's slap-bang in the middle of it all again? My fucking big brother Jackie, that's who.'

They were silent for a while. Then Daryl said, 'The ... thing that happened in Afghanistan . . . '

'Was the war, Boss. The thing that happened in Afghanistan was the war.'

'You didn't seem to think that when . . . ' Daryl gestured towards the shutters of the betting shop. Recalling Danny's visit of a few days ago.

'Aye, well, I was upset,' Fraser said. 'Look, Boss, there are rules that apply here,' he indicated the street, 'at

318

home, in everyday life. And then there are the rules of war, and I'm not talking about "rules of engagement" drawn up by some fucking lawyer in Whitehall or Geneva, but the real rules of war, which basically come down to two: personal survival and having your mate's back – '

'They were kids, Danny. What we did – '

'What we did was extract information. Information that saved people's lives. Okay, so they were what thirteen? Fourteen? But they were still old enough to carry Kalashnikovs. They were still old enough to blow up one of our guys. And, okay, it got out of hand. But we were in a high-stress combat situation. And we'd watched the previous day as someone stepped on an IED an lost his legs. Feelings were, understandably, running high,' Danny Fraser dropped his latest cigarette on the floor and ground it out with a heel, 'Take my advice, Boss. Forget about it. Go back to your life, your job. Go back to Tracy and your kiddie and forget about it.'

'What about you?'

Danny Fraser checked his wristwatch, then stood up, 'It's already too late for me.'

46

Pearson eyed the oblong of reinforced glass set in a metal door, the palimpsest of spray-painted gang tags, football loyalties and sexual obscenities. Momentarily, he hesitated. Watching his breath plume on the cold air. Hoping that coming here would not turn out to be the worst decision of his life. Then he reached out, opened the door and stepped into … the lingering odour of every lift lobby in every multi-story car park in every town in the country. The stink of every single underpass and back alley cut-through. The unmistakable reek of human urine.

Pearson went to the lift and jabbed the 'call' button. Staring up at the illuminated number '5' for half a minute. Punched repeatedly at the 'call' button. Watching the fixed an immobile number. Shook his head. Swore to himself, realising that he'd have to use the stairs. Mind you, he thought, the smell in the lobby was bad enough. The lift was bound to be worse. And he wasn't sure he could hold his breath for five floors. So, thrusting his hands into the pockets of his overcoat, he entered the stairwell . . . .

Earlier, in the interview room, Pearson had switched off the tape recorder and was slipping his jacket back on when he'd heard the sound of a chair being dragged across the linoleum floor of the corridor outside.

'You going to be alright with chummy here for a minute?' he'd asked Cat.

She had made a show of sizing up Gary Clark. A look halfway between disdain and menace, 'Yeah, I think I'll manage.'

Pearson had got up from his chair, winking at Clark, 'A word of advice, Mr. Clark,' nodding in Cat's direction, 'It's best not to upset her.'

He had opened the door to find a large man in uniform sitting on one of the moulded plastic chairs. Trying very hard for the appearance of having been casually flicking through the magazine open on his lap. And not having hastily retaken his seat only a moment before.

'Are you the prison officer who brought Gary Clark in? Mr. Murray, isn't it?' Pearson asked.

The screw closed the cover of the magazine and looked up, 'Aye.'

'Er, look,' Pearson scratched an earlobe, 'We're likely to be a while yet'. It was then that he'd clocked the title of the magazine: *Motor Cycle News*.

Murray had followed his gaze, 'Do you ride yourself?' he asked.

'Nah,' Pearson had shaken his head, 'I like my comfort too much. Definitely a car man, me.' And then, clearing his throat, 'Like I said, we'll be a while longer. Why don't you go and grab something to eat?'

Pearson had turned away. But, instead of going back into the interview room, he'd slipped his mobile out of his pocket. Standing at the end of the corridor, he'd watched Murray put on his coat and leave. Then he'd called Jack Morris. The phone had rung a half a dozen times, and Pearson had been about to give up, when the old man answered, 'Yeah, what?'

'This bloke you met at the car park. The Jock? The one who handed over the money to you?'

'Yeah. What about him?'

'You said he looked like he was in the services, right?'

'No. What I said was, that I've got someone who works for me that's ex-services, and this bloke had sort of the same look about him.'

'Yeah, whatever. What I'm asking is, could he have been a prison officer?'

At the other end of the line there was a long pause, then Morris sniffed, 'Could be. Look, when I said he had that look about him, I didn't mean I thought he was in the services now. He was some big, fat cunt.'

Pearson paused at the top of the landing. Puffing like a train. Sweating like a pig. Christ, I'm not dressed for step aerobics, he thought, unbuttoning his overcoat and loosening his tie. Taking a minute to catch his breath . . .

It was only after Murray had left that Pearson had finally placed him. The fat neck overhanging the collar, the beer gut straining the short-sleeved blue shirt, the keys in the ziploc bag on the belt loop of his black trousers, the shiny, steel-toe-capped shoes. It was the same obstructive prison officer who'd been in their interview with Tony Blake. Sitting on a stool against the wall and pretending to study form in the racing pages of a tabloid newspaper. And, all the while, earwigging.

'*Courtney,*' Blake had said, looking between him and Cat, '*she's mixed up in something nasty, right?*'

'*What?*' Pearson had asked. '*Mixed up in what? You talking about something she did with Michael?*'

'*She's in danger.*'

'*From who?*'

But Tony Blake had shaken his head, stared past them, and had had nothing more to say.

If what Gary Clark had told them was true, if Murray *was* in the pay of the Frasers, then this would explain Blake's reticence to say any more. Would explain his repeated glances in Murray's direction. Maybe he'd thought he'd said enough already. Enough to put himself in danger. It would explain, too, why he'd asked to talk to them again. But had then said nothing. Until his head had come up suddenly from the table and he'd confessed to the murder of Michael Morris. Perhaps he'd hoped that he'd be escorted by some other prison officer. But when it had again been Murray, he'd changed his mind.

Calculating that his best course of action to protect, not only Courtney Woods, but himself was to confess to a murder that, it seemed now, he may never have committed.

After their initial interview of Gary Clark, taking advantage of Cat nipping out for a quick fag, Pearson had approached Wendy Simpson. Asked her to arrange a meeting with the people who were pressurising her to provide information. He wondered again now whether he was doing the right thing. Then he opened the door and stepped out.

At this time of night, more than an hour after the last shop had closed in the adjacent retail centre, the top level of the car park was deserted. Pearson scanned the area. Shadows pooling between the few halogen lamps that remained un-vandalised. A mesh fence, erected recently to hinder the growing number of recent suicide attempts, sat on top of a low brick wall. And, to his right, framed against the glow of light pollution from the town, the silhouette of a waiting figure. Pearson walked over. As she turned to face him, he caught the look of surprise in Layla Gilchrist's eyes.

'Expecting someone else?' he asked.

'Detective Sergeant,' she said. Almost immediately regaining a measure of composure, 'How lovely to see you again.'

'I've got to admit,' Pearson said, 'You're not exactly who I was expecting either.'

She turned away and, for a while, they looked out into the night, saying nothing.

Finally, Pearson said, 'I thought you worked for the Security Services. Or is it a private company that has work contracted out to it by the Security Services?'

'Well, yes ... and no.'

'So, what happened? The Frasers offer you more money?'

'*Additional* money, Detective Sergeant. Additional money.'

'Tell me, Ms. Gilchrist. Where, exactly, *do* your loyalties lie?'

'Loyalty?' Gilchrist laughed, 'How quaint. I suppose I'd have to say that my loyalties lie entirely with myself.'

At the sound of a footfall on concrete they both turned. But the welcoming smile fell from Layla Gilchrist's face ...

47

The man who emerged from the shadows wore polished Doc Martens and black jeans. A leather coat over a grey crew neck jumper. Had cropped sandy hair, green eyes and a pale complexion.

Pearson recognised him immediately as the same man who had climbed from the car on the night he'd met Graham.

'Were you may be expecting somebody else?' he asked. Putting a cigarette in his mouth, 'my brother perhaps?' Taking a disposable lighter from his pocket and cupping his hands around the flame he sparked up. It took Pearson a second to place the accent – Scottish – and to realise that he was talking to Gilchrist.

'Only *this*,' he indicated the car park with the lighted cigarette, 'has Jackie's name all over it. A late-night meeting on top of a multi-story car park?' He shook his head, 'Jesus,' he took another drag on his cigarette, 'then again, he always did watch too much telly.'

'You must be Danny,' Gilchrist said. A hint of amusement in her voice.

'Danny?' Pearson asked, 'Danny Fraser?'

Danny Fraser glanced over. Once again assessing the threat. Once again dismissing it. Relegating Pearson to an irrelevance.

'Jackie's told me all about you,' Gilchrist said, 'You recently came out of the army. Isn't that right? Jackie offered you a job?'

Danny Fraser took the cigarette out of his mouth and studied the glowing tip, 'Aye. And what would that be? Waving handguns in the faces of drunks, maybe? Or chucking little girls off bridges?' He looked up, fixing Gilchrist with a stare, 'No, wait a minute,' he jabbed the lit cigarette in her direction, 'that was you, wasn't it?'

At the sound of a car engine they all turned. This, Pearson thought, is getting to be like fucking Piccadilly Circus.

'That,' Gilchrist said, looking over at the powder blue Bentley, 'will be your brother.'

The car pulled to a halt. The headlights went out and the engine died. Pearson waited for the driver's side door to open. Only . . . it didn't.

Looking back from the car, he saw that Danny Fraser now wore a pair of odd-looking dark glasses. Had, what appeared to be, a mobile phone in his hand. And suddenly he understood. But just that split-second too late. Pearson had squeezed his eyes shut, was turning his head away when he felt the punch to his chest as every breath of air was sucked out of existence ... and the world disappeared in a flash of excruciatingly white light . . .

It took a few seconds before Pearson was able to open his eyes again. A few seconds before the after-image of the panicked man behind the steering wheel faded from his retina. A few seconds before, despite himself, he was able to look over in the direction of the explosion. The windows were missing, fragments of glass lay strewn around the car, glittering in the light of the few halogen lamps. Surprisingly, most of the chassis was relatively untouched. Only in the area immediately around the driver's side had the paintwork scorched and blistered. But peering through the billowing smoke into the blackened interior, Pearson could see the smouldering and charred husk of what, only a few moments earlier, had been Jackie Fraser.

Pearson turned away. Layla Gilchrist, tears streaming down her face, was rubbing frantically at her eyes. Moaning something incomprehensible. Danny Fraser stood barely twenty yards away. His face impassive. His arms dangling casually at his side. The cigarette now discarded. Pearson caught, instead, the dull gleam of metal from a pistol in his right hand.

'Danny?' Pearson said. He slowly reached out a hand, feeling a bead of cold sweat run down between his shoulder blades, 'It would go better for you later if you gave yourself up – '

'You think so?' Fraser asked, 'D'you really think they'll let this – ' He swept a negligent arc with the gun. Taking in the wreckage of the car. The sobbing and blinded form of Layla Gilchrist. And Pearson himself, '– go through the judicial system?' He shook his head, 'D'you really think they want all their dirty little secrets out in the open?'

In the distance, Pearson heard the faint sound of approaching sirens.

'The explosion would've been called in by now, Danny,' Pearson said, 'It'll be treated as a terrorist incident. There'll be an armed response unit here in less than five minutes.'

Pearson wasn't really sure whether telling Danny Fraser *this* was such a good idea. It was, anyway, little more than a desperate bluff. And Danny Fraser was a former member of the Special Services. A former member of the Special Services who was now brandishing, what was very probably, an illegal firearm. A former member of the Special Services who had just blown his own brother up in his car. If he could kill his own brother without the slightest hint of remorse, what chance did he stand? Under his overcoat, the suit jacket, Pearson felt his sweat-soaked shirt clinging to his back. Even if armed backup *was* five minutes away, it would only take Fraser a split-second to pull that trigger.

'Danny?' Pearson said again, 'Could I have the gun? Please?'

Danny Fraser looked down at the gun in his hand. Turning it slowly this way and that. A look of mild perplexity on his face. Like it was some kind of alien artefact and he was puzzled as to how it had got there. Sirens. Closer now.

'They have this place . . . ' Fraser said, almost conversationally, ' . . . Detective Sergeant Pearson, isn't it?' When Pearson nodded, he went on, ' . . . You know, I think it's actually not far from here. Somewhere in the Essex

330

countryside, anyway. The official line is that it's an institute involved in research into the effects of combat stress and PTSD. In reality, it's a government-sponsored facility involved in human psychological experimentation. That's where *I'll* end up, Detective Sergeant.' He nodded to himself, 'Aye. And no one will ever hear of me again.'

Fraser lifted his hand. The gun went off. And, before he'd had time to register what was happening, Pearson was looking down at Layla Gilchrist's dead body.

'This lot … ' Fraser went on, nodding down at Gilchrist, like the staring eyes, the bullet hole in the forehead, the pooling blood, were the most natural thing in the world, waving the pistol in the direction of the still-smoking car, ' . . . will never see the light of day, Detective Sergeant. This will be written off as a sad accident. A report in a local newspaper, "Three *die in tragic car blaze at town centre car park*".'

For a second, Pearson stood paralysed. Certain of his imminent death. Debilitated by the suddenness of Gilchrist's murder. Incapacitated by the nonchalance of that phrase.

Years later, Cat Russell would remember experiencing that same numbing fear. Would remember standing among the press of spectators at the edge of the cordon. The blue-and-white police tape strung across in front of her. The uniform constable barring her path, '*I'm sorry, Miss. You can't come in here.*' Staring stupidly past him at Scene-of-Crime-Officers donning paper suits, unloading metal boxes from vans, assembling the framework of arc lights. Before the

331

unmistakable sight of Roberts in his oversize anorak had brought her back to her senses. And she had started the frenzied search of her handbag for her warrant card.

Once again, Fraser's hand moved through a lazy arc. The lights of the car park reflecting dully from the metal of the pistol. And for Pearson, time slowed. In that instant, looking down the barrel of that gun, Pearson knew he was about to die. He squeezed his eyes shut. And in that perfect silence of anticipation, he convinced himself that he could hear the sound of a trigger being pulled back. But, less than a second later, there was absolutely no doubt about the deafening report. The smell of burning flesh and bone. And the sudden, brutal impact of a body hitting concrete . . .

PART THREE

48

Well, we've been *here* before, Pearson thought. The Detective Chief Inspector's office. The visitors' chairs. To his left, Roberts. To his right, by the window, Cat. Pearson somehow back in the broken chair. The one in which the moulded plastic base had come adrift from the metal legs. At first, he had wondered why Roberts hadn't had it replaced, before deciding that he probably took a perverse gratification in seeing people struggle to keep their balance on the bloody thing.

On the other side of the desk sat Graham. Looking subtly different. The light brown hair still pulled back off of her face, but decidedly less frizzy. The freckles across her forehead and nose disguised by make-up. The eyes behind the steel-rimmed spectacles not a striking violet, but the soft brown of melting chocolate. The garish orange lipstick and nail polish replaced by an understated shade of bronze.

'Well, we've been here before, haven't we, Ms Graham?' Roberts asked, a flush in his cheeks, a barely suppressed rage in his voice. 'Not three months ago. On that occasion, you not only shut down my investigation into the murder, in the March of 1966, of sixteen-year-old Beverly Marsh, but also made certain that the enquiry into the death of Michael Morris was closed. And, as I said at the time, that was the real reason you were there. Wasn't it? To make sure we took the confession of Tony Blake at face value, and looked no further?'

On that occasion though, Pearson thought, Andy Curtis hadn't been standing in the corner of the room. The Detective Chief Superintendent wore his best dress uniform. His silver buttons specially buffed. His arms folded across his chest. Immaculately polished leather shoes squeaking as he glared balefully at them and rocked back and forth on his heels.

'Maybe this time, we can just cut out the bullshit?' Roberts said. 'This whole thing is about a power struggle between two different factions within the Security Services. Or at least, the Security Service and private contractors to which security work has been outsourced. Isn't it . . . Geraldine?'

Had there been the merest flicker of surprise in Graham's eyes? Roberts obviously thought so. 'Oh yes, DS Pearson has told me all about your little late-night conversation, Geraldine. At the very least, I think that you might owe us *some* explanation as to why your lot have been running around on our patch, waving guns about like a bunch of fucking cowboys? Not to mention detonating what amounts to an IED in a public place.'

Presumably, Pearson thought, given the presence of the DCS, not without at least the tacit approval of someone very high up in the Police Force. Though, given it *was* only Curtis, both the Chief Constable and the Assistant Chief Constable would obviously prefer to distance themselves from any suggestion of involvement.

After a momentary pause, an indication of some degree of indifference on her part, Graham licked her lips, 'I suppose that at this juncture in proceedings,' she conceded, 'it is probably incumbent on me to offer *some* element of exposition – '

'This is the part in "*Scooby-Doo*,"' Pearson said. Not sure himself whether this was an attempt to defuse the situation with a little humour. Or if he was only sublimating his own anger through sarcasm, 'where the monsters are unmasked ... to reveal that they were just ordinary people all along.'

'Only, I think in this case,' Roberts said, 'we might find that the opposite is true.' For a second or two the silence was broken only by the squeaking of Curtis's shoes.

'Why don't I kick us off?' Roberts asked. Graham *might* have nodded. In any case, Roberts didn't wait to find out. 'Somebody within MI5 has the idea to set up these ... "entertainments" at Westminster, or at least became aware of their existence ... either way, someone decides it might be useful to know who was there, what they were up to. Right? Just in case, say, that at some future date, one or other of these government officials should get it into their head to try and curb the powers of the security services? Meanwhile, the private contractor has the same idea. In their case, they're worried that a little pressure might be needed in order to – to put it in a language you might understand, Ms Graham – "institute policies that might otherwise prove unpopular enough to encounter political resistance"? In other words, to enable them to do something illegal. Stop me if I'm wrong.'

Graham nodded, 'Carry on.'

'Meanwhile,' Roberts said, 'someone decides that the original venue for these parties has become too risky. That the parties should be moved somewhere less ... "obvious". Who knows why they picked Southend? Maybe someone had a local connection? Maybe because it's a fairly easy commute into London? Or maybe they just like the fucking seaside? In any case, this is where the real trouble begins. The character of the parties changes. The clientele isn't just politicians and government officials anymore. It starts to include local councillors, businessmen, *criminals* . . . and the nature of the "entertainments" provided becomes less ... savoury, more degenerate, the paid "hostesses" replaced by vulnerable and, in some cases under-age, teenagers. Inevitably, it all spirals out of control ... culminating in the strangulation of Michael Morris.'

'Michael Morris was recruited by MI5,' Pearson said, 'By you. You *knew* that Layla Gilchrist was one of the people behind these parties. You *must* have been aware – or at least have suspected – the type of people who were at these parties? You must have known the kind of danger you were putting Michael in?'

'For Michael,' Graham said, 'that was part of the attraction.'

'And what about DI Carragher?' Roberts asked.

'Sean?' Cat blurted, 'How is – hold on, you're not going to tell me he was working for MI5?'

338

'Aren't I, Detective Constable? As I think I said previously, to say he was working for us may be overstating matters somewhat – '

'That was in relation to Michael Morris,' Pearson said, 'Who, as we all know, also ended up dead.'

'But,' Graham said. Ignoring Pearson's interruption, 'once again, Detective Inspector Carragher was ideal for our purposes.

'It's true DI Carragher may have had some issues; according to his psychological profile he was most certainly suffering Post-Traumatic Stress Disorder following his attempted murder during an undercover drugs operation in Toxteth. An attack which, according to the psychiatrist from whom he was receiving counselling, had a profound effect on both his psyche, and his sexuality.'

'His sexuality?' Cat asked.

'Quite so. In fact, DI Carragher admitted that the attack had left him sexually impotent. He went so far as to describe himself as "asexual" – '

'Sean told me he was gay,' Cat said.

'Well,' Graham said, the merest tinge of insinuation in her voice, 'I'm sure he had his reasons,' and then, to the room, 'We required someone who appeared approachable – '

'Corrupt, you mean,' Pearson said, 'or corruptible.'

'Indeed. DI Carragher was already under investigation by the Professional Standards department, albeit on charges that later proved to be fabricated, so it was then only a matter of making him appear as someone who – ' a look to Roberts here, ' – to put it in a language you might understand – "could be got at",' and then back to the room, 'Concocting an apparent cocaine habit, creating the impression that he had a gambling addiction – if you recall, you found a substantial amount of cash in his apartment – and then using what we knew as a lever to flush out the people involved in arranging those parties, while giving the impression that Detective Inspector Carragher would be willing to take money in return for keeping his mouth shut.'

'And along came Donna Freeman,' Pearson said, 'and threw a spanner in the works.'

'Yes,' admitted Graham, 'Donna Freeman was something of an "unknown variable".'

'Or,' Cat said, 'what any normal person might think of as a vulnerable young woman with mental health issues.'

'Someone else who met their death as a consequence of the activities of the British Government,' Pearson said.

'It's not something of which I'm proud, Detective Sergeant,' Graham said.

'And, what exactly, *are* you proud of in all of this, Ms Graham?' Roberts asked. 'Let's get back to these "parties" – though I've got to admit I find the term repugnant in this context – Layla Gilchrist didn't work for you, did she? And by that, I mean directly for the Security Services. That's the only way any of this makes any sense. She was working for this "private contractor", right? At least to start off with. Maybe even at the time she set up these parties in Westminster, or maybe it was later, but certainly when these parties were going on in this area. And you – and we're talking about the British Government again – wanted to find out what was going on, who was involved, what they knew, what you might be able to use to blackmail them? But, at no time did *anyone* involved spare a single fucking thought for these vulnerable kids. Did they? So, Michael Morris ends up dead. Even then you – or this private contractor – might have been able to cover it up. But one of the kids at the party – Courtney Woods – panics and calls her boyfriend – Tony Blake – to get rid of the body somehow. Blake, though, is not the hard man he wants everyone to think he is. His bottle goes and he dumps the body of Michael Morris on the beach. Which, of course, is where you come in. You turn up and make it plain, if not to us, then to people higher up,' Roberts paused to look over at Curtis, 'that we shouldn't look too closely into the case. Pressure is applied, Blake makes a confession, everything is hunky dory. Only there's other people involved now. Right? Unbeknown to you, not only is Layla Gilchrist working for the Security Services, but she's also working for the Frasers. In particular, one Jackie Fraser, a convicted rapist and drug dealer. And the person, we now suspect, guilty of the murder of Michael Morris.'

Roberts paused again. The only reaction from Graham the habitual blink.

'Donna Freeman and Ryan Yates torture and kill Clive Townsend,' Roberts said, 'In the process of which they find out exactly what's been going on. But there's people who don't want their involvement to get out. People who are worried they might be open to blackmail. Now, maybe this is Jackie Fraser. But maybe this is someone else. In any case, Donna Freeman is involved in a fatal fall from the pier bridge. Ryan Yates is killed in prison and, at first, it's made to look like the work of a fellow prisoner. And, finally we come to Danny Fraser. A man who had been employed as part of your personal protection. And the brother of Jackie Fraser. Don't your lot do *any* kind of candidate vetting, for fuck's sake? Hold on,' Roberts wagged a finger at her, 'that was something else that was outsourced, wasn't it? He was employed through this private company, wasn't he? You relied on them to make all the relevant background checks.'

Roberts scratched his cheek, 'So, let's recap, shall we? As a direct consequence of your actions, we have the murders of … Detective Inspector Sean Carragher, Michael Morris, Donna Freeman, Ryan Yates, Clive Townsend, Layla Gilchrist and Jackie Fraser. Plus, the suicide of Danny Fraser. Not to mention, the deaths that have occurred as an indirect consequence, such as that of Alicia Goode. And, in addition, you turned a blind eye to the sexual exploitation of minors.'

Roberts sighed deeply. 'Christ, even the apparent suicide of Sickert Downey, the former head of the Abigail Burnett Children's Home, is starting to look suspicious now … So, I'll ask you again, what exactly *are* you proud of in all of this, Ms Graham?'

342

Unable to meet his eyes, Graham looked down at the table.

A few seconds later Detective Chief Superintendent Andy Curtis cleared his throat and unfolded his arms. 'Given all you've been through this evening,' he said, 'I think it's best you all head off home now. They'll be plenty of time in the morning to write up reports.'

By which time, Pearson thought, the 'official' version of events would have been agreed. A template statement would have been devised, to which their own accounts would be expected to conform. Any contradictory evidence would have conveniently disappeared. And he thought, glancing across at Roberts, he would have time to come up with a story as to why he'd been in that car park in the first place.

When Graham and Curtis left the room. Roberts retook his seat behind the desk, looking exhausted, looking defeated. He shook his head, 'I think it's pretty clear who our new Assistant Chief Constable is going to be.'

He closed his eyes and leant back, placing his hands on top of his head. And that's how he stayed. For a good five minutes. Although to Cat, in that suffocating silence, it seemed longer. No one speaking. Both Pearson and she staring blindly into the middle distance. Then Roberts opened his eyes and slid out the top drawer of his desk.

'Looks like I picked the wrong fucking week to quit Polos,' he said. Without humour. Offering the pack of mints to each in turn. They both shook their heads. Roberts unwrapped the packet, popped one in his mouth and started to crunch noisily.

'So, what happens now?' Cat asked.

'Now?' Roberts wiped a hand down his face, 'Now, DC Russell, I suppose we *all* go home and consider our futures. Think seriously about whether we really want to remain in this fucking job at all.'

Cat swallowed, 'No, I meant . . . '

'I know what you meant,' Roberts said, 'Keep an eye out in the media for reports of any government ministers meeting with accidents, any unfortunate and tragic "suicides" of people who are retrospectively diagnosed with "severe depression" . . . '

'You really think it will come to that?'

Roberts sighed deeply again, 'Probably not. Wishful thinking. But no doubt there will be at least one member of parliament who stands down to "spend more time with his family" in the next few weeks. As for the rest ... the Home Secretary will announce that the Director-General of the domestic Security Service is to step down due to ill-health –'

'To live out the rest of his days on a final salary pension, no doubt.' Pearson said.

'Naturally,' Roberts said, 'The Deputy Director will then step into his shoes, and the new Director-General will then institute a series of measures aimed at the rationalisation and streamlining of the current departmental structure. As a result of which operations will be brought back in-house. And, in the process, *our Ms Graham* will get a "well-earned" promotion.' Roberts rubbed his chin, 'Maybe as much as a couple of grades up the pay scale. But nothing *too* vulgar . . . we are talking about the Civil Service, after all.'

49

Wearing her customary black trouser suit and white blouse, she scans the overcast sky uneasily, twists an elastic hair band over her dark, shoulder-length hair. Arranging it into a loose ponytail. Even in the dim interior of the car in which he now sits, even by the scant light of the single streetlamp twenty yards or so away, it is unmistakably Cat Russell. But the snapshot itself is disappointing; taken in bad light, with the camera on his mobile, and through a dirt-speckled front windshield, the image on the phone's screen is not quite in focus –

Headlights appear in his rear-view mirror; a dark blue Ford Mondeo passes and pulls up to the kerb. From here he is able to make out only the silhouettes of the two figures . . .

Inside the car, neither spoke. Neither of them having anything to say. What was there *to* be said? Neither moved. Both seemingly unwilling to finally call it a day. And Cat found herself, once again, surreptitiously studying Pearson's profile. Elbow resting on the door sill, fingers drumming absent-mindedly on the top of the steering wheel, Pearson stared out through the front windscreen. Then her eyes drifted up towards the darkened windows of her flat. For a fleeting moment she felt an almost irresistible urge to invite him in. To not be alone. To have him, have *someone*, spend the night, share her bed. She found herself, instead, unfastening her seat belt, opening the car door, saying, with no real conviction, 'See you tomorrow.' Not waiting for his reply.

A few minutes later, having thrown on a baggy t-shirt and jogging bottoms, Cat was sitting on the leather sofa in her living room. And more than halfway through the first, she suspected, of many glasses of red wine. The television was on, the volume just high enough to be company, but just low enough not to be intrusive. An ashtray, lighter and pack of cigarettes arranged in front of her on the coffee table. As weary as she had been, as miserable as she had felt, and despite the torment of the bottle of Malbec that she knew stood on the counter next to the fridge, Cat had by-passed the kitchen and gone, instead, straight to her bedroom. This, after all, was who she was; the habits, the routines, the rituals. She had removed her boots and placed them with the ranks of other black footwear in the bottom of her wardrobe, had taken off her black suit and hung it neatly alongside the rows of the many near-identical black suits. She had dropped her blouse and underwear into the laundry basket. The stripping off of the professional persona. Had chalked it up as a minor personal victory when, after a minute's deliberation, she had decided that she might, just this once, forego the shower. She had opened her chest of drawers, looking for a change of clothes, thinking after all, it wasn't like anyone else was –

And another thought had stopped her in her tracks. Dear God, had she *really* considered asking Pearson up? Had she *really* contemplated spending the night with him?

Now, though, sitting alone in her living room, the first glass of wine already starting to take effect, she was having second thoughts. Or were they third thoughts? Ever since the visit of the DC from Child Protection, she had found herself viewing Pearson in a different light. Since Fadziso Campbell had expressed a definite interest in him, she'd caught herself on more than one occasion secretly checking Pearson out. Despite herself, having to grudgingly admit that Pearson wasn't actually that bad-looking. That he did, indeed, have sort of nice eyes. And she had come to slowly realise that she might actually have genuine feelings for him . . .

No real surprise that it had taken the other woman's attraction – and the piquing of her own jealousy, she had to admit – before she became alive to her own emotions. To see Pearson as anything other than just a decent, steady bloke –

'*Don't knock it, girl. In my experience decent blokes are a rare commodity.*'

Anyway, who was she to judge? It wasn't exactly like she had a good track record of choosing men, was it? Or even choosing friends, come to that. Although, actually, she might be able to offer Sean as some measure of vindication. She had considered him a friend, a good friend, she had stood by him. Had defended him. Even when it had seemed that he had lied to her. That he had exploited their friendship, her loyalty, to get her to cover up for him. But, in his case, hadn't her evaluation of his character actually turned out to be pretty accurate? In the end, if what Graham had said was true, hadn't Sean Carragher only fabricated the persona of a dishonest police officer, and in so doing sacrifice his reputation, in order to unmask political corruption and child exploitation? Hadn't he only lied as circumstances demanded?

'*Sean told me he was gay.*'

'*Well,*' Graham had said, '*I'm sure he had his reasons.*'

Had Sean believed that she might have viewed their relationship as something more than just friendship? If what Graham had said was true, and Sean was impotent, that he thought of himself as 'asexual', had he regarded that particular lie as a kindness? Alone now in her flat, Cat blushed. From the tone of her voice, though, it was obvious that Graham at least believed that Sean had thought of Cat as some kind of sex pest . . .

Cat swirled the red wine around, watched the light of the television reflecting in its surface. Then she drained the glass. She had been right about John Hall too. Even if the truth behind their relationship *had* only come to her late in the day. Whatever way you wanted to look at it, he had taken advantage of her. He had used her as a lure for a suspected serial rapist, for fuck's sake. How could you *possibly* justify something like that? It had not only put her in danger, but had led, whether directly or not, to an attack that had very nearly broken her. Even his subsequent efforts to rectify the consequences of his reckless actions could only be seen now as being motivated by guilt. She had been taken in. But she had been little more than a child, even if at the time she might have thought of herself as an adult, and she had been vulnerable. Even now, she could still remember that first meeting in the Interview Room. Her reticence. Her embarrassment. Her shame. Shame. As if, somehow, it had been her fault. Like she might have been 'asking for it'. But she had known, even in that first meeting in Priory Park, the first meeting for nearly eight years, that he had been hiding something, had been lying.

That morning, their witness had come forward. '*Her* witness'. Because, somewhere along the way '*their* witness' had somehow become '*her* witness'. That epithet bringing with it the insinuation that he might not actually exist, that he might just be a figment of her imagination. The man she had seen as she knelt in the road by the pier bridge and probed Donna Freeman's neck for a pulse; the boots, the trousers, the bottom of a jacket illuminated in the glare of the car's headlights, the rest obscured by the night, the rain, and asking '*Can I help*?' The man she had directed to the female driver of the car in front of hers. The man she had later come to believe might be John Hall. There had been a call from reception. A man who might have information pertaining to 'that young girl who fell off the Pier bridge' . . .

They had interviewed a man in his late seventies who, on the night of Donna Freeman's death, had been taking his elderly Scottie dog for a walk. She had been 'making a fuss to go out,' he'd said, 'Wanting to do her business.' So, he had taken a chance. Hoping that they would be out and back before it started to rain. The sudden downpour had taken them by surprise. He'd heard the screech of brakes, the impact of the car with something solid – it was only later that he'd realised that it must have been the girl – and he'd tied the dog to a lamp-post and gone down onto the road to see if he could be of any assistance. He had hung around until the paramedics had arrived and, thinking he was maybe just in the way, had collected the wet and shivering dog and tucking her into his coat had simply gone home. He'd told his wife what had happened, and she'd said he should go to the police. She had said 'more than once' that 'anything he'd seen might be important. No matter how insignificant it might seem,' that that was what the police always said whenever they appealed for witnesses. So, 'ere he was, he'd said, 'to stop the missus bloody nagging,' and that was what he'd seen, for what it was worth. Had he seen anyone else about? they'd asked. Well, there *had* been someone on or around the bridge. When? At the same time, he'd heard the brakes, he thought. Yeah, maybe it *could* have been shortly before. Or after, possibly . . .

Could he describe this person? Well, it had been dark. And raining. And he had been concentrating on the dog rather than looking at other people. But he thought it *might* have been a woman. But he couldn't really say any more than that. That woman, they knew now, was almost certainly Layla Gilchrist.

It might have only been his unexpected arrival at the MIT that had led her to suspect that the witness had been John Hall, but, if she were honest with herself, she had felt a growing sense of paranoia, of being watched, ever since that text message asking if they could meet.

It had got to the point where she had caught poor, sweet Gilbert glancing over in her direction yesterday and she had felt a fleeting but intense feeling of menace . . .

He picks up the pack of Menthol cigarettes and disposable lighter from the top of the dashboard. Then, cupping his hands to hide the flame, he sparks up and takes in a lungful of smoke. He leans forward to tap the ash into the polystyrene take-away cup on the front passenger seat. That was the trouble with these new cars – no ashtrays. Did the manufacturers assume that nobody smoked anymore? Or did they just not want to take the chance of appearing to condone it? For a while he sits and smokes, contemplating the light in, what he knows is, the living room of Cat Russell's flat. Then he studies the glowing tip of the cigarette . . .

Detective Constable Peter Gilbert has come to realise that he doesn't really like smoking: the ash in the car, the smell on his clothes, the expense. Understands, too, that it is time to call it a night. So, he pinches out the cigarette and drops it into the polystyrene cup, turns on the headlights and starts the engine . . .

50

Cat Russell placed the disposable lighter and cigarette packet carefully back on the coffee table. She should feel angry. She should feel miserable. She should feel betrayed by the events of the last few hours. She drew again on her cigarette. Weirdly, though, Cat realised she didn't. Instead she felt … relieved. Like a huge weight had been lifted from her shoulders. The investigation into the events at the Abigail Burnett Children's Home, the untangling of her past association with John Hall, the visit of the officer from the Child Protection Unit, had all contributed to her coming to a decision. All that time spent in self-examination. All those weeks of brooding. All the agonising over whether or not she should stay in the Job. And all that time she'd been asking herself the wrong question. The issue was not whether she was doing the right job. But whether she was working in the right area of the job.

'There's a real sense of achievement when you make an arrest,' Fadziso Campbell had said when they had 'shared' a fag in the smoking area outside the nick.

'Yeah,' Cat said, *'The trouble with my job is, that even after you've made the arrest, sometimes it's hard to work out who the real victims are.'*

Or the real criminals, Cat thought now. If you were even able to make an arrest. Were allowed to make an arrest. If it wasn't all swept under the carpet in the name of 'national security'. Cat had joined the Police because, naively, she had thought that it was somewhere where she might be able to make a difference. Well, not much evidence of that, if the events of the last couple of months were anything to go by. Not much chance, either, that she might be able to forge any kind of career. Not where she was now. Detective Chief Superintendent Andy Curtis would always be looking for an opportunity to 'ease' her out of the force. Cat took another drag on her cigarette. It was time she moved on. A new unit. A clean slate . . .

Cat was pouring her second glass of wine as Pearson opened the front door of his flat, stepped into the hallway and flicked on the light. A few months ago, he'd decided to redecorate. He'd taken up the carpet and the yellowing newspaper underneath, only to reveal gapping grey floorboards spattered with various colours of paint. He'd had a go at stripping the wallpaper . . . but still hadn't quite finished the job. As a result, obdurate stalactites of anaglypta descended from the ceiling, a recalcitrant patch of the overpainted textured paper circled the light switch, and a border of scabrous and flaky lining paper clung to the top of the skirting boards. The exposed plaster gouged and scarred from his inexpert use of the metal wallpaper stripper. The only thing he came home to each night, the only thing he *would* be coming home to for the foreseeable, now his separation from Ruth was about to become official, was the unvarying daily delivery of junk mail. He stooped to pick it up and made his way into the kitchen, dumping his overcoat on an armchair in the living room on the way. He put his keys on the table and chucked the pizza, kebab, Chinese and Indian take-away menus into the recycling bin. Then he reached into the bin to retrieve the brown envelope. Its very ordinariness had caught his attention. No transparent window. No addressee. He flipped it over to check the back. Nothing. Even the unsolicited offers from local estate agents offering to buy your house came with a transparent window these days. Were usually addressed to 'The Occupier'.

Suddenly, he twigged what it was: the results of the forensic analysis carried out on the clothing of Beverly Marsh. Graham had promised him as much. During that late-night meeting a few days ago. Pearson wondered again whether he was under surveillance. Whether someone from MI5 had gotten into his place and installed monitoring equipment. Well, they'd be bored bloody stupid if they *had*. Fourteen or so hours of the fridge humming, the central heating system clicking on and off, the muffled sound of the stereo playing in the neighbour's flat. Followed by an hour of him flicking through television channels and swearing. He imagined someone sitting somewhere in a cold room with a pair of headphones on. Yawning. Fighting to stay awake. Not that you actually needed to get into a place nowadays. A high-powered lens, night vision cameras, directional microphones, you could, with the right resources at your disposal, watch someone from miles away.

Pearson dismissed the idea. With all that had happened since, the conversation with Graham had completely slipped his mind. And, if he were honest, somehow now the question of who had killed Beverly Marsh fifty years ago didn't seem all that important. All the same, Pearson found himself tearing open the end of the envelope and teasing out the contents. Inside he found two folded sheets of paper. The first page showed an entry on the national DNA database identified as a sample retrieved from the clothing of Beverly Marsh. The sixteen-year-old found murdered by the Crowstone on March the thirty-first, 1966. There had been a positive match between this sample, and one taken following the arrest of a man on a charge of driving while under the influence of alcohol. Pearson stared down at the name. Glanced up for a moment, across the kitchen, out of the condensation-streaked window, and into the dark night. Then he looked back down at the sheet of paper in his hand. Staring again at the name. As if, in those few intervening seconds, the name might have changed. And all of a sudden Pearson was back at that meeting with Graham . . .

'*There is another matter I can help you with,*' Graham said, '*the issue of your paternity? A simple match of your DNA run against the DNA sample taken from Jack Morris when he was arrested for drink-driving, of course, could establish any familial connection ... unfortunately, it's not quite that straightforward, is it?*' The agent had paused then, before adding, '*For you, that is.*'

Pearson knew then what the second sheet would contain. His DNA profile. As Ruth had rightly said, each serving police officer had to have their profile registered on the national database. The profile of the DNA sample collected from Jack Morris. And the results of a familial match run between the two. To all intents and purposes, a paternity test. And he knew, too, that that match would be positive.

Did he really want that final confirmation? Did he want that last, lingering, negligible doubt removed? Did he want absolute proof that he was related to Jack Morris? That he was the biological son of a murderer?

On the other hand, could he really trust any of this? Okay, so on the face of it, the documents looked legitimate. But they had been delivered anonymously, by hand, and in an unmarked envelope. Not that difficult, these days, to fake official looking documents. To create a passable facsimile of headed paper. After all, everything nowadays was produced by a laser printer. Could he trust Graham? Could he even trust the DNA database? Never mind faking documentation, it wouldn't be out of the question that MI5, with all its resources, might be able to hack a supposedly secure computer system and amend an entry.

The Security Services could easily have falsified the information. Hoping that Pearson wouldn't act on the knowledge that Jack Morris, his biological father, had killed Beverly Marsh. Or even that he might try to cover it up in some way. That this would give them some leverage over him. In which case, what *was* it exactly that they thought Pearson knew? What was it they were afraid would get out?

With that came a sudden realisation. If Jack Morris really was his father then Michael . . . was his half-brother, or half-sister, his half-sibling at least. Christ, how had that particular, obvious, glaring truth managed to elude him for so long?

Pearson made up his mind. If he *were* under surveillance, then he'd fucking-well give them something for their reports. He stepped across the kitchen to the gas hob, turned on the front ring, and pressed down the automatic ignition until it caught. Then he put the sheets of paper to the flame. He waited until the paper was properly alight, then he turned off the hob and went to stand by the sink. He held it in his hand until it was little more than ash. Then he let it fall into the sink and ran the tap . . .

51

Pearson stood in the quiet of his kitchen, his back to the worktop, cradling the recently made cup of tea. In the distance he could just make out the mournful call of foghorns in the Estuary. Of all the noises that characterised the town, the reverberation of jet engines coming into land at the airport, the thump-thump of music and the shrieking of passengers on the rides of Adventure Island, the shushing of the incoming tide on the pebbles of East Beach, this sound was, for him, the most evocative. He imagined himself on the bridge of some grimy tramp steamer; one hand on the steel chain of a foghorn, the other thrust into the pocket of a pea jacket, the prow cutting through the brackish brown water as kittiwakes and gulls circled its corroded metal superstructure. Heading downriver. Always downriver and away into –

Pearson's gaze fell on the black leather briefcase on the kitchen table. The briefcase he'd taken from Laurence in the hospital waiting room. Pearson moved across the room, placed his cup on the table and pulled out a chair. He sat down, opened the briefcase and took out the manila folder. The cardboard file now dog eared and curling from Laurence's fretful twisting and wringing. Pearson made a half-hearted attempt to flatten it out, before quickly admitting defeat and opening the cover.

A dozen or so pages of A4 containing Laurence's handwritten commentary. The interviews carried out with prisoners and staff. The scene-of-crime officer's report. The mental health assessment of Ryan Yates. The annotated transcript of the psychologist's interview. Pearson took a sip of his tea and began to read, cross-referencing each document with Laurence's notes . . .

John Hall had clocked the car as soon as he'd turned into the street. Had recognised the man behind the wheel in the sudden flare of the cigarette lighter. The young Detective Constable he'd seen in the Incident Room when he'd been talking to Pearson. The man he'd spotted on numerous occasions over the last few days. Parked up in the same place. His eyes fixed on Cat Russell's flat. So, Hall had driven past, gone around the block, before coming in from the other end. Finding a parking space twenty or so yards further up on the opposite side of the road. From where he had an unobstructed view of both the other vehicle and the front door to the shared property.

It had been a good few minutes now since Hall had watched the retreating taillights of the other car disappear around the corner of the street, so he picked up the phone again. Swiping back through the hundreds of snapshots held in its digital memory. Tracing the events of the last couple of days in reverse. Moving through a montage of countless images of the same person. Cat letting herself into her flat. Rummaging through her handbag. Lighting a cigarette. Cat exiting a blue Mondeo in the almost-dark of a late evening. Getting into the same vehicle in the police station car park. Cat getting into the Ford in the grey light of a dismal dawn. Twisting an elastic band into her shoulder-length brown hair as she surveyed an overcast sky . . .

Pearson went through the folder again. Making sure that he'd read every page. Checking that Laurence hadn't written on the back of one of the sheets. Then he opened the briefcase and looked inside. Just in case. Even though he absolutely *knew* it would be empty. There could be no other explanation: Laurence's investigation into the death of Ryan Yates was incomplete. His final entry had been the recording of the official arrest of Gary Clark and the subsequent arrangements for his transportation to Southend Nick for interview. But Laurence had obviously not finished his review of the psychologist's interview with Ryan Yates. The commentary, the underlining, the question marks, the marginalia were conspicuously absent from the last few pages. The section where Yates recounted the systematic torture of Clive Townsend. Pearson slipped the pen from the inside pocket of his jacket, turned over the last page on which Laurence had made notes and began to read:

'What is it you want to know?' Ryan asked.

'Everything,' Donna said.

'Everything?'

'Everything *he* knows about the parties,' Donna said, 'Where they were held. Who arranged them? Who went to them? Who else is involved – '

And then Donna Freeman was pressing the knife into his hand. And Ryan could feel her hot, sticky fingers, could feel its sweaty metal handle . . .

John Hall was familiar with the received wisdom, had read the cod psychology, was well acquainted with the popular misconception of the shrine. The secret rooms; the dusty lockups on the out-of-town industrial estate, the chill, empty garages with oil-stained concrete floors. Knew only too well the widespread and erroneous notion of what they contained. Photographs pinned to a set of corkboards, perhaps, surrounded by the melted stubs of votive candles, the artefacts of infatuation. The trophies collected from undetected late-night break-ins; the recently worn underwear swiped from a laundry basket, the earring snatched from a bedside cabinet, the lock of hair retrieved from a brush, the lipstick-smudged cigarette end taken from an ashtray.

As a serving police officer, of course, he understood that even these seemingly isolated, these apparently secluded locations still carried a very real risk of accidental discovery. Even a simple physical photograph album; secreted in the bottom drawer of the desk in a locked private study or concealed in a loft space accessible only via a pull-down extendable ladder, might still be stumbled upon by pure chance. It was for this reason that the smartphone, made secure by biometric technology, had become for him the chosen repository, the portable digital reliquary, of his own particular obsession.

He swiped back through more photographs. Giving most no more than a cursory glance. It had been just as he had told Cat at their meeting in the car park. Ten years ago, he had been given a tip off. He *had* handed over money and received a name in exchange. That name *was* Daniel Angus Fraser. At that time, Fraser *had* been in the building trade. He *had* had access to the sort of vehicle that, according to several of the victims, had been driven by the assailant. His family *was*, and still are, involved in various criminal activities in the Durham area. His older brother, Jackie, *was* a convicted rapist. The Cathy Russell of that time had fitted the profile of previous victims. Okay, yeah, maybe he had used her as a decoy. And maybe trailing her home from all-night student parties, observing her from the shadows of the bar as she served behind the counter of the 'Queen's Head' and following her on her evening run, in the hope that Fraser might strike and he would be there to catch him red-handed, might be seen, in retrospect, as a bit of a risk. But hadn't he admitted that? Hadn't he held his hands up? Quite literally. Hadn't he explained that, if it wasn't for the car accident, he'd have been there to protect her? Even if it was a lie. But she wasn't to know that. Was she?

Hall swiped back through the images. The photographs he had taken over the now seven years and nearly six months since Cat had left the University in Durham and returned to Southend. That had been another lie, of course. At that first meeting in Priory Park. Telling Cat that he had heard her name only recently, during a late-night conversation in a hotel bar, where he just happened to be attending the same seminar as someone who had previously worked out of Southend Nick. He'd known much earlier, of course, that Cat was in the Job. In fact, almost as soon as she'd joined the Force. It wasn't that hard to work out that she'd become a police officer, was it? After all, it was him who had put the idea in her head. And that was when he had started making the four-hundred-mile round trip to sit behind the wheel of his car in this same street. Telling his wife he had to work, that he wouldn't be home, or not telling her at all and just not bothering to go home. He had watched Cat leave her flat in the early morning, followed her over the course of the day, and watched her returning to her flat at night. All the while snapping photos on his phone . . .

And so, he came back to that photograph. The picture to which he always returned. The image that had started it all. Even now he had no clue as to the reason. No idea why it had such a profound significance for him. Why it should hold such a fascination. It wasn't even as if it was a good likeness. The central figure ever so slightly out-of-focus. The edges blurred from camera shake. If you didn't know the subject, if you weren't acquainted with the young Cathy Russell . . .

It might have been anybody. Even the look wasn't typical for the time; the black mini-skirt, the grey silk top, the long, straight dyed black hair had only been adopted for a short while – sometime in the first few weeks he had observed her – and then discarded. But there was something about it. Something seductive. Something fascinating. Something irresistible. He had known then that he had *had* to have her. And that had been another lie. On that particular night he hadn't followed her in the car. The road hadn't been extra busy on his way up to the roundabout. The traffic lights hadn't been against him. There had been no collision. Instead he had waited in the woods . . .

But hadn't he made it up to her? Since then. Since that momentary loss of control. That part, at least, had been true. He *had* been allocated the sexual assault case at short notice. And he *had* walked into that interview room and been horrified by the result of what he had done . . .

But hadn't he *more* than made it up to her? Hadn't he been the one to support her through the most traumatic experience of her life? Hadn't he been the one who had nursed her through the resulting mental crisis? Hadn't he been the one who had given her an education? Hadn't he taught her about philosophy, music, literature and the classics? And what thanks had he got?

Hall dragged his eyes from the photograph. Stared out through the windscreen. At the corner where, a few minutes earlier, the other car had turned right onto the main road. The young DC, though, really was of no consequence. He doubted Cat had even noticed him. But the DS – Pearson – now, he was a different matter. He'd seen, during that meeting, how Cat had looked at him . . .

For a while, Hall watches as snowflakes flutter down from a strangely orange sky, settle on the roofs of cars, the rutted and icy road. He takes in the flickering blue light of television sets in warm front parlours, the amber glow of street lamps reflected from the chromium ornamentation and partially covered windshields of stationary vehicles. Finally, he turns his attention from this silent, frozen world . . . to the light which still burns in the living room of Cat Russell's flat.

Sitting at his kitchen table, Pearson had shut the folder. Had slipped his pen back into his inside breast pocket, having not written a word. Was staring down at the tatty cardboard cover. Had, in fact, been staring at it for some minutes. The half-empty cup of now cold tea forgotten. Trying to make some sense of what he'd just read. Wondering just what he should do next. And feeling the need to talk to somebody. He shot his cuff to check his watch. The old-fashioned Timex on a battered leather wrist strap. The only thing he had belonging to his father. The man he had believed was his father. Up until now. Already too late for Cat, he thought. Probably. Looking up, he caught the reflection of himself in the darkened window. Once again, everything suddenly dropped away, and all became clarity. And he experienced that same sensation of being somehow outside, looking in . . .

Pearson squeezed his eyes shut. Waited for the feeling to pass. Then, opening his eyes again, he snatched up the folder and his keys, and pushed back his chair . . .

52

Pearson slammed the driver's side door. Pressed the electronic fob to activate the central locking system. The Mondeo's heater had barely had time to warm the car in the short drive over here, the dashboard thermometer registering the outside temperature as sub-zero, and in his anger, his haste to leave his flat he'd forgotten his dark woollen overcoat. Despite this, he took a few breaths to calm himself. Glanced up at the night sky. Reflected light illuminating low clouds. A flurry of snowflakes caught in the light of the sodium streetlamps. His breath condensing on the cold air.

He weighed the manila folder in his hand. There had been another manila folder, of course. The folder in the Richard Lennon case. A folder containing the transcripts of historical counselling sessions which, had they been followed up, might have had a material effect on the outcome of the investigation. He had handed that folder over to Roberts. And, presumably, it had been passed up the chain of command. Until it ended up in the possession of MI5. Where it had been promptly buried. He wasn't about to part with this folder so easily.

Finally, Pearson looked over at his brother-in-law's club. There was a single light shining at a first-floor window. Otherwise the place was in darkness.

'*Make him tell us,*' the ghost of Donna Freeman whispered inside his head, '*make him tell us ... everything. Make him tell us.*'

The neon sign was dimmed. The lights off. The double wooden doors at the entrance locked and bolted. He had stood in that bar in the past. Drinking a bottle of lager. Eating a bag of cheese and onion crisps. And he hadn't had the faintest fucking idea of what had really been going on. The private parties. The exploitation of under-age, vulnerable teenagers by older men. The asphyxiation and subsequent murder of Michael Morris.

A few months ago, he had stood in that bar and had the brief, but overwhelming, feeling that his life was not his own. That he was acting out a script. That his every action was being directed by someone else. And since his meeting with Graham, that feeling had returned. And along with it, the sense of being watched. Of his actions being scrutinised and evaluated. That he was being judged.

'You're a copper, Frank.' Ruth had said, *'You've always been a copper. Whatever happens you can carry on being a copper. It's what you do. It's what you are.'*

Except, he hadn't been much of a copper lately, had he? He'd suspected that Terry Milton was up to something, was hiding something, months ago. And he hadn't done anything about it. Hadn't, at the time, wanted to do anything to upset Ruth. Hadn't wanted to do anything that might disturb her already delicate state of mind. So, he'd let it slide. Turned a blind eye. So, he'd been as much to blame as anybody . . .

Now, he knew for certain. Milton was, as he'd put it himself, 'up to his nuts' in this. Now, Ruth was in a better place. Had given Terry his marching orders. Now, at least, he

370

could do something. Terry Milton held the key to the whole case. Was the connection between Layla Gilchrist, Clive Townsend and the men they were organising the parties for? He would have been – and Pearson gave Milton the benefit of the doubt here, even if he wasn't quite sure he merited it – if not actually participating in what had been going on, then at least present, in order to safeguard his own interests. So, he should be able to identify the people involved. He would make fucking sure Milton identified the people involved.

Pearson felt calm now. No point in going in heavy-handed, no matter what he thought now of Milton. Terry was, essentially, a coward. Would, without a doubt, cave in at the first sign that Pearson knew what he'd been up to. He only had to show him the evidence, confront him with the truth, and Milton would spill the lot.

And perhaps it was because he was preoccupied, because his mind was on other things, that he didn't notice the approaching car. Its headlights off. Bars of light reflecting along its bodywork. Perhaps it was because his ears were numbed, because of the howling wind, the deadening effect of the snow, that he didn't hear the accelerating of its near-silent electric engine, the grit crunching beneath its tyres . . . .

There is a sound of tyres on compacted snow. The brief flash of brake lights. Red taillights fading into the night. Then … silence. Time passes in the almost-dark of a city street lit only by sodium lamps, the muted neon displays in shop windows, the light escaping between cracks in the closed curtains of upstairs rooms. Snow falls on a motionless figure. A man.

Lying among a confusion of churned snow, filthy slush, and strewn gravel. His eyelids flutter. He is alive. Barely. Though, shivering, cold, wracked with pain, he is unable to move. He can hear a sound. Faraway, it is scarcely audible. The piteous whimpering of a distressed and wounded animal. And he recognises his own voice. He is aware of the blood seeping and pooling beneath him on the frozen tarmac. Sees it steam slightly in the chill air. Sees the crystals of snow slowly turn scarlet and then melt away. A gusting wind howls again between the parked cars. In exhaust pipes. Swirls and eddies the drifting flakes of snow. Flaps open the cover of the discarded manila folder. Riffles the edges of the sheets of paper inside, before lifting them and urging them along the street where they come to rest against the tyres of stationary vehicles. Wrap themselves around the bottom of street lamps and road signs. Lodge in the grills of drains. And if, over the course of the next few hours, it was to snow heavily, then rain perhaps, the paper might grow damp. Might become little more than a soggy mush. Might finally disintegrate and be swept away by the brushes of a municipal street-cleaning vehicle. The snow intensifies, becoming a blizzard, and continues for an hour. Two, perhaps. Then, abruptly, it stops

. . .

A few words from the author

I had thought to include here a lengthy explanation of certain aspects of the trilogy. A justification for why, I believe, this trilogy goes well beyond being mere crime fiction. In the end, though, I decided against it. So, instead, for any who might care to take part, here is a quiz.

In each book in the trilogy I have included the name of a footballer. A clue here: they have all played for the same team, and it just happens to be the team I support.

In each book I have included the name of a song by a band who's first hit was in 1978. The first song title was included in 'Burned and Broken' as a sort of thank you because the buzzy guitar riff intro had allowed me to instantly re-connect each day with Donna's character.

Finally, I am, and always have been, a massive Bowie fan. I have included numerous references to DB in each book. See how many you can spot.

Good Luck

Mark Hardie, August 2019, Southend-on-Sea, Essex.

Printed in Great Britain
by Amazon

32512939R00225